Portia would not trust him to keep his word, but she was willing to take him to her bed? What sort of logic was that?

Mateo snorted in disgust. Women's logic—the sort tailor-made to drive him mad.

And therein, perhaps, lay part of the problem. For until she'd pressed that deliciously curved body up against him he hadn't allowed himself to think of Portia as a woman. First he'd painted her as a scheming opportunist, and even once he'd realized he was mistaken still he had not truly looked at her. Instead he'd overlaid her with a picture of the unassuming, unfailingly supportive young girl he'd once known.

In reality, she was neither. She was still as he'd remembered and expected, but she'd grown, too. No, he had not expected to encounter strength, steel and determination. She'd become a woman of fascinating layers. And were this any other time and circumstance he'd enjoy nothing more than slowly peeling them away.

* * *

Tall, Dark and Disreputable
Harlequin® Historical #1086—April 2012

Tall, Dark and Disreputable

DEB MARLOWE

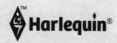

Harlequin®

TORONTO NEW YORK LONDON
AMSTERDAM PARIS SYDNEY HAMBURG
STOCKHOLM ATHENS TOKYO MILAN MADRID
PRAGUE WARSAW BUDAPEST AUCKLAND

Recycling programs
for this product may
not exist in your area.

ISBN-13: 978-0-373-29686-6

TALL, DARK AND DISREPUTABLE

Copyright © 2009 by Deb Marlowe

First North American Publication 2012

This edition published by arrangement with Harlequin Books S.A.

For questions and comments about the quality of this book
please contact us at Customer_eCare@Harlequin.ca.

www.Harlequin.com

Printed in U.S.A.

To the Biaggi's Bunch...

You all already know why—
and that's what makes it beautiful!

Chapter One

Berkshire, England—Summer 1821

Ribald laughter and drunken babble spilled out into the night. The owner of the Spread Eagle Inn took cheerful part in the bonhomie as he shooed his last customers into the dark. He stood a moment, listening as they scattered, secure in the knowledge that they would be back tomorrow and that the satisfying weight of coins in his apron pocket would only grow heavier.

Inside his taproom, quiet settled over the abandoned tables and peace wrapped itself around the place in lieu of the dissipating curtain of smoke. Mateo Cardea alone had not stirred when the innkeeper called. Here the fire burned warm, the ale was good and the accommodating wench in his lap ran soft fingers through his hair. He should have been blissfully content.

He was not.

The lightskirt slid a finger around his ear. She leaned in close, her brassy blond hair tickling his jaw, her other hand trailing a whisper-soft caress against his nape. Mateo could feel the tough calluses on her fingertips. He closed his eyes and imagined the touch of them against his other, more sensitive areas.

Arousing as the image might be, Mateo still could not summon the enthusiasm needed to climb out of his chair. Ridiculous. A few paltry coins and the girl was his for the taking, yet the thought did not dredge up more than a faint stir of desire.

The yawning innkeeper ambled back into the tap-room. He cast a glance at Mateo and crooked a finger at the girl. 'Get these chairs atop the tables, Etta, and I'll help you sweep up,' he said, not unkindly. The girl gave a soft groan of protest, but rose up and out of Mateo's lap. She trailed a finger over his shoulder and down the length of his arm as she went. Mateo recognised the gesture for the promise it was and briefly waited for an answering surge of interest.

It did not come. Inside him there was no room for such clean and simple things as peace and desire. *'Dio nel cielo,'* he breathed. Oh, but he was tired of the unfamiliar burn of anger in his gut and the caustic flow of resentment in his veins. For weeks he'd been like this, since he'd first discovered his father's shocking betrayal.

All of it gone. Everything he'd spent his life working for, planning towards, gone with the reading of a few cold words. Years of biting his tongue, of endless explanations, of patiently coaxing his father to more modern business practices, and still the old man had not trusted him in the end. Mateo was in disgrace and, for the first time in a hundred years, control of Cardea

Shipping had fallen outside the family. It was more than a man's pride could bear.

His indifference was more than the strumpet could bear. She had worked her way back over to his side of the room and into the dark corner behind him. Now she leaned against him, blocking the heat of the fire, but warming him none the less when she bent low to encircle him in her arms. Her impressive bosom pressed soft against his back.

'Are ye even here, tonight?' Etta asked, demanding the return of his attention. 'What are you thinkin' of, that's got your mind so far away?' She stiffened a little and drew back. 'Some other woman, p'raps?'

Mateo smiled. 'I am not so foolish, sweet.' With a sigh of regret he acknowledged the need to evade her interest and retire upstairs alone. Tomorrow held fair promise to be the worst day of his life and no amount of mindless distraction tonight would help ready him for it.

'What is it, then?' she demanded, circling round to the front of him again, her bottom lip forming a perfect pout. 'Something important, I hope,' she said low in his ear, 'to be distracting you from the bounties at hand.'

He disentangled himself and drew her around to his side. Taking the girl with him, Mateo crossed the small distance to the bar. Here the innkeeper tidied up, trimming the wicks on cheap tallow lamps and polishing the worn wooden counter with pride. Mateo took the furthest stool and gestured for the girl to perch next to him.

'No, tonight I have been lost indeed—thinking of fathers, and of sons. Do you know,' he continued in a conversational tone, 'that my father once caused a city-wide riot over a wh—' Etta straightened in her seat and he cleared his throat '—over a celebrated courtesan?'

She relaxed. 'He never!'

Mateo smiled at her obvious interest. Even the innkeeper sidled closer to listen. 'Oh, but he did. It happened in Naples, long ago. La Incandescent Clarisse, she was called, the greatest beauty in Europe. Endless poems were written to the soft pink of her lips, to the sweet curve of her hips. Playwrights named their heroines for her, artists worshipped her as their muse. Men followed her carriage in the street. My father was only one of many caught firmly in her spell.'

'What happened?' The girl's face shone bright and she had briefly forgotten her practised seduction.

'The inevitable.' Mateo shrugged. 'La Incandescent got with child. All of Naples held their breath, fascinated to hear who she would name as the father.'

'Who was it?' she breathed. 'Not your da?'

'After a fashion. You see, Clarisse could only narrow down the field. The father of her child was either *my* father, or Thomas Varnsworth.'

'No!' The innkeeper gasped.

'Him what's the Earl of Winbury?' Etta asked, amazed.

'The old Earl, rather,' Mateo replied.

The innkeeper could not contain his shock. 'But his daughter lives—'

'Yes, I know,' Mateo interrupted. 'Shall I continue?'

They both nodded.

'Upon hearing the news, Lord Thomas—for he was not the Earl yet—and my father got into a terrible row.

They fought long and hard, nearly destroying La Incandescent's apartments, and still they raged on, until the fight eventually spilled out into the streets. Spectators gathered. Someone spotted the tearful Clarisse and the rumour spread that La Incandescent had been harmed. The crowd grew furious, for Clarisse was a favourite of the people, and soon the two men found themselves fighting for their lives.'

'And all over a strumpet?' the innkeeper said in wonder.

'Hush, you,' the girl admonished. 'Let him finish.'

Mateo shifted. Too late he worried about raising the tavern wench's expectations, but that thought set off another surge of bitterness. It had been a woman's damned expectations that had ruined his life. Portia Varnsworth had once expected to marry him. Mateo's father had expected him to go along with the idea. Mateo might have expected somebody to consult him on the matter, but no one had bothered.

Etta, however, appeared to have taken the tale as a challenge. She raised a brow and tossed him a saucy grin. 'I'm summat well known, myself, in these parts,' she said.

'Indeed?'

'Oh, aye,' she purred. 'Would you like to know what I'm famous for?'

'He don't need to know now,' grumbled her employer, 'and not in front o' me. What ye do upstairs is yer own business. Down here, it's mine. Don't ye want him to finish his tale? And you've a taproom to straighten first, in any case.' He nodded for Mateo to continue.

'Ah, yes, well, my father and Lord Thomas were

arrested—for their own protection. They spent two days in a cell together and came out the best of friends.'

'And the lady? Clarisse?' Etta leaned closer.

'When they were released, she had gone. She left Naples and disappeared. No one ever knew where she went, although rumours abounded. My father and Lord Thomas made a vow to find her and searched for years.'

She stilled. 'Did they? Find her, that is?'

'No,' he said soberly. 'Not to my knowledge. But they never stopped looking, either, until their dying days.'

Her eyes shone in the dim light, bright with unshed tears. 'That's the most romantic thing I ever heard.' She sniffed.

The innkeeper snorted. 'Then I would say you were in sore need of a little romance.' He nodded towards Mateo. 'He might be the one to give it to ye, but first—'

'Aye, I know, I know, the taproom,' Etta grumbled. The weight of her gleaming gaze felt nearly solid on Mateo's skin. 'I just mean to give him a taste of what comes after.' She slid down from her stool and reached for him.

Mateo saw the stars in her eyes. The girl's mind tumbled with fancies and dreams and he knew that he had perhaps not been so wise in his choice of tales. It is no bad thing to create a vision of things that might be, but of a certainty he would not be the one to bring her grand ideas to fruition.

He stilled as her arms went around him. He had no wish to damage her feelings. A woman had brought his world to a crashing halt, but he would not take his revenge on this, her artless sister. He sent a swift plea to the heavens for something, anything to distract the girl and extract him from the awkward situation of his own making.

The knob on the taproom door rattled. A floorboard creaked in the passage outside. Mateo jerked to attention along with the others as the door opened swiftly and his name echoed through the empty room. He stared, speechless, at the figure framed in the shadowy entrance and he knew that in the future he would be more careful in what he wished for.

A breeze wafted over Portia Tofton's flushed cheeks as she approached the Eagle. The night air was cooler than she had expected. She didn't care. She had her indignation to keep her warm, her dead husband's pistol to keep her safe and a fervent desire to shock the wits out of Mateo Cardea to keep the purpose in her step.

Coming to a halt in front of the inn, she cast it a look of loathing. The beady eyes of the building's painted namesake returned her glare. The raptor's outstretched talons glittered in the moonlight, sending a shiver down her spine

Mateo had arrived in the village today; word was out and spreading fast across the county. Weeks it had taken for him to take ship and make his way here, but had he come to her? She snorted. Of course not. Apparently not even the loss of his family legacy was enough to tempt him to her side. Despite the urgent wording of her request he had holed up in the most disreputable tavern for miles around. No doubt he'd spent the day drinking, carousing, and who knows what else, while she had been left to twiddle her thumbs.

How utterly predictable.

No. Portia squared her shoulders and took a step forwards. Such treatment might be standard in her old life, perhaps, but it was not at all acceptable in the new. She was a widow now. Her husband's death had granted her a new freedom and independence that she meant to take full advantage of. Heaven knew—and everybody else did too—that it was more than he'd given her while he lived.

She raised a fist to knock loud and long upon the tavern door, but noticed it stood slightly ajar. She put her hand on the knob and paused. Gone were the days that Lady Portia Varnsworth—or even Mrs. James Talbot Tofton—meekly did as she was expected. She'd had enough of men ruling her life. Though her brothers might try, there was no one left with the authority to order, bully—or, worse, ignore her. And Portia meant to keep it that way. She wanted nothing more than her independence, the chance to be in charge of her own destiny. She'd thought she had it, too, until that wretched solicitor had come calling.

But no matter. She had a grasp on the situation. One even exchange with Mateo Cardea and she would have her freedom—and her home—safe again. It only wanted a little courage and a good deal of determination. Sternly she reminded herself that she had an ample supply of both. Boldly she pushed the outer door open and let herself in, steeled to face—

Empty darkness. Silence.

'Is anyone there?' Some of her bravado faded a little as she stepped forwards into the gloom. Portia paused to take a good look, curious to see the place servants and villagers whispered about. The ante-room appeared perfectly ordinary at least, certainly not like she'd imagined a reputed den of debauchery and iniquity. Disappointed, she continued forwards.

A doorway sat at an angle to the right. From beneath it shone the faintest glow of light—and from behind it she caught the low murmur of voices. She crept closer.

There. Faint but unmistakable: Mateo Cardea's wicked chuckle.

Portia stood helpless against the intense shiver of reaction that swept through her. As a young girl she'd spent hours tagging after Mateo and her brothers. She'd lurked in hallways and corners, listening for that infectious sound. Five years older than she, Mateo Cardea had been an ideal, the unsuspecting object of her first consuming love. An absent smile from him had held the power to light up her day, but it had been his rich laughter, full of mischief and exuberance, that had set her young body a-tremble.

Not that he had ever taken notice. Despite their friendship, she'd never been more than background scenery to him, a secondary character in the drama of his young life.

She was determined that things would be different now. All day she had sat, waiting for him to come, seething when he did not. Until—as the hour grew late and her temper grew short—she'd finally decided that this time she would begin with Mateo as she meant to go on. She would force him to look at her, to see her, to truly recognise her for the woman she was. Mateo, her brothers, indeed the whole world—it was time that they all took a second look at Portia Tofton.

With a purposeful and careful tread she approached

the door. But he was not alone. Feminine tones mixed with his, and then both faded away. Portia's face flamed. Etta was as notorious as the Eagle itself. Of course Mateo would be with her. Everyone else had been—including Portia's own husband.

She was a different woman, now, though. She would not sit idly by and be ignored. She turned the latch as quietly as she could and paused once more. The manner of her entrance must lend itself to the image she wished to convey. She wished to appear a woman of self-possession and authority. *A woman he could desire*, whispered some deeply buried part of her. She shushed it. Above all, she would not be a supplicant.

She shifted her weight, hoping for a strategic glimpse into the room before she entered. A board creaked loudly underneath her, but Portia did not heed it.

It was he. Her stomach fluttered in recognition. How well she knew that rogue's twist of a wry grin, the tangle of inky, wind-tousled curls, and the spark of wickedness dancing in a gaze as warm as her morning chocolate. Her pulse tumbled nearly to a stop, then rushed to a gallop as her mind made sense of the rest of the tableau before her.

Mateo Cardea at last—but perched on a stool, the infamous Etta entwined around him tighter than the Persian ivy Portia had coaxed up the walls of her arbour. She gripped the door handle until her knuckles whitened. God, but it was the old hurt all over again. How many times in a woman's life could she withstand such a whirlwind of pain and humiliation?

One too many times. But this would be the last. She breathed deeply and willed her spine straight and her voice steady. With a flourish she swept the door open and stepped into the taproom, trampling her heart underneath each tread of her foot. 'Ah, here you are, Mateo,' she called. 'As ever the scapegrace, I see, seeking pleasure when there is serious work to be done.'

A rush of anger pulled Mateo off of his stool and out of the circle of Etta's arms. In an instinctive reaction his knees braced, his toes flexed within his boots to grip the floor and his breath quickened to match the sudden racing of his pulse. It was an old impulse, standing fast to face his enemies—except this adversary was neither a ship of the line bent on impressing his men nor a fat merchant clipper ripe for the picking. Instead it was a slip of a girl in a sky-blue pelisse.

He stared as Portia Tofton sauntered into the taproom as if it belonged to her. But this was not the shy, round-shouldered girl he recalled from his youth. From her head to her curvy figure and on to her dainty little toe, this was a woman to be reckoned with. Her stylish bonnet beautifully framed the look of cool amusement fixed on her face. Mateo's jaw tightened even as she removed it, letting it swing by ribbons of shaded velvet.

For so long he had imagined this confrontation. In his mind he had rehearsed his collected entrance into her presence, practised the biting words with which he would consign her to the devil. Now it would seem she had connived to rob him even of that satisfaction.

His fists clenched. An air of assurance hung about her as she stepped into the candlelight. And why not? She thought she had him right where she wished. Heedless of propriety, unmindful of the great wrong she had done him or perhaps just without regard for his feelings, she stood there, all expectation, smiling up at him.

That smile made him wild. Fury set his temples to pounding, but he would be damned before he would let her see it. 'Peeve!' he called. 'It is you, is it not?'

Her expression of triumph dimmed at the use of the old nickname. Relentless, he pressed his advantage. 'But I see that much is the same with you, as well, my dear.' He shook his head sadly. 'Still, after all these years, you are pushing yourself in where you do not belong.'

If he had hit his mark, she hid it well with a toss of her head. 'Come, let's not be rude, Mateo,' she cajoled.

He nearly choked. 'Rude? You conniving little jade! You would count yourself fortunate should I stop myself at merely rude!'

'I don't think the occasion warrants it.' She cast a quick, curious gaze about them. 'This is a place of… conviviality, is it not?'

He had not thought it possible for his anger to grow hotter. But the roiling mass of resentment inside him ignited at her words—and his control slipped further as the flames licked higher. Incredulous, he gaped at her.

He pushed away from the bar, away from her. Retreating back to the dying fire, he glared at her. 'Conviviality,' he scoffed. 'Is that what you expected from me? Damn you English, and damn your deadly, dull-mannered ways,' he said thickly. 'And damn me if I will greet with equanimity the woman who has usurped my life's work, and then—as if I am but her lackey—calls me to her side with a damned insulting peremptory summons!'

Her eyes narrowed and she took a step towards him. 'Mateo—'

'Stop,' he ordered. 'By God, I am not one of your reserved English gentlemen! Come within an arm's reach of me and I won't trust myself.' He turned away from her and gripped the stone mantel over the fire. 'Never in my life have I struck a woman, but you, Portia Tofton, tempt me beyond reason.'

Perhaps he had gone too far. At the bar, the innkeeper made a slight sound of protest. Etta watched with avid interest. But Portia barely reacted.

'Ah, Mateo…' she sighed '…I'd forgotten how incredibly dramatic you become when you are angry.'

She could not keep the slight mockery from her tone—and that was all it took. The last of his restraint tore away. Everything this infuriating chit did and said only fuelled the blowing gale of his anger.

'Dramatic?' he ground out. 'I am betrayed. I am robbed of the future that I have laboured all my life for. I am a laughingstock where once I was a respected businessman. And I am *furious*. What I am not is *dramatic*.' He whirled around and advanced on her with menace alive in his step. His voice, gone rough and threatening, reinforced the truth in her words and the lie in his. But Mateo was beyond caring. Hell and damnation, but she pushed a man too far! And she was—at last!—a bit frightened. God help him, but he wished to frighten her.

She stood her ground, though her eyes widened, and her fingers crushed the velvet of her ribbons. 'I believe you have let the Cardea temper and your own imagination run away with you,' she said. 'I sent an *urgent* request for you to come and discuss this situation. There is a vast distance between urgent and peremptory.'

'Ah, it is my mistake,' Mateo growled. 'Yes, I am sure your urgent need of a long and thorough gloat required my presence. Well, I can assure you, I feel your triumph keenly enough without such a humiliation.'

'But I—'

He swung his arm in a sharp gesture and cut her off. He was close enough now to clearly see the puzzlement in her great brown eyes. Good, then. There was one question that had hung between them for years. He would answer it one last time and put an end to this entire farce. 'We've both trod this ground before, have we not? It was not enough that you and our fathers sought to manoeuvre me into marriage? But I won that battle—so now you must find a new way to steal my future. Once again you have played a game without informing me I was a participant—and just as before you will find that I refuse to act as the prize.'

She gaped up at him. 'What are you saying?'

'Do not play the innocent with me, Portia, not after you have conspired to steal all that I value,' he growled. 'Perhaps it is not so inappropriate for you to be here tonight, after all. It is a fitting setting for you to learn that I will not be bought like a whore, no matter the bait that you dangle in front of me.'

Portia gasped. Behind him, Etta echoed her. The innkeeper dropped his cloth and took a step towards the corner of the bar. 'That's enough, now.' He cast a conciliatory eye in Portia's direction as he came around and approached them. 'I don't claim to know what there is between the two of you, but the gentleman was right the first time, Mrs Tofton. You shouldn't be here, let alone at this hour. If word got out, your credit would suffer, and so would mine.'

All of Portia's colour had faded at Mateo's last heated words. As the innkeeper's objection penetrated, her flush returned with a vengeance. Her chest heaved as an angry red wave crept upwards from beneath the standing collar of her pelisse. 'I'm sorry for it, sir, but surely the damage is done.' She cast a neutral glance at Etta and then regarded Mateo with the sort of loathing his crews reserved for an empty rum casket. 'And well worth it, I must say, for suddenly I find several things have become clear.'

She looked away and this time it was she who took a step back. 'I never thought—I can scarcely believe—' She dropped her head, placed her hands on her hips and actually paced back and forth a few steps, seemingly lost in thought. Some of Mateo's ire began to fade as he took in her air of bewilderment and the forgotten bonnet swinging against her knee.

She stopped suddenly, caught at the apex of her trajectory. Her chin lifted and at last he caught a glimpse of answering anger in her gaze—but there was hurt there too, and something bleak and sad.

'I wished you to come because I needed your help.' She spoke low. 'I thought it possible that you might have some insight into why your father and mine would have acted so contrary to expectation and good sense. I know *nothing* of why your father made the choices he did. I'm sorry he died, but I was as shocked as you were to hear the contents of his will.' She paused. 'My father is dead, too, Mateo. And my husband, as well. Together they have left me in a dilemma as terrible as yours.'

Her words doused the burn of fury inside of him, but she was not done yet. At her side, her fists clenched. 'I came here tonight to chide *you*, for I was unable to fathom why I had to ask you to come to sort this mess out in the first place, and why you would dally so long once you set out, in the second. But now I see.'

He watched her pull her bonnet on with shaking fingers. 'I had no notion that your opinion of me had sunk so low, but truly, it matters naught. I *ask* you, please, to come to Stenbrooke tomorrow.' She tied the strings with short, jerky movements. 'You are both right. This is neither the time nor the place. But if you will come tomorrow, we will discuss this business.' She swept the room with a glare that included all three of them. 'Business, and nothing else. I trust I make myself clear?' With an all-encompassing nod, she turned on her heel and strode out of the taproom and into the night.

The towering heat of his anger had faded to mere embers. She had cut the legs out from under him. Still, Mateo managed an involuntary step after her. The tavern owner deliberately put himself in his path. 'Mayhap, sir, you don't have all the facts you need,' he said gently.

'Aye, I fear you're right in that.' Mateo stepped back, scrubbed a hand from brow to jaw, and cocked an enquiring eye to the man. 'She tells the truth, I think?'

The innkeeper shrugged. 'They do say as she's one for straight dealing, hereabouts.'

'I would say it is either truth she's given us,' Mateo paused, 'or a beautiful performance.' He sighed. 'I feel like the Mariner—discovering the world has shifted and the sun is rising in the west.'

'A woman'll do that to a man, eh?'

'I fear so.' Mateo glanced back at Etta. 'Look at me. Knocked off my pillar of righteous anger in the space of a few minutes—and damned if I'm not exhausted from the fall.' He reached beyond the man to grasp his ale and drained it in one long haul. 'I am for bed,' he declared. 'It seems I've a mess to straighten in the morning.'

The innkeeper nodded his approval. 'I'll see that you are not disturbed.'

Mateo shook his head. 'It's far too late for that, my friend, but I thank you just the same.'

Chapter Two

A glorious morning dawned the next day, spilling sunlight into the breakfast room at Stenbrooke. A breeze drifted, rewarding early risers with the taste of heavy dew and the fresh scent of green and growing things. Never had Portia felt more out of harmony with the start of a beautiful day.

For once immune to the call of her gardens, she stood at the window while her breakfast grew cold behind her and the light limned the fair hairs on her arm with gold. The parchment in her hands glowed nearly transparent, grown worn with time and tears and frequent handling. And though she hid the letter when her elderly butler came in to shake his head over her untouched plate, he would have been hard pressed to read the faded ink in any case. Portia, of course, had no need to read it; its message had long ago been etched into the darkest corner of her heart.

Philadelphia, 11 July 1812

Your curst brother has arrived safely, Peeve— it began without preamble—*bringing with him details of this preposterous scheme our fathers have hatched between them. I cannot believe they have risked him at such a time of conflict between our two countries, and I am inclined to agree with Freddy when he wonders what put such a maggoty idea as marriage in their brains. I know we spent a good deal of time in company together when last I was at Hempshaw, but surely they must realise that was years ago and we were only friends, besides?*

In fact, I feel that I owe you a most profound apology—for this must be my father's doing. He is grasping at straws because I mean to sign a letter-of-marque bond. It's a surety he'd rather see me occupied with a wife and marriage than a privateer's cruise. I am deeply sorry to have caught you up in such a muddle but what must we do to break free?

Stand firm, I suppose, is the only answer. I pledge to do my part here—for at last I have got my own ship and she is the fastest schooner, with the sweetest lay in the water that you've ever seen. I mean to make my fortune with her, Peeve, though I promise not to target any ship that carries your brother back to you. In any case, I'm sure you've your own plans you don't wish me to

*disrupt. Stand fast, dear girl, as I mean to, and
there is little they can do to force us otherwise.*

'What's this?'

Portia started as the door opened again behind her.
Over her shoulder she watched as Dorinda Tofton, her
cousin by marriage and companion, entered on the heels
of the butler.

'Vickers tells me that you are neglecting your breakfast again, Portia,' Dorinda chided. 'He also suspects
that you are mooning over a letter. Has *that woman* sent
another of her hateful missives? I thought we'd seen an
end to this nonsense! I won't have you harassed—'

'No, Dorrie,' Portia interjected before her companion could get herself too wound up. 'I was just going
through some old correspondence.'

'Oh. Well. You're all right, then?'

Portia hesitated. 'Of course.'

'Good.' She shot a brief glance out of the window
before focusing on the food spread out on the sideboard.
'Will you please come and have some breakfast then,
dear? I can see that we are in for a beautiful day, but
you know how I feel about you disappearing into the
gardens without so much as a piece of toast in you.'

For a long moment, Portia did not answer. The letter
she held was the last communication she'd had with
Mateo Cardea until last night—and even after so many
years it still held the echo of her youthful shock and
dismay. With gentle fingers she folded it up and tucked
it into her bodice. Right over her heart she placed it—
where she would wear it as a reminder and a shield.

'Portia?' Dorinda paused in the process of making her own selections and eyed her curiously.

She turned. 'Yes, of course. I was just sitting down to finish.'

Dorinda took a seat and tucked into her coddled eggs with relish. 'What do you mean to tackle today, dear? The damaged bridge on the Cascade Walk?' She frowned. 'Or did I hear you say that the dahlias were in need of separating?'

Portia smiled. Only politeness led Dorrie to ask—she neither shared nor understood her charge's passion for landscaping. 'Actually, I mean to stay in this morning.'

Dorinda brightened noticeably. 'A wise choice. The sun is quite brilliant today. You know how harmful it can be to one's complexion.' Dorrie's own milky countenance was her pride and joy—and Portia's significantly browner one counted as a chief worry. She set down her fork and took up her teacup. 'Perhaps,' she began, her word choice seeming as delicate and deliberate as the stroke of her finger over the fine china, 'we might begin to pack some of our winter things? We might even consider starting on the books in the library.'

Portia set down her toast.

'It's only sensible to be prepared.' Dorinda sounded as if she were coaxing a reluctant child. Her voice lowered. 'We're running out of time, dear.'

Portia was a woman grown. She'd been married—and then widowed in spectacular fashion. She'd run this estate entirely on her own for years now. Never had she shown herself to be fragile or weak, and especially not since the day she'd first received the letter tucked into her bodice. Bad enough that her father and brothers had always treated her like a nursling—when Dorrie followed their example, it made Portia long to act like one.

But this was not the time for such indulgences. Instead of treating Dorinda to a screaming fit, she caught her gaze and held it. 'There is no need to pack, as I've told you repeatedly. We are going nowhere. We will proceed exactly as planned.' She leaned forwards. 'Even better, we begin today. Had you not heard? Mateo Cardea has arrived in the village. I expect he will call on us today.'

'He's here at last?' Dorinda nearly dropped her teacup. 'Oh, but will he co-operate?' she fretted. 'I know you recall him fondly, but there is this business with his…well, his business!' She reached over and laid her warm hand over Portia's. 'I want you to be prepared. I know you have not wished to consider it, but when you put this admittedly odd circumstance together with what you've told me about the marriage scheme your fathers tried to force on both of you… It's just that it's entirely within the realm of understanding…' She exhaled in exasperation. 'Portia, he's likely to formulate *ideas*. And none of them are likely to paint you in a favourable light.'

Portia felt the heat rising in her face. Dorrie had raised this concern before, and she had refused to believe such a thing of Mateo. Unfortunately, Mateo had been all too willing to believe such a thing of her. Bitterness churned in her belly. So much for the friendship she had valued so highly and for so long.

But admitting it also meant confessing her entirely improper, late-night visit to the Eagle, and that was a pot that Portia had no intention of stirring. 'If he is so disobliging as to think so of an old and dear friend,' she said with heat, 'then he is not the man I thought him to be.' She drew a deep breath and squared her shoulders. 'And I will just have to set him straight.'

'Oh, if only we'd bought that French muslin when we had the chance! The sage would have been so flattering on you, dear.'

Portia frowned. 'I begin to worry that you are the one with *ideas*, Dorrie. And if that is the case, then you can just rid yourself of them straight away.'

'Well, forgive me, but he's a man, is he not? And if you mean to ask for a man's help, then you've got to use every weapon in your arsenal—and give him every reason to agree.'

Portia rolled her eyes at the familiar refrain, but Dorinda had not even paused to take a breath. 'I confess, I'm so nervous about meeting him! I know you count him an old friend, but in all of these years there's been not so much as a letter between you. I—'

She stopped as Portia slapped both hands on the table and stood.

'Please, Dorrie! Stop or you'll have me tied in knots along with you.' She straightened. 'I have what Mateo wants. He can help me get what I want. It will be as simple as that.' She ignored her companion's huff of disagreement and stepped away from the table. 'I'll be in the library, settling the accounts, should you need me.'

It took only minutes at her books for Portia to regret her decision. A bundle of frayed nerves, she fidgeted constantly in her chair. She could scarcely believe that Mateo had laid the blame for his troubles at her door. They had always been at ease in each other's company, accepting of the other's foibles, keepers of the other's secrets. It should never have been so easy for him to believe the worst of her.

She put down her quill and rested her head in her hands. He'd casually crushed her fledgling feelings so long ago. It should come as no surprise that he did it again, and so easily. A conniving jade, he'd called her! Even her husband's betrayals had not cut so deep into the heart of her—perhaps because they had been expected.

She stared blankly at the housekeeper's note complaining of the rising cost of candles. A bitter laugh worked its way out of her chest. Beeswax could become as dear as diamonds and still not jolt her as deeply as the sight of Mateo Cardea's arms around the Eagle's Etta. The sight had been a jagged knife to her heart and to her faith in her friend. And Mateo had only twisted the blade deeper when he made his suspicions clear.

Abruptly, she pushed away from the desk and crossed to the window. Staring out over the beauty she had coaxed from the earth, Portia forced herself to acknowledge the truth. Through a span of years, a disastrous marriage, neglect and isolation, some part of her old schoolgirl self had survived—and she still suffered an infatuation for Mateo Cardea.

It must end here and now. Any lingering softness or longing must be locked tight away. She thought she might go a little mad if Mateo also thought of her as helpless and weak. So she would meet him as a woman—composed, controlled, in charge of her own life, and to some extent, his as well.

She could not suppress a smile at the thought. Of all the men in her life, Mateo might be the only one she had never been able to best or ignore, but she had the whip hand over him now. Keeping it might not be easy, but it could prove to be a great source of satisfaction.

With a flourish, Portia threw open the casement. Breathing deeply, she acknowledged the subtle siren's call of the gardens. Abruptly, she decided to answer. Turning, she strode out of the library, and headed for the stairs. 'Dorrie!' she called. 'I've changed my mind! I'm going out!'

In general, Mateo's mood suffered when he found himself landlocked for any length of time. It seemed some part of him always listened, yearning for the time-less thrum and endless animation of the sea.

Today, though, the beauty of the day and the peace of the country conspired to silence his craving. A wonderful mosaic of woodland and farmland comprised this part of Berkshire. His mount stretched out beneath him, light on his feet. The faintest breeze blew across his face. It all made for a pleasant enough morning, but not enough to distract him from his pensive musings.

Dramatic, Portia had called him. Hardly the worst label that had been handed him. Hell, he'd been called everything from rascal to reprobate. But through months of war and a longer struggle to keep a business literally afloat, he'd always maintained his reputation for cheerful roguery. Even through the heat of battle, his crew teased time and again, he'd kept a fearsome grin on his face and his wit as sharp as his blade.

That had not been true in the last months. He'd been on the verge of a major business coup when he'd been struck hard by the grief of his father's passing. That unexpected tragedy had been difficult enough to deal with, but swift on its heels had come the reading of the will, and, with it, the added afflictions of anger and betrayal. They made for unfamiliar burdens, but Mateo had embraced them with a vengeance—as anchors in a life gone suddenly adrift.

He and his father had always had their differences. Leandro Cardea had been a serious and driven man, determined to live up to the ancient merchant tradition of his family. Mateo's lighthearted manner had at times driven him mad, as had his ideas for the business. Their disagreements had been loud; their heated debates, on the future of shipping and how best to steer the business in the hard years after the 1812 war with England, had been legendary. Mateo had been constitutionally unable to submit to the yoke of authority his father wished to confine him in, but despite different temperaments and differing opinions, he had thought they always shared the same end goal: the success of Cardea Shipping.

He did not know who he was without it. His first steps had been made along the teeming Philadelphia docks. He'd spent his childhood in that busy, dizzy atmosphere, learning arithmetic in the counting houses and how to read from warehouse manifests. He'd grown to manhood on board his father's ships, learning every aspect of the shipping business with sweat and tears and honest labour. His adult life had been comprised of an endless search for new markets, new imports, new revenue. For years he had worked, struggled and prepared for the day that he would take the helm of the family business.

And now he never would. So, yes—he had grabbed on to his anger with both hands and held tight. But it was an unaccustomed affliction, and it had grown heavier and more burdensome with each passing week. It would be a relief indeed to set it aside, but was he ready?

Not quite. Portia had been convincing last night. Something inside him wished to believe her, but he had a need to question her closely, and a rising desire to compare stories.

I need your help, she'd said, and she'd mentioned something about her own dilemma. It set his mind awhirl, with curiosity and, worse, a growing sense of suspicion. His father's heavy-handed manipulation blared loud and obvious, but could Portia truly have been unaware of her part in it?

As he'd already done hundreds of times, Mateo dragged his memory for details of the thwarted marriage scheme Leandro Cardea and the Earl of Winbury had attempted nearly nine years ago. Their timing had been preposterous. Mateo had been completely occupied with his sleek new schooner, and the opportunity for fortune, glory and adventure that privateering would give him and his crew. The notion of a marriage had been his father's last, desperate attempt to steer him from that course. Ever the rebel, Mateo had laughed at the idea—and at his father's clumsy choice of a bride.

Portia Varnsworth? A girl-child she'd been, with

plenty of pluck, but no more appeal than a younger sister. At the time he'd hoped she'd been just as incredulous as he. He'd written to her with that assumption, and certainly her response had reassured him. She was far too young to contemplate such a thing, she'd replied, and entirely too caught up with a landscaping project on her father's estate. And there was the Season for her to look forward to the following year. Mateo had sighed in relief and promptly forgot the entire scheme.

But he had thought of her occasionally, over the years. He remembered her shy smile and her willingness to listen. He'd been surprised and curious at the news of her marriage, and sympathetic when he'd heard of her husband's death. Had anyone asked, he would have confessed to remembering her fondly.

Until the day he'd sat in the solicitor's office and heard that his father had left the controlling interest in Cardea Shipping to her. Instead of leading the family legacy into the future, he would be working for Portia Varnsworth.

Mateo's shock had been complete. Doubt and suspicion had sprouted like weeds in his mind. And if he hadn't been so angry, he would have laughed at the—once again—impeccable bad timing of the thing.

At the thought he urged his mount to a quicker pace. Whatever the outcome of this meeting, *someone* had to quickly take control of Cardea Shipping. Ahead must be the lane that would take him to Stenbrooke. He took the turning, but after only a few minutes' travel he found himself distracted. Gazing about him, Mateo realised that, of a certainty, there was one thing about his childhood friend that had not changed.

Portia Tofton, née Varnsworth, was a gardener. Digging, planting, pruning, cutting, Portia had never been happier than when she was covered in muck. Looking about, it became clear that she had continued to indulge her beloved pastime here at Stenbrooke.

The lane he followed led first through a wooded grove, immaculately kept and dotted with the occasional early-blooming clump of monk's hood. Eventually, though, the wood thinned, giving way to a sweeping vista of rolling hills. Ahead the path diverged. To the left, over the tops of a grouping of trees, he caught sight of a peaked roof. On the right nestled a jewel of a lake, edged with flowering shrubs and spanned by a rustic stone bridge.

Mateo marvelled at the beauty of the scene. Then he spared a moment's empathy for the hardship some sea captain had endured in transporting the obviously exotic specimens.

He shook his head. The landscaping work here was awe-inspiring. Surely Brown or Repton had had a hand in it. Had Portia kept this up herself after her husband's passing? But of course she had. Care and attention to detail were evident in every direction.

It was ongoing even now, he noted, catching sight of several labourers grouped on the far side of the bridge. Standing thigh-high in the lake, they were repairing one of the arches, judging from the steady ring of hammer against stone. He watched them idly until he reached the fork in the lane, and then he turned his mount's head in the direction of the house.

Until suddenly his brain processed what his eyes had just seen. He hauled on the reins, startling the animal, and spun him swiftly around. Raising a hand, he cast his best weather eye towards the lake again. Yes. One of the labourers had moved to the edge of the stone pedestal and into view. A labourer in skirts.

A sharp bark of laughter broke free. Yes, he mused, men did die. Enterprises failed, empires grew and nations were born. Mateo had learned that lesson the hard way. One had only to look about with an unjaundiced eye to know that change and upheaval were the only persevering truths in this life.

Perhaps that explained, then, why he should be struck with unexpected delight at the odd tableau before him. It was something of a relief to discover that some things never did change.

The ghost of a smile flitted about his mouth. It was even more of a relief to once again find pleasure in a simple, unexpected moment. He let the stranglehold on his anger slip—just a little—and spurred his mount towards the lake.

Chapter Three

'That's done it now, Mrs Tofton.'

Portia's ears still rang from the blow of the mallet. Her foreman's voice sounded tinny and distant, though he loomed close by her side.

'You can let go. That's the last one.'

She did, shaking out the strain in her arms and stepping back. The damaged pedestal of her stone arch bridge was nearly repaired, she saw with satisfaction.

'Aye, that does it,' Newman echoed her sentiment. 'A bit of mortar and it'll be right as rain.' He turned as another man splashed up. 'We'll not be needing another block after all, Billings. You can throw that one back in the cart. We're nearly done now.'

Billings turned, but cast a resentful eye back towards the bridge. 'Can I be gettin' back to the orchard now? New branches don't train themselves.'

'Yes, of course.' Portia grasped her water-logged skirts and started back towards shore, as well. 'Thank you, Billings. I am sorry I had to tear you away from your trees.' She sighed. 'Perhaps next year we shall be able to hire some more permanent labourers.'

'Aye, well, and if you do, let them waddle after Newman here. I'm fine alone in the orchard, but if you be wantin' a crop this year or next, you'll be lettin' me get on with me work.'

'Oh, go on, you old crosspatch,' she said, smiling over her shoulder at him. 'Newman, can you finish up on your own? I suppose I must get back to the house and change before our company arrives.'

'You've left it a bit late.' Billings shifted his burden and spat casually into the water. 'Leastaways, you did if your company's dark, broad as that yonder oak and near as tall.'

Portia's gaze followed the thrust of his chin towards the shore before the impact of his words truly hit her. With a gasp, she splashed to a halt and dropped her skirts. A horse stood tethered near the pony cart they had used to transport stone and supplies, and striding down the slight incline towards the water came Mateo Cardea.

Tall and strong, with sun glinting off his dark curls and shining boots, he advanced with a purposeful tread. Portia's mouth gaped open as he failed to stop at the shore's edge, but the chiselled lines of his face were set and determined. Without hesitation he strode right into the water and towards her. She stared, noting his furrowed brow and the large straw hat dangling from his fingers.

Water sloshed around her knees as he drew to a halt in front of her. Her breath caught.

And then he smiled.

Unfair! The cry emanated from the vulnerable part of Portia's soul, the one that she had spent just this morning locking away. It was a nonsensical notion, but the sudden pounding of her heart felt eerily like the bang of a fist on a closed door.

Where was the angry, brooding man who'd hurled insults at her last night? She searched his face, but the stormy countenance and dangerous gaze had fled like clouds before sunshine. And left only the visage that had fuelled her adolescent dreams for years.

The real irony was that it was a face that might have been made for anger and brooding. Bold, dark eyes flashed under arched brows and amidst a longish, angular face. The great Cardea nose might have overwhelmed any other man's features, but on Mateo was balanced beautifully by his wide, sensual mouth and irresistible tangle of curls. Masculine splendour shone down on her, warmer than the rays of the sun. And suddenly Portia wobbled, as weak in the knees as if she truly had spent too long in the heat.

Mateo stepped close and grasped her arm.

Billings snorted as he sloshed past them. 'Coming through, Mrs Tofton.'

Newman followed without comment, and without turning his gaze in their direction. Portia barely noticed. She watched, mesmerized, as Mateo's other hand lifted, rose and disappeared above her head. She jumped, startled at the gentle touch of his fingers moving in her hair.

'Forgive me,' he said softly. 'But—' Brown and capable, his hand hovered before her face, holding a large chip of stone. Comprehension dawned, along with a flush of embarrassment. She suppressed it and watched him toss the thing into the water. Grasping the straw hat where it dangled beneath their arms, he offered it up. 'You'll want your hat, Peeve,' he said quite casually. 'Your nose is turning red.'

She lost her fight with the advancing tide of warmth. And just the thought that he might notice turned a simple blush into a spiralling wave of heat. She tried calling herself to task. She'd meant to demonstrate her complete indifference to his anger, to present a picture of a woman occupied with her own pursuits, fully capable of commanding her own destiny. She had *not* meant to blush like a girl at his first words or to meet him standing knee-deep in the lake.

But this was the Mateo of her youth—and somehow their bizarre situation seemed fitting. He towered over her, one eyebrow elevated, a matching wry grin pulling at the opposite corner of his mouth. Portia drew a long, shuddering breath. It struck her hard—that oh-so-familiar gleam in his dark eyes, full of good-natured mischief and just the smallest hint of irony.

She pulled abruptly away from his touch and struck out on her own for the shore. 'Don't call me that, please.'

He followed, literally in her wake. 'I will not, of course, if you dislike it. But I assure you that today at least, I meant it only in affection.'

'Nevertheless.' Portia climbed the springy bank, bent down and grasped her shoes.

'Shall I call you Mrs Tofton, then?' he asked with a quizzically raised brow.

She heard the unasked question. He wondered why she did not use her hereditary title. And deliberately she did not answer. 'That is my name,' she answered in the same tone. 'But why don't you just call me Portia, as you used to?' She summoned a smile. 'I beg your pardon for meeting you in such disarray. My foreman said we had to act quickly to prevent further damage to the bridge, and I'm afraid I cast all other considerations aside.'

She lowered her gaze as he drew close, and caught sight of his ruined footwear. 'Oh,' she gasped, 'your boots!' She glared up at him. 'Whatever possessed you, Mateo? There was no need of that.'

'But it was necessary—after my display of spectacularly bad manners, I feared you would strike out for the opposite shore at the sight of me.' He still held her floppy hat. With delicate movements, he lifted it high. Moving slowly, as if he worked not to frighten her, he settled it on her head.

She stood stiff and ram-rod straight. He followed the line of ribbons with his fingertips and began to tie them under her chin.

'I suppose I could not have blamed you if you had,' he spoke low and his jaw tensed. 'I owe you an apology, *cara*. No matter the situation, I should not have lashed out at you like that.'

She flinched at the old endearment. He was too close. She was too flustered. She'd wanted him to look at her, *see* her, but she'd imagined it at more of a distance. Portia's heart began to flit inside her chest like a bird in a cage.

She pushed his hands away and stepped back. 'I'm perfectly capable of tying my own ribbons, thank you,' she said irritably. She breathed deep, needing to regain control of her wayward emotions and the situation. *You aren't a love-struck young girl any more*, she reminded herself fiercely.

'There is no need for an apology.' There, that was better. Her tone, at least, sounded tightly controlled. 'The circumstances are highly unusual. I suppose anyone might have jumped to the conclusions you did.'

His dark gaze roved over her. He said nothing for a long minute, just watched her closely while she fiddled with half-tied ribbons. 'Ah, but I begin to see now,' he said. 'Anyone might have suspected the worst, but you didn't expect it of me.'

Some heavy emotion weighted his voice. Guilt? Sorrow? She wished she knew which she would have preferred it to be.

'And that changes much of what I thought would pass between us.' His brow furrowed as he stared down at her. 'And what do I do with you now, I wonder?'

Portia stiffened. 'Not a thing! It's not your place to *do* anything at all with me. In fact, I'd say the shoe was quite on the other foot.'

He winced. 'I deserved that, did I not?'

'And far more.' She raked her gaze down the length of him. 'Hard as you may find it to believe, Mateo, I've had important things on my mind—and not a one of them involved a scheme to trap you into marriage.'

He returned her speculative gaze. 'Do you know—I think it would have been better for me, had you been the villainess I suspected you to be.'

How was she supposed to answer that?

'Portia! Are you down here still?'

The shrill call saved her from the necessity. She glanced up and caught sight of a glimpse of colour through the trees. Many times over the years, she'd had reason to be grateful to Dorrie, but she could recall nothing like the great tide of relief that swept through her now.

'Portia?'

'Here, Dorinda!' she answered with a wave as Dorrie erupted from the trees at a trot.

'Portia,' Dorrie called, urgency alive in her expression, as well as in the unusual quickness of her step. 'Vickers tells me a rider was spotted...' Her gait faltered. 'Oh, yes. I see I'm too late.'

Portia fidgeted as the heavy weight of her companion's gaze fell on her.

Dorrie let out an audible moan. 'Oh, Portia, dear! How could you?'

From beside her came an unexpected, but completely familiar sound. From this broad-shouldered hulk of a sea captain came an almost boyish snort.

Portia's eyes widened. How many times had she heard that exact sound? Hundreds, if not thousands. It triggered a whirlwind of old emotion: exasperation, irritation and fleeting camaraderie. Visions danced in her head, of infuriating pranks, of whispered *risqué* stories she'd tried desperately to overhear, and of the pair of them united, usually to get one of her brothers either into or out of trouble.

It was a sound from her past. But today it ignited a great, yearning well of hope for the future. The old Mateo Cardea would have helped her in an instant. Perhaps he was still in there somewhere.

And perhaps he would enjoy getting to know the new Portia Tofton.

Her heart pounding, she moved forwards, beckoning Dorrie closer. 'It's just a little lake water, Dorrie,' she cajoled. 'And you're not late, but just in time to meet Mr Cardea. Come, and I will introduce you.'

Mateo watched Portia hurry away. A great wave of guilt and confusion had swamped him at her earlier words. He allowed it to fade a bit, allowed it, even, to be replaced with a wholly ungentlemanly sense of satisfaction. He'd rattled her. Good.

He had a sneaking suspicion that it would be in his interest to keep Portia unsettled. And a little rattling was no more than she deserved. After all, she'd rocked his moorings loose last night. And she'd done it again today, too, without even so much as trying. Ah, but the picture she had presented just now had been priceless! Pink-cheeked, covered in rock dust and knee-deep in water—*Dio*, but she'd been the most beautiful sight. He'd seen the contentment on her face and the glint of mischief shining brighter than the gold flecks in her eyes, and he'd forgotten his purpose.

What was he to do now? He closed his eyes. Exactly what he'd intended, he supposed. Her artless confusion and hesitant manner convinced him of her innocence, but changed nothing, really.

Mateo had arrived in England with a purpose. He'd meant to rebuff Portia Tofton, thwart any attempt at manipulation and get his company back. Failing that, he meant to say a last goodbye to his old life—and move on to the new. Old expectations were of no more use than a leaky skiff. A clever man knew when to abandon them and move on.

'Mateo, may I introduce my cousin and companion?' She approached again with the new arrival in tow. 'Miss Dorinda Tofton.'

'*Piacere*, Miss Tofton.' Mateo bowed respectfully over her hand. 'It is indeed a pleasure to make your acquaintance. My old friend is fortunate indeed to be surrounded by such beauty.'

'Oh, yes,' Miss Tofton agreed with a sweep of her hand towards the lake. 'Is it not the most charming prospect?'

'Nearly as charming as her companion.' He delivered the compliment smoothly, but with just the right touch of sincerity. A flush of pleasure pinked her pale cheeks, but she did not grow uneasy.

'And almost as pleasant as a reunion with an old acquaintance.' Miss Tofton knew how to play the game. She glanced over at Portia and her brow creased once more. 'Please do not allow the manner of our greeting to dishearten you, sir. Though it may not look it, we have been awaiting your arrival with the utmost anticipation.'

'Yes, yes, Dorrie.' Portia grew impatient with the fussing. 'I do thank you for coming today, Mateo. We must talk of your company, of course, and I have something of the utmost importance to discuss with you.'

She called out suddenly to the men preparing to leave in the pony cart. 'Billings, Newman! Just a moment, please!'

She turned back to Mateo. 'Dorinda is right, though; I really must change before we speak. Perhaps you would care for a stroll about the gardens?' Mateo caught the significant glance she shot towards her companion and wondered what it foretold. 'I would love you to see some of Stenbrooke before we discuss our…troubles.'

She smiled sweetly before he could protest. 'We'll bring your mount along to the stables, and you can get acquainted with Dorinda.' Her hand swept towards the bridge. 'It's quite safe now, and there are some lovely vistas on the Cascade Walk.'

Again, he was given no chance to respond. In a flash she was gone up the hill and climbing into the cart. One of the labourers hitched his hired horse to the cart and jumped on the back as it jerked to a start.

'Well…' Miss Tofton sighed as she waved them off '…it's an unorthodox reception you've had, to be sure, Mr Cardea, but as Portia tells me you've been acquainted since infancy, I gather you won't be too surprised by it.'

Curbing his impatience, Mateo laughed. 'Surprised that Portia let a landscaping project distract her from every other concern? Not at all, ma'am.'

She glanced askance at him. 'I see you do indeed know Portia well.'

He gestured towards the lake and they set off at an easy pace. 'Perhaps it surprises you that a half-Italian merchant sea captain should be on intimate terms with the family of an English earl?'

Her denial came quickly, and, if he were any judge, in sincere terms. 'Not at all,' she assured him. 'Portia has explained how close your fathers were. I have to say, I was more than a little jealous when she spoke of the visits back and forth your families undertook. It sounds infinitely more exciting than my own childhood.'

'I admit it was great fun, in most instances.' He

smiled down at her. 'And I will tell you, over the years, in all the months we spent together, there were always constants,' he said. He held three fingers up. 'During each and every visit, my father and Portia's would spend at least one evening drinking and recounting the story of La Incandescent Clarisse.' He folded down one finger and laughed at the sight of her rolled eyes. 'Yes, I see you are acquainted with the story.'

He ticked off another finger. 'At least one of Portia's brothers would rake up a scrape that I would be forced to rescue him from.' He raised a brow. 'Again, you do not look shocked.'

The last finger he wagged in her direction. 'And three—whenever Portia went missing, we all knew to look in the gardens.' He dropped his hand and sighed. 'I have only just finished telling myself that in a world of chaos, it is most comfortable to know that some things do not change.'

Miss Tofton tucked her hand a little more firmly into the crook of his arm. For a few moments they walked in silence and Mateo welcomed the cool comfort of the shade as the path led them through a grove of birches.

'I confess it is a relief to hear you speak fondly of Portia and her family,' her companion said after a few minutes. 'I realise that you have not had a chance to discuss…things, but I am very grateful to think that we might have your help.'

Curiosity quickened his pulse. But as so often happened with women, his silence had encouraged Miss Tofton to continue. 'One thing I know from experience, Mr Cardea, and I would ask you to remember, is that a woman alone does not have an easy path in this world.'

'None of us alone do, ma'am.'

'You are right, of course, but I profess that it is particularly hard for a woman; we have so many more obstacles and fewer options, you see. A woman in such a situation must display more courage, resilience and determination than a man.' She let go of his arm and crossed over to a pretty little bench. She ran her fingers over the scrolled ironwork, but did not sit. 'Portia in particular is strong in many ways, but vulnerable in others. She's had a difficult time of it since her husband died. Aside from the obvious repercussions, there's been the unfortunate notoriety…' She shook her head. 'And debt—you would not believe some of the indignities she's been exposed to in settling James Talbot's debts.'

Debt Mateo could well believe. Even as a young man, J. T. Tofton's tastes had run towards high stakes, fast horses and loose women—tastes that a mere squire's son could not often indulge. But notoriety, indignities? The companion's words and manner suggested something more than a husband who lived a little beyond his means. A sharp spike of curiosity peaked inside him, followed by a faint sense of shame.

'You will be happy to hear, perhaps, that one area in which she has stood fast is in her belief in you, sir.'

'Indeed?' Shame quickly outpaced any other reaction.

'Yes. You must excuse me, but with no personal acquaintance of you, sir, I counselled her to proceed cautiously. I thought you might naturally have wondered if Portia had any prior knowledge of or design in your father's actions.'

'Naturally,' he echoed weakly.

She pierced him with her stare. 'But Portia stood staunch in your defence and has claimed all these weeks that you knew her better than to suppose so.' Her expression darkened. 'I hope you will deserve her faith in you, sir.'

As a warning, it was most effective. Mateo fought back another surge of guilt and tried instead to focus on just what all this might mean: for him and for Cardea Shipping. 'I hope I will, too,' he said. He held out his arm once more. 'Shall we go back and find out?'

Portia changed quickly to dry stockings and her prettiest day gown of palest yellow, the one that Dorrie said made the most of the dreaded sun-kissed streaks in her hair. On the verge of leaving her room again, she gasped. Her hair! She'd nearly forgotten. Bending over to peer in the mirror, she moaned at the liberal coating of rock dust.

Well, she was not going to ring for her maid and wait an eternity to be re-coiffed. Instead, she took up a brush herself and stroked until her arm was tired and her plain brown locks were clean and shining. A quick high knot, a tuck of the wayward strands that would soon be working free in any case, and she was off, tripping down the stairs and rounding the turn at the bottom towards the back of the house.

Vickers stood outside the dining room, giving low-voiced instructions to a footman. Portia nodded and, trying not to give the appearance of hurrying, she headed straight for the morning room, where double doors led out to the veranda. They stood open, bathing the room in sunshine and warmth. Despite her urgency, she could not resist pausing on the threshold.

Here. This exact spot—her favourite. Her eyes closed. She loved to stand here, poised at the juncture of inside and out, balancing on the common point between untamed nature and domesticity. Beeswax and baking bread scented the air behind her, the earthy smell of the sun-soaked lawn in front. In between. Neither here nor there. The perfect metaphor for Portia Tofton.

Voices sounded ahead. Her eyes snapped open and she crossed to the stone balustrade. There. They had reached the ha-ha; Mateo was assisting Dorrie over the stile at the far end of the lawn. Portia watched closely as they approached. Could she do it? Could she make him understand what all of this meant to her?

Carefully, she tried to gauge Mateo's mood. Certainly he appeared relaxed as he talked easily with Dorinda. Portia stared, transfixed as the breeze tossed his curls and he laughed out loud. Their words were indistinct, lost in the crunch of gravel underneath their feet as they crossed the path, but as they approached her spot on the edge of the veranda, his tousled head rose. He looked up and met Portia's gaze.

They grew closer, and he continued in his steady regard, until gradually it turned into a slow survey, down the length of her and back up. Something shifted inside of her, a thrill of awakening excitement, long gone but not forgotten. She gripped the balustrade beside her.

'Portia,' he said gravely as they reached her, 'I was just telling Miss Tofton how impressed I am with your gardens.'

Dorrie smiled. 'And I was just about to tell Mr Cardea how much more impressed with Stenbrooke he would be, had he seen it before all of your hard work.'

Mateo's brow furrowed. Portia could see his mind working, remembering. 'It was not in good shape, then?' he asked, but he said it as if he already knew the answer.

Portia merely shook her head.

'You know,' he mused, 'at first, as I rode in, I could only think of harried crews of seamen struggling to keep your more exotic specimens alive to make it in to port.' He smiled. 'But I also thought to myself that one of the great landscapers must have had a hand in all of this.'

'Yes,' Dorinda said firmly. 'She did.'

'Oh, don't tease him, Dorrie.' Portia smiled and lifted her brows at the pair of them. She wanted Mateo at his ease for this interview. 'Thank you for giving me a moment to repair myself.'

His gaze travelled once more over the square neckline of her gown. 'It was my pleasure.'

Her pulse jumped. 'Come,' she said. She gestured to the elegant table and comfortably padded chairs set up in the shade. 'Please, join us for some refreshments. This is one of our loveliest spots.'

'Thank you.' After he had seated them, he took his own chair and cast a smile at Dorinda. 'When you mentioned the state of the place, I suddenly recalled the time when Portia's aunt passed on and we all discovered that she would inherit this estate. It wasn't until just now that I remembered that it was supposed to be a run-down old spot. Her brothers teased her unmercifully.'

He turned his gaze to Portia and she noticed tiny

lines at the corner of his dark eyes. 'Brothers do tend
to believe in the right to cruelty towards their siblings,
no? And in Portia's case, I believe they regarded it as a
sacred duty. Especially when they heard the estate was
to come to her on her marriage. They spent hours specu-
lating how decrepit this place would become before
Portia found someone to marry her.'

Dorrie choked back a laugh. 'Well, marry she did,
and a good thing it was for me too,' she said staunchly.
'I've hardly been as comfortable and happy in my life
as I have since Portia graciously took me in.'

Portia returned her fond smile, but Dorrie continued.
'And despite their meanness, her brothers were not that
far off the mark. Of course, I was just a visitor then, but
the house and grounds were both in a terrible condition
when Portia and James Talbot moved in.'

Perhaps Portia should not be watching Mateo so
closely. Tension throbbed through her until she thought
he must be able to sense it. But if she had not been
paying such close attention, she might have missed
it. There. Just the smallest wince at the corners of
Mateo's eyes. Not a smile line, either; it showed up at
the mention of J.T.'s name. She had the fleeting thought
that it resembled pain—or perhaps she only thought
so because of the stabbing clench of her stomach that
occurred for the same reason.

He hid it well, by turning his gaze about him. Despite
her anxiety, Portia felt a thrill of pride. She could not
be falsely modest about the beautiful prospect; she'd
worked too hard to achieve it.

'Do you mean to say that this—' he gestured '—is
all your design?'

'It is,' Dorrie answered for her. She glanced at Portia and then graced Mateo with a determined smile. 'And since there is yet no sign of the tea cart, why don't the two of you walk along the front of the house? Portia can tell you about the changes she's made.'

'A tempting notion, Miss Tofton, were this a social call. But it is not. Portia has stated that she had no notion of my father's intentions and I've offered my apology for jumping to conclusions, but I would like to hear the particulars, if you please.' Mateo paused, his lips pressed tightly together.

'Ah, the devil!' he finally exclaimed, pushing away from the table. 'This is a damnable snarl we've found ourselves in and whether it goes your way or mine in the end, we need to get it untangled—and the sooner, the better.' He sighed. 'But I suspect that first we must find out how we ended up here. To begin with, I'd like to hear more of the dilemma you mentioned last—'

Portia jumped to her feet. 'Please, Mateo?' she interrupted before Dorrie could catch a hint of her late-night activities. 'I promise your questions will be answered. And, in fact, there may be a solution to make both of us happy. But if you will bear with me, I'd like to start by showing you some of the history of this house.'

'Portia…' He sighed. '*Cara*, for me, this is already painful enough. I just wish to be done with it and truly there is some urgency…'

She turned a pleading gaze on him and he trailed to a stop. She thought he meant to balk—but then he heaved a sigh.

'For a moment,' he relented. 'And then, Portia, we talk.'

Grudgingly, he stood and offered his arm. She

took it, and then led him on a slow revolution about the house. She spoke ardently as they went, trying to convey her passion along with a picture of the estate as it used to be. And trying to subdue the hum of passion that coursed through her with every step.

But it was difficult. Her head might know how useless and more, how stupid, it was to fall into old patterns. Her heart might shrink, fearful of trusting the man who'd scorned her first, fledgling love and bruised her tender, young soul. But her body—her traitorous body didn't care. It lit up for him, surging with awareness, trembling with intense response to his nearness.

How could it not? He was Mateo, and he was beautiful. Not the right word, perhaps, for a sun-browned example of strong and robust manhood, but the one she chose none the less. It was the beauty of character that he possessed—stamped into his laughing dark eyes, moulded into the kindness, the confidence and the absolute assurance of his manner. It called to her, just as it always had. And she could not answer.

So she talked instead of the choking ivy that they'd had to tear down, the sagging columns that had barely supported the first-floor balcony, the gradual replacement of the casement windows and large sections of the slate roof. She used every excuse to pull away, to walk ahead and remove herself from danger.

To her relief, he paid close attention, questioning her about the house and grounds, and when they circled back to the veranda he took his seat once more with a shake of his head.

'I admit to being suitably impressed,' he said to Dorrie as he held Portia's chair. 'Portia's descriptions are so vivid that I can nearly see the sad state of disrepair that she first encountered here. The enormity of what you've accomplished is humbling.' He gazed about at the tranquil scene. 'I can only imagine the hue and cry and mess of reconstruction. It must have taken an army of labourers.'

Dorrie chuckled. 'That's exactly the remark that all visitors make.'

Conversation was interrupted by the arrival of the refreshments. Portia poured: tea for Dorrie and coffee for Mateo. Strong, hot and sweet—she recalled exactly how he liked it. The quirk of his lips told her that he noticed. He sat back with a sigh of satisfaction.

'I'm glad you realise the scope of the work we've done here, Mateo,' Portia began, ignoring her own tea. 'We started with the neglected fields first, and the orchards and the dairy. Once we had an actual income, we began on the house and the gardens.' She leaned forwards. 'But we've never had an army of hired workers. Everything we've done has been through the effort of our small staff and tenants. We've all worked hard and made something useful and beautiful. I know that you, of all people, understand what happens when people share goals, work and rewards.'

He stared. She thought he looked curious and a little resentful. 'I think I know what you are trying to say, Portia. You've done an admirable job here.' He pressed his lips together once more. 'I suspect you mean to retain your control of Cardea Shipping, but before you decide, I ask that you listen to me, please—'

She cut him off. 'No, what I'm trying to convey is that we are a family, Mateo. All of us here at Stenbrooke.' China clinked as she pushed her cup to the side. 'And that is why I need you to help me save it.'

Mateo sat upright, jolted out of his customary lounge by the startling unpredictability of Portia's words. In fact, that was not remotely what he'd been expecting her to say. He'd thought she'd been laying the groundwork, preparing him to accept her as the head of *his* company. Instead—

'Save Stenbrooke?' he asked. 'From what? Explain please.'

Her pretty face twisted with pain. 'You've complained that your father betrayed you. I find myself in complete sympathy, for mine failed me.'

'I'm going to require a more thorough explanation than that.'

'First I will tell you one last time—I have had no hand in your misfortune. I had no earthly idea of what your father was about, to will me controlling interest in your business.'

'It is true, Mr Cardea,' chimed in her companion. 'I was here when her brother's solicitor arrived bearing the news. I can testify to her utter shock.'

'I panicked, in fact,' Portia said. 'I thought something dreadful must have happened to you.'

Mateo saw sincerity in her eyes and an urgent need to be believed. 'I'll accept that—since we've met again, I already strongly suspected it. But what does it have to do with Stenbrooke?'

'Nothing yet.'

Mateo caught his first glimpse of hesitation. He leaned forwards.

'I was bewildered, but Anthony's man didn't have

any answers. I sent a letter with him back to Hempshaw, thinking my brother would have them—or at least have news of you.'

'And did he?'

She shook her head. Mateo watched several heavy strands of her honeyed hair fall from confinement and curl against the slender column of her neck. 'No, neither. So I immediately sent a message to you, asking you to come and help me decipher this mess.' Her gaze fell away. 'I realise it might have been short, and perhaps awkward. That was precisely how I felt, considering how long it had been...and especially considering the nature of our last contact.'

Her hand rose and hovered near the bodice of her gown. Mateo recognised her obvious unease and thought back to her letter. It had indeed been curt and cryptic—and it had helped fuel his rising fury and suspicion. He sighed. It didn't matter now, he supposed, but he was surprised at the intense relief that came with the knowledge that she had not conspired against him.

'It was only a day or so later that yet another solicitor came calling—but for a very different reason.' Portia exchanged a pained look with Miss Tofton. 'He carried with him a deed of conveyance and informed me that Stenbrooke was no longer mine.'

Mateo shook his head. His brain hurt from the sudden shifts in this conversation. 'How can that be?'

'That was exactly our reaction,' Miss Tofton said indignantly.

'It could be—' and now Portia's voice rang with bitterness '—because of my rotten blighter of a husband.'

'Portia!'

Mateo felt inclined to echo her companion's gasp of shock.

'I beg your pardon, Dorrie, but you are well aware of my feelings and Mateo might as well be, too.'

'But to speak so of the dead…' She shuddered.

'Will not bother him in the least,' Mateo assured her. He turned to Portia. 'Please, go on.'

She nodded. 'As you said, Stenbrooke came into my possession on my marriage. It was meant to be secured to me and my children in the marriage settlements. Somehow, my father failed to see it done.' She fought to keep her resentment from overpowering her. 'I have no notion how my father could have neglected to take care with the single most important thing in my life, but the fact remains that he didn't. Stenbrooke therefore became my husband's property, according to law.' She paused. 'And I had no idea. It was an oversight that no one saw fit to inform me of.'

Drawing a deep breath, she continued. 'J.T. knew of it, obviously. He used the estate as a stake in a card game. He lost my home over a hand of faro—another fact that he neglected to tell me before he went and got himself so ignominiously killed.'

There was not enough room in Mateo's head for all his myriad reactions to this conversation. A whirlwind of conflicting thoughts and feelings set his temples pounding. Ridiculous, then, that the one at the top was an ugly sense of satisfaction that perhaps Portia had not loved her husband.

'I am sorry to hear it,' he managed to say.

'Oh, but you don't even know the worst of it!' Miss Tofton exclaimed. 'This new owner is craven. He didn't even have the decency to face Portia; he merely sent along a newly hired solicitor to deliver the news. And that dreadful man was in turn evasive and cruel. He said that his employer is an experimental agriculturist who is always in search of new ground for his research. He said it was quite likely that all of this would be ploughed under if ever he got his hands on Stenbrooke!'

Mateo narrowed his focus, and watched Portia intensely.

'I want you to help me,' she said simply.

He exhaled sharply. 'And how do you expect me to do that? Portia, you must know why I've come. I want to make arrangements to buy back your interest in Cardea Shipping.'

She shook her head. 'I won't sell it to you.'

He closed his eyes and tried to ignore the twisting of his stomach. 'Perhaps just the Baltimore office, then. I started that branch myself, in the face of my father's opposition. I confess, I don't have enough ready capital of my own to buy you out completely, but I could likely manage just the one office.'

She shook her head again.

Now there was anger churning inside of him along with everything else. 'Portia—'

'No.' She interrupted him yet again. 'There will be no sale.' Tension shone apparent in the thin line of her mouth and in every stiff angle of her body. 'Instead I propose a simple trade. Stenbrooke for Cardea Shipping.' Her hands gripped the end of the table until her knuckles whitened. 'Buy Stenbrooke, Mateo, and sign it back over to me. Give me my life back, and I'll give you yours.'

* * *

Portia clenched her teeth, her fists, and every muscle at her command as she waited for Mateo's answer. He would agree. Of course he would. He had to.

His gaze, staring so boldly into hers, broke away. He exhaled sharply and pushed back from the table, crossing over to the stone balustrade. Leaning heavily, he stared out over the garden and beyond for several silent minutes. Portia's head began to ache with the strain.

'Why do you not go to your brother for assistance?' he asked at last.

'I have,' she said, helpless against the bitterness that coloured her tone again. 'Nothing there has changed since we were children. I am still the youngest, the baby of the family, and a woman besides. What need have I to live alone on my own estate?' She rose to her feet and crossed over to the potted *rosa rugosa*. With quick, sharp movements she began to pick fading leaves off it, keeping an eye on his bent, still form all the while.

'Anthony cannot spare the expense, and if he had that sort of ready income, he'd be honour bound to put it into his own estate. He sees no reason why I should not be happy to pack my things and move back to Hempshaw. His countess is overrun, you see, exhausted from birthing four boys in six years, and could use a bit of help with keeping them in hand.'

Mateo let loose a sharp bark of laughter, although there was little humour in it. 'That is Anthony all over.'

'Yes,' she said flatly. 'But I won't have it. I am tired of being let down by the men who are supposed to have my best interests at heart. I want my home, Mateo. I want my independence.'

'At the very least she should be allowed to use the London house,' Dorrie complained. That had been her favourite plan for their future. 'But her brother is adamant about saving expenses and has leased it out.'

Finally Mateo turned and looked at her.

'The rest of the world would no doubt agree with my brother,' she said. 'But I had hoped that once you were here, and saw what we've done, you would understand. We've both had everything we wanted in our grasp, only to have it snatched away.'

His expression was carefully blank, but she could see the tension in the stiff line of his jaw. 'I don't have enough to purchase an estate like this.' He gestured about him.

'Perhaps not, but between the two of us, together in possession of a company like Cardea Shipping, surely we could, ah, liquidate some assets?' Her spine had gone as rigid as stone, but she would not plead, even now. 'I realise that the prospect is not pleasant, but it must be better than the alternative.' She let the unspoken threat hover.

But Mateo's head had come up. 'I suppose it could be done. We've the *Lily Fair* just in at Portsmouth with a cargo of flax-seed and fine walnut. And the agent there is as good as any we have in the company. The cargo itself will fetch a fair price, but once she's unloaded, we could put it about that we'd like to sell her.' His hands clenched on the balustrade behind him. '*Dio*, but I hate to give her up. She once made the run from Philadelphia to Liverpool in sixteen days, just two off the record.'

He stared unseeing at the terrace. 'Her captain will be fair disappointed. I'll have to reshuffle, offer him something special to keep him and his crew content. I'll have to see her refitted, renegotiate with the insurers.' He sighed then, and met her gaze. 'But there's no doubt she'll fetch a fine price—perhaps enough so that with what I have set back, we won't need to sacrifice any others. I'll start the process.' He grimaced. 'And with both of our signatures upon the papers, there can be no questioning the order.'

He abandoned the balustrade and began to pace, his expression lighter than she'd yet seen. 'There'll be no need for me to linger, though. With her reputation, she'll sell quickly. Our agents can handle the rest. And all you really need is funds. My own ship is waiting. A few days to draft up the exchange, leave instructions for proceeds from the sale to be sent to you, and I can be on my way.'

'No,' Portia said yet again.

Mateo stopped. He pivoted on his heel and turned to face her.

'You must stay,' she explained. 'My brother is seriously annoyed that I will not let Stenbrooke go. He tells me there is nothing to be done and has forbidden his solicitors to aid me in this. After all the strife following his death, my husband's solicitor will not even admit me any longer.'

Now she was on her feet and moving. 'I have serious questions about the validity of this conveyance, but no one will give me any answers. I broached the subject of buying the estate back with the new owner's solicitor, but he would not even agree to present the idea to his employer. This whole transaction seems cloaked in mystery, and no one will see it.' She turned away, allowing sour frustration to leak into her words. 'I am shushed like a child, patted on the head and ordered to pack my things.' She spun back. 'I am sick to death of it.'

She watched Mateo draw a deep breath. The excitement drained from his face even as it began to settle into an expression of exaggerated patience.

'I'm afraid you don't understand,' he began. 'There are business matters—'

She fought back a gasp. 'Don't you dare!' She could not believe it. How did he dare to patronise her after all she'd told him? 'Do not even think to speak to me in that reasonable tone! I've reached my limit, Mateo. I tell you now that I do not care what pressing business awaits you in Philadelphia. It has become painfully obvious that no one will take me seriously in this matter. Well, I am done being bullied, silenced and ignored. Clearly I need a man to aid me in this—and *you* are the only viable candidate.'

Anger flashed in his dark eyes and his jaw clenched. He moved away from the balustrade and began to pace from one end of the veranda to the other.

'You will stay and help me with this matter until Stenbrooke's deed is in my possession. Only then will I give you Cardea Shipping.' Though she suffered a pang of guilt at his resentment, on that she must stand firm. 'I am sorry to have to insist, but every other avenue is blocked.' She tossed him a bitter glance. 'I suppose I should not have hoped for sympathy. I doubt you have any notion how it might feel to be left without choices.'

'Until now?' he ground out.

She raised her chin.

'And you would be wrong in any case,' he continued bitterly. 'You knew my father.' He heaved a sigh of resignation. 'He was a good man, as I know you will agree, but a hard one, as well, and one absolutely committed to his own path. You cannot imagine the frustration I have felt, the times I thought I must be crushed under his thumb. And now I find myself back in the same position.' He raised an eyebrow at her. 'Albeit, under a smaller, daintier thumb.'

Portia's breath hitched. She'd been a fool to hope that they could get through this without harming each other's feelings once again. But she *would* be free at last. She was determined. She was also fully aware of the great irony here; that the one man she must force to help her gain her independence was the only one she'd ever truly wished to give it up for.

She straightened her shoulders. 'I would not place you in such a position if I could think of another way. So I suppose it is you who must decide. In the end you will get your legacy back, but you will have to wait, and I am afraid you will have to adjust to the weight of my thumb.' She summoned her courage. 'So—what will it be? Will you allow my hand on the rudder? Or is it too great a price to pay?'

His eyes glittered. 'You may have the upper hand here, Portia, but I must insist that you keep your hands off my rudder.'

Careful. His pride had already been dealt a massive blow. She must handle this delicately, but the thought of surrendering her fate into the hands of another man made her reckless.

'This is a crucial point, Mateo. We act as equals, or we do not act at all. I will not blithely turn this over for you to handle, while I sit at home. If you cannot accept me as a partner in this, then you will not get Cardea Shipping back.'

It was incongruous, the sight of him and his restless energy and gathering ire. He drew the eye, demanded attention, and looked completely out of place here in the midst of her green and tranquil haven. She blanched as he spun on his heel and approached her. The storm clouds were back, gathering across his brow.

'So you do not trust me with your business, Portia?' he asked in an acid tone. 'No doubt you think I'll be distracted by a stray wench and forget the weighty matters at hand.' He frowned. 'Careful, *cara*, you begin to sound like my father.'

'Nevertheless.' Her chin thrust even higher. 'What is it to be, then? Will you accept my terms? Or is the price too dear?'

'Almost, it is,' he growled. 'Almost, you tempt me to fling your offer back in your teeth. But I will do it. As you knew I would. I've no choice, really, do I?'

His words cut the taut line of tension running up her spine. She collapsed, sinking back onto the support of the balustrade. Relief and a fierce, hot joy blossomed in her chest.

'Give me a name,' he demanded. 'Where do I find this man and his deed of conveyance?'

It took a moment for her to gather her thoughts. A great weight had been lifted from her. For the first time in months she felt…light. Hopeful. Happy. She sucked in a breath, wanting to smell and taste and wallow in it.

'Portia? Dear, are you all right?' Dorinda eyed her with concern.

She breathed out. 'Of course. Mr Rankin is his name,' she said to Mateo. 'He has offices in Newbury.'

'How far?'

'Less than an hour's ride.'

'I'll see him tomorrow. You can be sure that I will only ask questions, scope the lay of the land. I'll not make a single decision,' he said sourly, 'and I'll call when I return to tell you of the outcome.' He turned away from her and sketched a brief bow in Dorrie's direction. 'Miss Tofton, it was a great pleasure to make your acquaintance.' Without hesitation he turned and strode for the steps.

'But…Mateo, wait!' Portia crossed the veranda in a hurry and leaned over in the exact spot he had so recently vacated.

'No. By God, I have no patience for any more today.' He paused and looked up at her. She recoiled at the annoyance and frustration suddenly visible in the depth of his dark gaze. 'I do not know how you do it, Portia, but always you poke and stir in just the right spots to send my temper flaring. I leave now, before either of us gets burned.'

Abruptly silenced, she pursed her lips and watched him stride away.

Chapter Four

Better a serpent with two heads than a man with two minds. It was advice that his *nona* had always delivered earnestly to his female cousins. Mateo had suddenly developed a more perfect understanding of what she had meant.

He'd been horrified at Portia's flat refusal to sell him back her portion of Cardea Shipping, and then he'd nearly shouted out his pleasure and relief at her proposal. Of course he had. It was a good solution—one that he would likely have come up with, had he found himself thrust into her unenviable predicament.

Cardea Shipping would be his again. Soon enough he'd have the freedom of the open sea before him, and the streets of Philadelphia underfoot. And then, at last, the autonomy to steer the business where he believed it needed to go. He clenched his fists. The family's docks would be a hive of activity again, their warehouses full to bursting. And those who had long scorned his ideas and lately laughed at his misfortune would soon be eating their words. He would prove to the merchant community of Philadelphia at last that they must let go of their past to secure their future.

His elation would be complete—were it not for the delay. Time was of the essence. Cardea Shipping had been on the brink of their most important venture in years when his father had died, and Mateo was going to have to hurry to salvage what he could of it. He could only hope that this business with Stenbrooke would go quickly.

And truthfully, something else had him swallowing a bilious rush of anger, even as he left the gloom of the inn and stood blinking in the bright morning sun. In his head he understood and even empathised with Portia's position, but he could not completely subdue the small, ugly ball of resentment churning in him.

She didn't trust him—and, oh, how that stung. The wound of his father's mistrust still lay open and now she rubbed it raw.

Purposefully, Mateo breathed deep and brushed such small thoughts aside. Where was his mount? The sooner he set this devil's bargain in motion, the sooner he'd have his business back on course.

He turned back and opened the inn door. Impatient, he called for the innkeeper. Abbott, he'd discovered the man's name to be, an irony which he found to be humorous on several levels.

'Abbot!' he called. 'I thought you'd sent word to the stables?'

The man came from the kitchens, brushing his hands on a stained apron. 'Yes, sir, I did. It'll be just a minute, though. We had a late customer come in. He was up early and bespoke my last nag for hire. I've sent to the livery in town for another.'

'How long?' Mateo asked.

'Any minute. Lads could be saddling him up right now, even.'

'I'll wait outside.'

Cursing the delay, he stepped back through the door. A rider circled around the building from the direction of the stable. On *his* mount, no doubt. Mateo watched him pass, a man of roughly his own age, dressed in the universal buff breeches and long brown coat that served as the uniform of a country gentleman. Only his hair, dark and a good deal longer than fashion currently dictated, made him stand out. He tipped his hat and Mateo swore he saw the hint of a smile as he passed. Damned impudence.

He left the empty courtyard and headed for the stables. Dew lay heavy on the ground this morning, sparkling off the blades of grass and beading like diamonds on tiny spider webs stretched between them. It brought to mind the dazzle of light bouncing off the water of the lake yesterday and the vision of Portia—full of sunshine and mischief—emerging from it.

Hard to believe, but she'd looked more enticing in the full light of day than in the flattering shadows of the inn, and that was not a claim one woman in a hundred could make. A child of Apollo, that one, with the sun captured in streaks through her tawny hair and golden flecks glimmering from her dark eyes. The sight of her had been a blow low in his gut, stimulating both a stir of desire and another flare of heated anger. His reactions to her were bizarre. He couldn't explain them to himself, let alone to her.

So he decided to learn from her example instead. Look at what she'd done with that bridge. She'd pitched in and helped repair it with her own two hands, even knowing that it might shortly belong to some damned farmer with a gambling habit. Surely she'd been full of worry, doubt, and, yes, anger. But she'd set it all aside to attend to what needed to be done.

Just exactly as he was going to have to do.

He rounded a corner and came into sight of the stables—and stopped short.

Of course he would. Right after he finished wringing her neck.

The reason for his mount's delay became suddenly apparent—she sat perched on top of a restless bay mare, resplendent in a rich brown habit with golden frogging in a military style. The animal tossed its head, shifting in her eagerness to be away, but Portia controlled her easily, never losing her smile or pausing in her conversation with the inn's groom who stood dazzled, grinning doltishly up at her, holding in one hand the lead of Mateo's patient, and apparently forgotten, gelding.

Irritation blossomed yet again. Hadn't he told her he would go alone and report back to her? It should be enough of a concession that he had cast himself in the role of lackey. Hell, he'd agreed to her proposal and ignored her overbearing arrogance. He'd let her relegate him to a subordinate, though she had to know that it grated every nerve in his body to do it. And she couldn't summon enough patience to wait a couple of hours at home?

He unlocked his knees and started forwards again. 'What in the name of Triton's forked tail are you doing here?'

He'd used his captain's voice, authoritative and designed to scare the slack out of hardened sailors. It spooked her mare instead. The bay reared and tried to bolt. Though she'd been caught by surprise, Portia reacted smoothly, bending lithe and low over her mount's neck. Graceful and at every moment in control, she allowed the animal to dance, gradually gathering her in and soothing her to a trembling halt.

As the mare calmed, Portia straightened. Mateo expected her to snap back, or at least resort to the high-handed manner she'd adopted yesterday, but she only watched him with a clear gaze. 'I'm going with you,' she answered simply.

Mateo drew a deep breath. Her calm helped him to keep his. 'Why?'

Her steady gaze did not waver or retreat. 'Because I need to.'

An echo of her words rang in his head. *I am tired of being let down by the men who are supposed to have my best interests at heart.* They were a pair, weren't they? He—fighting the old, stifling sense of suffocation—and she—battling a well-deserved feeling of helplessness.

He sighed. 'You understand that I will do the talking,' he said.

The mask of anxiety about her eyes faded away. Mateo watched it disappear and was struck by a sudden thought. In their every encounter he'd wondered what had happened to the old Portia. Now he knew that those lines of worry were the first glimpse he'd got of her.

He didn't like it. He much preferred the bold, confident Portia over the shy, reserved version.

Frowning, he mounted quickly. 'Let's be off, then.'

They set out, Portia keeping her mare pulled in to his gelding's shorter stride. Neither spoke and Mateo was just as glad. He did not want to feel any sort of preference for Portia Tofton. It could only be dangerous, given the awkwardness in their past and the volatility of their present. The old ease that they'd felt together was gone. Long ago they had taken comfort in each other's company, had often ridden out together like this, in companionable silence. But everything had changed.

Everything about their current situation rang problematic, but it was more than that. He was acutely aware of her, in a manner he had not expected. Like a man was aware of a pretty, vibrant woman. Or like a man on top of a powder keg warily eyed a burning brand.

Mateo spurred his mount to a faster pace. He would set aside his emotions, make the necessary transactions and he would be gone. As she said, in this fashion they would both get what they wanted. And then they would move on.

Horatio Rankin kept them waiting. It had to be a calculated move on his part, for his dour clerk had at first assured them that Mr Rankin was free. When he'd come shuffling back from his master's office, though, the clerk had sourly informed them that they would have to wait. And wait they had, for nearly an hour.

Portia was not annoyed in the slightest. She was feeling quite in charity with the world, and most particularly with Mateo Cardea. It seemed nothing had changed between them, and everything had. Out of the pack of her brothers and their friends, he'd always been the one to treat her with consideration, the one who had taken her seriously. It was the reason why she'd pinned her hopes for Stenbrooke on him, and he had lived up to all of her expectations.

She watched him wander from one corner of the dingy office window to the other and back again, the embodiment of restless motion, and she knew that Mateo had not changed. Worse, she knew that the feelings she'd once harboured for him had.

She'd been a girl all those years ago, and she'd wanted him with a girl's vague yearnings for a boy. Now she was a woman, a widow. Her eyes followed him, alive and vibrant with suppressed energy and impatience, the only thing worth watching in this bleak and barren space, and this time she knew just what she yearned for.

It would not do. There was too much unsaid between them, and in any case she could feel the resentment simmering just under the surface of his calm civility. This situation might not be of her making, but she still stood as the figurehead of all that had befallen him. No. It would be better all the way around if they just finished their business and parted ways.

He sighed in exasperation and bent low, his hands on the window sill as he stared at the bustling activity outside. A tiny smile played at the corners of Portia's mouth. In the meantime, she would allow herself to enjoy the view.

She started as he cursed suddenly and whirled to face

the silently scribbling clerk. 'By all that's holy, can you not check to see what is delaying the man?'

The scratching of the man's pen stopped. The small sound was replaced by his long-suffering sigh. Casting Mateo a look of extreme annoyance, he slid from his high chair and creaked his way down the hall.

Once he'd gone, Mateo smiled and dropped himself on to the bench next to her. Portia returned his smile. She enjoyed the warm feel of him next to her nearly as much as she'd appreciated his backside view.

She cocked her head at him. 'Rankin is a horrid little man,' she said. 'He's likely trying to goad us.'

'Aye, I began to suspect as much,' said Mateo. 'But I thought we should discuss the question—why? He cannot know exactly what we wish to discuss, and even if he did, why should he seek to unsettle us? Or perhaps he only hopes we will leave? But again, why?'

Portia shrugged. 'I put it down to his ill nature.'

'Surely there is more to it than that? And I give him what he wants, eh? The old one will report that my temper is heated to boiling.' He scrubbed his hands vigorously through his dark curls. 'So—do I look the part?'

She laughed. Impulsively, she reached out and loosened his respectable stock. Tilting her head, she ran a considering gaze down the front of him and then reached out and undid the top button of his waistcoat. 'Now you do.'

She glanced up and her smile faded. Mateo stared and it was not laughter she saw now in his eyes. His smile had faded, taking those tiny, irresistible lines with it, and leaving something intense and speculative that heated her from the inside.

She dropped her hands away from him. 'Thank you for bringing me along.'

'It is nothing.'

'No,' she said firmly. 'It's not.' But it would be better if he did not know just how grateful she felt. 'I know that you wish to do the talking, but I do have some questions I'd like Mr Rankin to answer. I was curious about a few things before, but his treatment of us only sharpens my curiosity.'

'Yes?' He looked suddenly alert. 'What questions do you have?'

Portia breathed deep. 'I'd like to know exactly when J.T. lost ownership of the house. Why did the new owner not take possession immediately? Or why not after J.T.'s death, when every other gamester he'd borrowed from or lost to made claims against the estate? He's been dead for nearly fifteen months. Why wait until now?'

Mateo shrugged. 'Perhaps the new owner did not hear of your husband's death right away.'

She looked wry. 'If he was in England, then he would have heard of J.T.'s death,' she said scornfully.

He sat straighter. Portia could see the questions in his eyes, but she was in no way prepared to answer them. Not here. Not now. She shook her head. 'And it does not explain why he did not make his claim immediately upon winning.'

Mateo sat back and allowed his gaze to return to the dingy window and the unceasing activity on Northbrook Street. 'You are right, I believe. There are too many questions here.' He stared intently down the hallway where the clerk had gone. 'Our decrepit friend has been gone a long time.'

Portia stared as he abruptly rose from his seat.

'Something is not right here,' he said.

She jumped to her feet and followed as he strode suddenly down the hall.

Mateo tried to ignore his sense of foreboding. Likely this Rankin was only passed out from drink, or just the small sort of man who built himself up by irritating and belittling others. He prayed it was some such simple explanation and not a complication that would cause a delay and destroy his company's best chance for the future.

An ornate door on the left looked out of place in this dusty corridor. From behind it came the sound of small, frantic movements and the faint sound of cursing. Portia came up behind him as he reached it. He placed his hand on the knob and cast her a faint look of enquiry. At her nod he pushed it open.

Chaos reigned inside. They stood on the threshold of a small, comfortably appointed office, but comfort was clearly not on the itinerary today. Papers and files were strewn everywhere. The elderly clerk knelt on his knees at the bottom of a filing cabinet, searching frantically through its contents. From behind a richly carved desk piled high with scattered documents rang another loud curse.

'Damn it all, but it *must* be here! Where the hell else would it be?'

Mateo cleared his throat.

The clerk jerked about. Up over the desk rose a set of sandy eyebrows and a pair of small, narrowed blue eyes.

'Well, well, Mrs Tofton,' Mateo mused. 'It does appear that we have come at an inopportune time.'

The piggish eyes were joined by the rest of the man. Mateo caught the scent of alcohol, noted the red, bloated face and ample belly and was reminded strongly of his sea-cook's stories about Davy's drunken sow.

'Yes, yes—a most inconvenient time.' He waved a dismissive hand and attempted an apologetic expression. 'So sorry, but you'll have to come back another day.'

Mateo narrowed his gaze. 'Oh, I do not think it will be so easy, Mr Rankin.'

Just like that the solicitor's barely conciliatory air disappeared. He whirled on his clerk. 'Useless old fool!' he hissed. 'I told you to get rid of them!'

'Ah, but you cannot blame your assistant.' Mateo glanced askance at Portia. 'Anyone will tell you that I'm a most inconvenient fellow.'

She nodded in pleasant agreement. Rankin merely sputtered.

'We are here about Stenbrooke.' He let his gaze roam over the mess. 'We'd meant to discuss a sale of the estate, but I have a feeling there might be some difficulty with that.'

Mr Rankin not only looked like old Davy's sow, he apparently shared her stubborn characteristics. 'I'm not prepared to discuss the business today, sir, with you or anyone else. You'll have to leave.'

Mateo merely leaned against the door frame and crossed his arms. 'Mrs Tofton, something tells me that there is no need for you to start packing.'

Rankin actually grunted. 'She's to be out by Michaelmas.' He turned his narrow little gaze on Portia. 'That's four short weeks,' he said nastily. 'If you haven't started packing, you'd best hop to it.'

'I'm not so sure about that, Mrs Tofton. It would appear that Mr Rankin has misplaced something.' Mateo arched a brow in Portia's direction. 'Would you care to make a wager on it? I'm betting he's lost the deed of conveyance to Stenbrooke.'

'I don't think I'd care to take that bet,' said Portia casually.

A snarl of frustration ripped across Rankin's face. 'Perhaps I have mislaid the document. But that doesn't change the fact that the place no longer belongs to her.'

Mateo stood straight. 'Do you know, I think your brothers would have some colourful cant phrase to describe what Mr Rankin is trying to sell us—a bag of moonlight, would they label it?'

He hid a smile as she considered. 'A bag of moonshine, I believe. Or they might say that Mr Rankin is trying to bamboozle us.' She cocked her head at the solicitor. 'And I do believe that they would be right.'

Musing, Mateo glanced at Portia again. 'Two women alone might have appeared to be an easy target. Perhaps the document never existed.'

Portia pursed her lips. 'He did have the deed last month.'

'It could have been a fake.'

He saw hope flare in her eyes, but then her brow furrowed. 'Much as I'd like to believe that, it did look official enough to me.' She frowned. 'I believed it to be J.T.'s signature. Both Dorinda and I examined the deed, and I asked Mr Newman to look it over, as well. We were all convinced.'

The clerk rose, groaning to his feet. 'Did Mr Rankin not leave you a copy, when he came out to see you, ma'am?'

'Keep quiet, Dobbins,' the solicitor ordered.

Everyone ignored him.

Portia shook her head. 'No, should he have?'

'Well, it's usual in these cases, but not required,' the old man mused. 'Certainly at one point there were three copies of the thing, right here in this office.'

Mateo waved a hand. 'But if none of them can be produced, there is no proof. Stenbrooke will remain yours.'

The solicitor abruptly slumped into his desk chair. 'Mr Riggs will see me drummed out of the county for this,' he moaned.

Mateo could not help but notice that the clerk did not greet this pronouncement with any sort of distress.

'But wait…' Rankin straightened in his chair. 'Perhaps his courier mistakenly took it back with him. Yes, of course!' He slapped a hand on his desk and cast a look of triumph at Mateo and Portia. 'It must be so! So sorry,' he smirked, 'but I'll be in contact with Riggs and soon enough I'll have your copy and one for the courts. I'll file it at the quarter session and that will be an end to it.'

Portia took a step into the room. 'Who is Riggs?' she asked. 'The name on the deed was Averardo.'

Mateo stilled. Rankin's expression fell again.

'Enough!' Mateo barked, suddenly impatient. 'I have had my fill of these games. Mrs Tofton, who is the local magistrate? He can sort through this mess better than you or I.'

'No!' Rankin reached out a pleading hand.

The clerk's mouth twitched. 'The magistrate threatened to ride him out of town on a rail himself, should he catch him in another questionable bit of business.'

'Shut *up*, Dobbins,' Rankin growled.

'Let's go,' Mateo said to Portia.

'Please!' Rankin called. He stepped around the desk. 'You'll put my livelihood at risk, all for a misplaced piece of paper?'

'Yes,' Mateo said over his shoulder. 'And with the same amount of pleasure that you have shown in displacing Mrs Tofton.' He placed his hand on Portia's elbow and stepped towards the door.

It was the clerk who spoke out. 'Ma'am, I'm thinking you'll want to hear his end of it.'

Mateo glanced over his shoulder.

Rankin's shoulders slumped. 'Come back,' he said with a wave. 'I'll tell you.' He looked up sharply. 'But you'll have to agree not to run telling tales to the magistrate.'

Mateo raised a quizzical brow at Portia. She nodded. Together they turned back, and he swept a pile of files from a chair for her. She arranged the heavy skirts of her habit, and once she was seated, he perched on the edge, firmly telling himself to ignore her sweetly spiralling scent. 'Let's hear the whole of it,' he said.

Rankin took his seat again. He shrugged and darted a look of ill-concealed dislike at Portia. 'There's not so much to tell. Everyone knows her husband was a gambler and a wastrel.'

Portia flinched. Mateo leaned forwards, scowling. 'The whole of it, where you are concerned,' he growled.

Rankin returned his glare. 'It's simple enough. Her husband used the estate as a stake in a card game. And lost. My client is someone who I have collaborated with before, handling his business matters in this part of the country. He sent the deed over by courier, along with signed statements of witnesses who were present when Mr Tofton lost his estate.'

Next to him, Portia tensed further. Her fists clenched in her lap and the elegant column of her neck tightened. Mateo had to blink and stop himself from running a soothing finger down the slender length of it.

'I looked everything over carefully. It was all in order. So I travelled over to Stenbrooke to deliver the news,' concluded Rankin.

Mateo listened with only half an ear. His brain was sifting through the man's words, hearing everything that he did *not* say, but his gaze was still caught by the contrast of Portia's creamy skin and thick, honeyed hair. He could see her pulse, beating steadily right at the tip of a richly curling lock of hair. The curl fluttered, shifting just the tiniest bit with each beat of her heart.

The clerk, still hovering at the filing cabinet where his employer had flung him, cleared his throat. Loudly. Then he did it again.

Mateo jerked his gaze away. 'Is there something you'd like to add, sir?'

'No,' Rankin answered for him—and viciously. 'Absolutely, there is not.'

'He come back from the lady's estate chortling over their reactions,' the clerk said defiantly. 'Those ladies were shocked and devastated, and he enjoyed every moment of it.'

'Hold your tongue, old man.' The threat in Rankin's tone was clear.

'I've held it long enough,' the clerk replied. He focused his attention on Portia. 'I am old,' he said simply. 'I worked thirty years for my last employer, but they sent me out to pasture, wanted new blood. I took this job because I thought no one else'd have me. But I can't abide the sick feeling it gives me.'

He raised his chin. 'Don't want to retire; I'd likely go mad with boredom. I'd like a nice, quiet position, though.'

Mateo's mouth quirked. 'It just so happens that Mrs Tofton is the controlling owner of a fleet of merchant ships. I'm sure she could find you something to your liking, should you have something she'd like to hear in exchange.'

Rankin stood. 'That's enough! I've told you what I know—you can't go stealing my employees right out from under my nose.' He cast a malevolent look at his clerk. 'Even if they are traitorous dogs.'

Portia stood suddenly. 'I've had as much of your company as a lady can tolerate, Mr Rankin.' She turned to the clerk. 'Mr…?'

He bobbed his head. 'Dobbins, ma'am.'

'Mr Dobbins. I am certain we could find a quiet task verifying manifests or something similar. I'm sure we could round up a raised desk, a cushioned chair and an increase in pay. Does that sound to your liking?'

The clerk's eyes lit up. 'It does indeed, ma'am.'

She shot a dark look at Rankin, and then held her

arm up invitingly to Dobbins. 'Then let us go, sir. I'm quite anxious to hear what you have to say.'

'Now, just a minute!' Rankin objected, starting around his desk once more. 'I won't have—'

Mateo stepped in front of the man. 'You won't have an office, a business or all of your teeth, should I hear another word from you. Or another word about you, either. As of this minute, this affair is none of yours.' He grasped the man by his oversized waistcoat and pulled him in close. 'Do I make myself clear?'

Mateo pushed him away. Without another word he hastened after Portia and the clerk. They'd reached the outer office and were just stepping into the bustle of the street when he caught up with them.

'Well, Mr Dobbins, I'd like to hear just what you can tell us. Now, before we go any further.'

'Perhaps we could find a spot to sit down?' Portia interrupted. 'Poor Mr Dobbins has had quite a morning. I can feel your arm trembling,' she said kindly to the man. 'There's a bench in front of that bookshop, down the street. Can you make it there?'

'Surely I can, Mrs Tofton, thank you.'

They set off. At the clerk's shuffling gait it took several long minutes to reach the spot. Mateo was bursting with impatience again by the time they arrived. All thoughts of Portia's elegant nape and appealing new confidence aside, his mind was already drifting towards the sea, to the difficulties he was going to have to face back in Philadelphia. He needed to wrap this transaction up, and quickly, before he actually gave into temptation and touched that dancing curl of honeyed hair.

'Smartly, Dobbins,' he ordered once the old clerk

had settled on to the bench and leaned back gratefully into the warmth of the sun. 'Let's hear what you have to offer.'

'Aye, aye, sir,' Dobbins said with a flash of humour in his eyes. He sighed. 'Rankin told you the truth, ma'am.' He smiled at Portia. 'Just not all of it.'

'What is it that you thought I needed to know?' she asked softly.

'Just what you started to find out for yourself. The client Rankin mentioned was Mr Riggs. He's a scientific type, an agriculturist—always trying to find a way to get a bigger, faster crop, or the harvest in quicker. He has a great tract of land outside Marlborough. Longvale, it's called. But he also searches out small parcels of land in different areas and uses them in his experiments.'

'Mr Rankin told my companion that his employer would likely plough Stenbrooke under, but Riggs was not the name on the deed.'

'Exactly, ma'am! Riggs leased a bit of land from Rankin, then asked him to keep an eye out for more in this area. Oh, he found him a few lots, but he skimmed a little cream off the top of the deals, if you know what I mean.'

'And Riggs found him out?' Mateo asked.

'He did. But he told him he would not turn him in—not if he handled this Stenbrooke case, fast and quiet-like.' He looked to Portia. 'Averardo is the one who won your estate at cards. I don't know why he didn't handle the conveyance himself, but he sent the documents out to Riggs, who sent them on to Rankin. Sent them by courier, in fact, and that fellow stayed here while Rankin set the conveyance in motion. Mighty curious man, that courier. High-handed, I'd call him. He asked a lot of questions of Rankin, once he come back from Stenbrooke.'

'What sort of questions?' Mateo demanded.

'Oh, he wanted to know who was with Mrs Tofton, and how did she take the news, that sort of thing.' Dobbins patted Portia's hand.

'And do you believe the courier took the deed with him when he left?'

'Must have done. It's not in that office and there's been no chance to file it with the courts. Won't reconvene until quarter day.'

Mateo felt a surge of hope. All he needed was to find this Averardo before the next quarter day, before there was any chance of that conveyance being recorded. It would be simple enough then to make the man a generous offer. The deed and any copies would be destroyed and Stenbrooke would remain Portia's as if the conveyance had never happened. Most importantly, he could be out of England and on his way to Philadelphia, with no need to wait for another deed to be drawn up, no need to involve clerks, solicitors or courts at all.

Mr Dobbins had reached a similar conclusion. 'You'll want to find Averardo, should you wish to buy Stenbrooke back,' he told Portia.

'Do you know where we might find him?' she asked.

'I don't know the first thing about him. Mr Riggs is the man to ask,' Dobbins spoke kindly.

'Yes, thank you, Mr Dobbins. I've heard of Mr Riggs and his work.' She smiled at the old man. 'Now, what are we to do with you?'

Mateo fished out his purse. 'Are you familiar with Portsmouth, Mr Dobbins?'

'I know where it is,' the clerk replied cautiously.

'Then take this.' Mateo gestured and counted out a fistful of coins to the man. 'Make your way there and in Union Street you'll find offices for Cardea Shipping. Talk to Mr Salvestro—he's the agent there. Tell him that I—' He stopped and cursed inwardly. 'Tell him that *we* sent you. We'll write ahead so you'll be expected. By the time you arrive, they'll have a satisfying position set up for you.' He raised a questioning brow. 'Will you have any difficulty with that?'

'None at all, sir!' Dobbins replied happily.

Portia stood, smiling brilliantly. 'That's settled, then.' She held out her hand to Dobbins. 'Welcome aboard, Mr Dobbins.'

Chapter Five

Perhaps Portia should have felt disheartened. Her simple plan to regain Stenbrooke had suddenly become more complicated. The Michaelmas deadline had acquired a new significance and now she had Mr Rankin working actively against her, instead of just callously executing his duty.

She wasn't in the least disheartened, however. Oddly, and against all reason, she felt elated. Rankin had been vile and rude, it was true, but he had a long way to go before he could match the habitual coarseness of her late husband. Rankin's discourtesy had barely moved her—and it was not only because of her more than passing familiarity with a bully's behaviour.

No—it was because she'd faced it with Mateo at her side. He'd always done that for her, boosted her confidence with his own. Her father, perpetually surprised that he'd fathered a girl after so many strapping sons, had always treated her as if he'd expected her to break, or perhaps just to break into tears. She'd always thought he'd be equally horrified at either occurrence. To her brothers she'd been a nuisance, or an occasionally amusing target, and as for J.T.….well, she was not going to ruin her good mood by recalling anything about him. But Mateo had always treated her with a simple acceptance, and she had come to crave that heady feeling of equality.

Today she'd had a taste of it again—and she wanted more. She bit her lip to keep from grinning. Watching him stride up Northbrook Street ahead of her, she knew that that wasn't all she wanted.

Mateo was different in nearly every way from the other men in her life. He just seemed so much *more*. Darker and more handsome, without doubt—also strong enough in character to stand up against the unscrupulous and confident enough to extend a little kindness to the unfortunate. Mateo had never, she felt sure, dragged someone down to lift himself up.

Instead, the opposite held true—he exuded an incredible masculinity that was impossible to ignore. Perhaps it came from being a ship's captain and the air of command that went with it. Perhaps it was the intriguing dichotomy of knowing that his large, calloused hands were equally comfortable gripping the top rigging of a merchant sloop or a lady's hand amidst London's grandest society. Whatever its origin, his appeal was a smoky, nearly tangible thing, reaching out to her and setting her blood to surging until she feared she couldn't contain her response. Despite the difficulties ahead, she felt hopeful and light.

Unfortunately, Mateo's temper was not pulling in tandem with hers. Since they'd parted from Mr Dobbins he'd been silent and withdrawn. Lost in contemplation, he'd walked beside her, but without touching her, until his absorption and his longer pace allowed him to gradually draw ahead. He had not even noted her absence, and though she knew he did not deliberately ignore her, and while she could certainly appreciate once more the pleasing prospect of broad shoulders, tight trousers and tall boots, she was not inclined to allow it to continue.

Already he'd reached the side street that led to the livery. 'Mateo,' she called as he made the turn. She was still a good distance behind him.

He did not pause.

She quickened her step. 'Mateo!' She reached the corner. The crowd was thinner here, but still the street was busy. 'Mateo! If you pull much further ahead, I'll lose sight of you completely.'

She saw his head turn and his step falter. He cast about for her and spun on his heel. She waved at him and he strode rapidly back to her.

'My apologies, Portia.' He offered her his arm.

'Since I'm to benefit from your contemplation, I suppose I will forgive you,' she said lightly.

'Hmm.'

'Are you thinking of the trip to Marlborough? It's a good nineteen miles, nearly twenty by the time we reach Longvale, but we'll be on the Bath road for most of the trip. We should make it there in a morning's drive.'

'Hunh.'

She tried again. 'J.T.'s curricle is still in the carriage house at home. If the day is fine, and you don't mind riding in the open, we could make use of it.'

No response. Perhaps she should try another tactic. 'My ears are purple, your nose is green and since I'm a widow now, I'm contemplating having a torrid affair with a rakehell of the first consequence. I know you've connections to the nobility through your cousin Sophie and that you've made a few forays into London society over the years. Can you recommend anyone who might do?'

'Mmmph,' was the entirety of his reply.

Portia nudged him with an unladylike jab of her elbow. 'Mateo!'

He glanced down at her. 'Yes?'

She rolled her eyes and gave up. 'Are you fretting about how to deal with Mr Riggs? There isn't the slightest need.'

'Is there not? I hesitate to disagree, *cara*, but I have a bad feeling we are about to become mixed up in what your brothers would call a cavey business.'

They'd reached the livery. Portia nodded her thanks as he held the door wide for her to enter the dingy office. 'A havey-cavey business, they might label this,' she corrected. 'While my father would storm about, calling the whole thing a damned hum.'

His eyes widened. 'But he would not approve of you repeating it,' he chided.

'Well, I don't approve of how he handled my inheritance, so we'd be even. In any case, I suppose that the question of whether they would be right or not depends on what Mr Riggs has to say.'

The livery attendant was a boy of about fourteen, sleeping soundly on the one rickety wooden chair. Mateo shook him awake and sent him off to ready their mounts. 'I don't know what caves have to do with any of it,' he grumbled as he offered her the questionable chair.

'I'm sure I don't, either,' she said with a smile. The office was wooden, nothing more than a lean-to attached to the side of an ancient barn. Sun shone through cracks in the boarded walls and ceiling, highlighting the straw dust in the air and touching the shabby room with a hint of magic. Mateo perched himself on an empty barrel and gave every indication of going off into deep thought again.

'But are you not interested in what I have to say about Mr Riggs?' she asked. 'I assure you I know exactly how to handle him.'

'Indeed?'

'Indeed. I am in possession of the perfect weapon, one that will guarantee he will tell us everything we ask.'

'Are you?' he asked with mild interest, running a discerning eye over her sitting form.

'Yes. You see,' she said, lowering her tone and leaning forwards, 'I am intimately acquainted with his mama.'

He choked back a surprised laugh. 'Do you know, that is exactly the sort of thing that might weight the ballast in our favour?' He smiled at her with tepid approval. 'I swear, I've never met a lady so naturally up to every rig.'

Mild interest. Tepid approval. Up to every rig? What utter rubbish. Portia watched his attention wander again and clenched her fists in frustration. There was nothing *mild* about her response to Mateo. Quite suddenly, being treated as an equal became woefully inadequate. She wanted to be seen, to be treated, to be *wanted* as a woman.

Her eyes narrowed. But how to go about it? The old Portia wouldn't have had a clue; would never have attempted it, in any case. She'd do what she'd always done as a young girl, duck her head and accept her own inadequacy.

But that girl didn't exist any more. Like a sharp blade she'd been forged by fire and honed by hardship. Portia was no longer content to wait for what she might be given; she was ready to go after what she wanted.

She stood. Gathering her skirts, she straightened and threw her shoulders out. She took a step forwards, positioning herself so a shaft of sunshine caught the golden frogging on her habit, setting her chest ablaze.

He looked up. 'Well, there's no hope for it,' he said cheerfully. 'I suppose you'll have to come along to Marlborough.'

She froze. Her heart fell and she let her skirts follow it to the packed dirt floor.

'You'd meant to leave me behind?' she whispered.

He nodded.

The gathering cloud of ire inside of her must have shown on her face, because he hastened to add, 'But only because I can travel more quickly alone.'

Speechless, she picked up her skirts again and headed for the door.

He stopped her just as she reached the threshold. 'Portia?' He took her arm. 'Where are you going?'

'We passed a gunsmith, just down the street,' she

snapped. 'I feel the sudden need to purchase myself a firearm.'

His mouth quirked. 'Does someone need shooting?'

She jerked her arm from his grasp. 'Yes. You—for being a great, irritating lout. And me—for being a great, naïve fool.'

'*Cara*, come back.' His tone rang smooth and caressing. And also insincere and patronising. She knew he didn't mean anything at all, calling her *beloved*. She'd heard him use the term with his cousins, with her cousins. She was sure he'd used it once with a scullery maid from her father's kitchens. But she *wanted* it to mean something when he said it to her. 'Surely it cannot be as bad as all that.'

He really did need shooting.

'Tell me,' he said, stepping closer. 'What is the trouble?'

The trouble was that he stood too close yet again. Sensation rippled from the top of her head and took a swirling detour round the front of her, raising her nipples to stiff peaks. She shivered and all the fine hairs on her nape and along her arms stood on end, straining towards *him*, no doubt.

'The trouble is that I have been silently singing your praises,' she grumped.

He grinned. 'It does not sound so bad.'

She crossed her arms in front of her. 'It is. All morning I've been thrilled because we were acting as equals in this endeavour. Now I see I was mistaken.' She turned away again. 'You are no different from any of the men in my family—dismissive and in no way inclined to believe that I have a brain and an idea how to use it.'

'No—not so!' he exclaimed. He grabbed her hand as she tried to walk away again. 'I was rude, it is true. I am most sorry, Portia. Of course we are equals, just as you asked. Partners in this damned rum.'

'Hum,' she said. Which was exactly what her body was about, humming, even while her brain was slowing, ceasing to function altogether. Warmth, thick and rich, spiralled from their clasped hands, crawled up her arm and slid downwards, settling low.

But Mateo had grown serious. 'Truly—I thought only of speed,' he said earnestly. 'You must understand, it is very important that we finish this as quickly as possible.'

Disappointment nearly choked her. Aghast, she could only marvel at her own stupidity. Of course he wanted to be done and gone quickly. Of course his interest in her was only mild at best. She'd come a distant second to adventure nine years ago. She placed further behind his business interests now.

Mateo reached up and squeezed both her shoulders in what was meant to be a comforting grip. Letting his hands slide, he grasped both her elbows and pulled her close. 'Now,' he said with a warm smile, 'was that all that was bothering you?'

It was the smile that did it. She wished he'd snapped at her. She wished he'd agreed that she was a woman, and of no use. But he stood there, smiling that easy, encouraging smile and she couldn't help herself. It blended into all the countless other times he'd teased her, heartened her, made her feel special and *alive*.

Fondness swamped her, along with exasperation and a great flood of hot and molten desire.

'No,' she said. She gripped his arms tight, stood on her toes and leaned in until her breasts pressed against the hardness of his chest.

His eyes widened, and then darkened. His heart beat against hers, quickening to match the racing tempo of her pulse.

'There's more,' she whispered, right before she leaned in further and kissed him.

She'd caught him by surprise. But experience and a seaman's instinct to seize life's bounty as it came had him quickly entering into the spirit of the thing. And perhaps there was another reason, as well. The thrum of a familiar chord sounded in the back of his mind, a twang of awareness and want that he'd been ignoring. He listened to it now, and let his tension melt away, returning her eager kiss, deepening it, in fact, and sliding his hands along the length of her trembling arms. Tenderly, he pulled her in and wrapped her in his embrace.

For several long, delicious moments he indulged them both. Her mouth was sweet, their kiss languid and deep. But then, at last, he settled his mouth against the white, endlessly tempting turn of her neck. And the chord thrummed deeper, more primitive and carnal. Inside him it echoed like a growl of satisfaction. *Mine.*

He had to acknowledge it then, the sense of recognition that had struck him when first she barged into the tavern the other night. It overwhelmed him, sweeping over him like a great wave over his bowsprit, leaving him muddled with longing.

He couldn't think, couldn't formulate a thought past his need to see her as overcome as he. Slowly his lips and tongue travelled, dancing over the pulse point at the base of her elegant throat and on to the one just below her ear. She let out a whisper of a moan, a sound of pure pleasure. The resonance of it, low and throaty, vibrated against his searching mouth and sent a surge of lust straight through him.

She turned her head, capturing his mouth with her own, moving her hands along a sensual path around his ribcage and across the breadth of his back. She trailed naughty fingers down to his buttock, making him writhe against the slow, soft circles she drew there.

Not a nymph, then, his Portia, but a siren, full of mischief and devilry of the most appealing kind. He measured the weight of her breasts in his hands, stroking his thumbs over nipples already peaked in desire. His erection strained further and he pressed it against her. Let her feel what she did to him with her bold mix of confidence and need.

He stilled, his caressing hands slowed. The sudden realisation of where she had come by such confidence struck him like a blow. J.T. *Dio*, she'd been married to that snivelling boy. He'd had the teaching of her, had the right to put his hands all over her, in just the way Mateo did now. And more.

No. It was an image that he could not endure. He kissed her again, purposeful, urgent and hot. He was desperate to drive the image of J. T. Tofton from his mind, the memory of him from hers.

But the heavy fabric and high neckline of her habit frustrated him. He ran his hands along the length of her, delighting in the sweet turn of her waist, rejoicing in the abundant curves of her breasts. He pulled her close, wrapping himself around her, as if in that way he could claim her, make her his own.

She pulled her mouth from his, breathed his name in his ear. Her voice rasped, husky with need.

Portia. He stiffened, torn reluctantly away from desire once more. This was Portia in his arms, tempting him, driving him wild and making him forget.

But he ought to remember. No matter how much he burned for her, he needed to remember who she was and why he was here. Remember that only yesterday he'd accused her of the vilest betrayal. Remember that people were depending on her. That others looked to him for their livelihoods and on top of that responsibility he also carried the weight of a centuries-old family tradition.

How weary he was of carrying so many burdens. He yearned to dump them overboard, leave them behind as so much flotsam and return to the discovery of this new and intriguing facet of his relationship with Portia. But could he do it? No doubt it was exactly what his father would have expected him to do.

He pulled away. Stepped back.

'We cannot,' he said, holding on to her hands, meeting the question in her eyes with regret. 'This has to stop.'

Her eyes filled. She ducked her head. 'Does it?' she asked the floor.

'It does,' he affirmed. He let her go and retreated across the tiny office. 'I'm sorry.'

She raised her head then and took a step towards him. 'I'm not.'

'No,' he said again. 'Portia...' he turned her name into a caress '...my impetuous Peeve, you do not understand all the issues I am faced with.'

'Then tell me,' she said simply.

He ran a hand along his jaw. How to make her understand? Turning away, he braced a hand on the door frame and looked out over the small courtyard and the street beyond. But it was the thought of Philadelphia that occupied him, and a clipper he saw in his mind's eye, heavy in the water as she fought an icy sea.

'First I have to make you understand how things are at home.' He sighed. 'Twenty years ago, Philadelphia was the greatest seaport in America. Our ships, builders and seamen were famous, our reputations earned us the greatest respect. But war and blockades, the rise of other ports, shifting markets, they have nearly broken us.' His head dropped. 'You have been to my home. You know how all of my family is involved in Cardea Shipping, in one way or another. If the ships do not sail, if the warehouses sit empty, then my uncles and cousins and their wives and children do not eat.' He shrugged. 'Yet our port has fallen into an unprofitable pattern of revival and depression that must be broken.'

'And you have an idea how to do that?' She sounded interested, despite herself.

'Everybody does,' he snorted. 'Many of my competitors have turned their backs on the sea altogether and now they ship coal from the interior on crude, box-like boats.' He shuddered. 'I have done what I can, what my stubborn father would allow me to do. I have searched out new markets. I fought to establish a presence in Baltimore's rising hold on foreign goods.' He paused to look over his shoulder and catch her eye. 'Now Cardea Shipping is on the eve of its most important venture.'

He breathed deep. 'Ships from Philadelphia were the first to break the monopoly of the East India Trading Company. Twenty years ago there were forty of our vessels engaged exclusively in regular trade with the East. It is a difficult market, yet the rewards are great. And I mean to revive it.'

He gripped the frame hard in his passion. 'Any day now the *Sophia Marie* will be beating her way home. Near a year and a half she's been gone. My cousin Giorgio captains her—he and her crew will be weary from the long trip from the northwest and the difficult journey around Cape Horn, but her holds will be stacked high with the deep-piled furs that the Chinese adore. I have a warehouse stocked high with the ginseng they crave.'

He turned back to face her. 'The risks are high in a voyage like this, but the odds become more favourable for a caravan of ships. For several years I have toiled, putting together this enterprise. I have spoken endlessly, cajoled shamelessly and forced compromise on a handful of uneasy, rival merchants. I've battled my father and risked my reputation putting this arrangement together. It was to be the biggest opportunity of my lifetime.'

He could see the comprehension in her eyes. 'Until the reading of your father's will.'

He nodded. 'Until I was no longer the head of Cardea

Shipping, nor even the eventual heir to the business. I was only a man whose own father had passed him over, whose father had given control of his business into the hands of a woman a continent away rather than see his son take over.'

'Oh, dear. Oh, Mateo,' she breathed. 'I am sorry.'

'You can imagine the value my judgement holds now. The caravan, the entire Eastern enterprise, began to unravel. My investors have fallen away. The insurers will no longer do business with Cardea Shipping until they hear from *you*.'

She bit her lip, but he pressed on. 'Do you understand now why I must finish our transactions as quickly as possible? Cardea Shipping began generations ago in Sicily. My grandfather brought it to the New World. All my life I've planned to carry on the tradition left by countless Cardea men. This was meant to be the making of the business, setting us up for success for years to come.'

She exhaled slowly. 'I begin to see just why you were so angry with me.'

'I was laughed out of port, Portia, for losing my business to a woman,' he said bitterly. 'I am anxious to restore my reputation, yes.' He met her gaze with a hard, direct stare. 'And what do you think would be said of me, should it became known that we…' he gestured '…were involved.'

'That you were a man of great good taste and refinement?'

He did not smile. 'No; and you are naïve to think so. I have no wish to for ever be the man who prostituted himself to regain his legacy.'

She shrugged. 'It happens every day in the aristocracy.'

He began to grow impatient. 'It does not in my world. And even were we to remove that consideration, still it would not be a good idea.'

Mute, she looked away from him.

'Your father and mine might be gone,' he said, folding his arms in front of him. 'And I have more than a passing suspicion that my father's mind was running along exactly these lines, but do you think I would betray their memories so?'

She waved a dismissive hand. 'There is no betrayal between consenting adults. You don't need an excuse, Mateo, a simple "No" will suffice.'

He should let it go. Clearly she was ready to do so. But for some reason his mind kept scrabbling around and around the idea. 'I only consider the gossip that would arise about you. We were raised as a family in spirit, if not in blood. Your opinion of me must be abysmal indeed if you think I would dishonour that tradition and treat you so shabbily.' Oh, *Dio*. He greatly feared that he was trying to convince himself, not her.

She looked at him squarely. 'You are being dramatic again, Mateo. And you forget that I have been out in society a little. I did pay attention, you see. Married and widowed women have gentlemen admirers all the time.'

'Is that what you want? A gentleman admirer?' he asked bluntly. 'Because your kiss told me that you are more interested in a lover.'

She stiffened. Perhaps he should not have been so crude. But she straightened her shoulders and met his gaze. 'And if I was? You are free and so am I. There would be nothing shameful in such a…relationship.'

She put on a brave front, but he could see the start of tears swimming in the depth of her dark eyes. The sight caused his stomach to clench. 'I do not mean to hurt you,' he said gently. 'It is more than evident that I desire you, *cara*. Perhaps it is because of our history, but I cannot regard you so casually.' He took the risk and approached her again. He caught her hand. 'It is not in me to love you and leave you,' he said softly.

She said nothing, only gazed up at him, hunger in her gaze.

And a warning clanged sharply in his head. 'No— it could be nothing else. We've explored this avenue before, Portia.'

'I know.' He could barely hear the words.

A sudden fear set him to say, 'I am too restless for married life. You, of all people, should know that, Portia. I cannot even stand still for long! Nothing in my life has prepared me for such a thing. I would be abysmal at it.'

'I don't recall asking you,' she snapped.

He raised a brow.

'A kiss!' she nearly shouted. 'I wanted a kiss. I've had it. I thoroughly enjoyed it. But that is all.' She wrenched away from him. 'Men! A lady asks for an inch and they fear you mean to steal a mile!'

Had he been wrong? 'I am sorry,' he said. Again.

'Yes, I know,' she said bitterly. 'And you are not ready to be anything else. I understand. But all of this talk, if you ask me, is the true damned hum. We could have "dallied" seven times by now and no one would have been the wiser.'

He let loose a short bark of laughter. 'Of course they would. People know. They always do.'

As if to prove his point, the attendant and a groom at that moment appeared in the courtyard outside, leading their mounts. Trying to silently convey the full weight of his regret, Mateo extended his hand and led her out to meet them.

But when the groom had gone and they stood alone next to her restless mare, he gave in to temptation once more and touched that wayward lock curling so prettily against her nape. 'Can you see how a dalliance,' he said quietly, 'no matter how tempting, would not be wise?'

She looked up at him, her brown eyes shining, but did not answer.

'You have Stenbrooke to get back to and I must make haste back home. A quick finish to our business and then we must say goodbye once more.' He wrapped his hands about her small waist and lifted her easily into the saddle. She hooked her leg over the pommel and settled in.

It was then that the idea hit him.

'Unless,' he said suddenly, 'unless you would consent to sign Cardea Shipping back over to me, right away? Before we track down this man who's won your estate?' He gripped her leg in his excitement. His mind raced with the possibility. 'It would not be as effective as leaving for Philadelphia right away, but if I were returned to the helm I could get word back, perhaps send the factor from Portsmouth back to start with the insurers...'

Mateo looked up. 'I would not leave you, of course,

until our business was complete.' He let all of the naked need he felt show in his expression. 'I know I have disappointed you, *cara*, and more than once, but you must know that you can trust me to keep my word. Please, would you consider it?'

Her expression had gone carefully blank as she looked down at him. 'No,' she said. 'I would not.' She spurred her mare forwards, and left him behind.

Chapter Six

The ride home passed silent and uncomfortable, but mercifully brief. It wasn't until they'd reached the boundaries of Stenbrooke that Mateo spoke to her. He spurred his mount up next to her mare. 'I'd like to speak to Miss Tofton when we arrive, if I may.'

'Of course.' Portia nodded. She purposefully curbed her bay's passion for being the lead in every group, keeping her reined in close, but Mateo had nothing further to say. When they reached the house he helped her dismount, but also curtly informed the groom to keep his gelding ready, as he would not be staying long.

Portia was spared the need to send a servant for Dorinda; she came running lightly down the staircase as they entered the hall. 'Well,' she asked, breathless with excitement, 'did it go as planned?'

Mateo snorted. 'It did not, Miss Tofton. And I begin to detect an unpleasant pattern. It would appear that nothing in this business is fated to go as planned.' He shot an enigmatic look in Portia's direction. 'I will let

Portia fill you in on the details, but we've had several obstacles placed in our path.'

Undaunted, Portia returned the look, but he had turned back to Dorinda. 'If you please,' he said, 'we'll need your help in overcoming them.'

'We will?' asked Portia.

He ignored her. 'We will be travelling to Marlborough tomorrow morning. As it is a good deal further than this morning's jaunt, I would ask you to come along as Portia's chaperon.'

'I don't need a chaperon,' she protested. 'I'm a widow, not a green girl!'

The expression he turned on her shone distinctly ironic. 'I think it would be wise.'

She folded her arms. 'And in any case, Dorrie is not a good traveller.'

'I believe Mr Cardea is right,' Dorrie interjected. 'I will manage. It wouldn't look well for the two of you to be roaming the countryside unescorted.' Though she looked flustered at the idea, she summoned a smile of approval. 'Not everyone will be aware of your long-standing friendship. And people do talk.'

He sketched a formal little bow of agreement. Portia didn't like it a bit. Was this to be her punishment then? she wondered. Was she to be treated with cold formality because she had refused his self-serving request?

'But the curricle—' she began.

'Is not large enough for three,' he interrupted. 'I shall arrange the transportation.' He bent over Dorrie's hand. 'If you could be ready to depart early in the morning? At eight, perhaps?'

'Of course,' she answered.

He bowed once more and turned on his heel. On the threshold he hesitated. 'It's possible we might be forced to spend the night on the road,' he said over his shoulder. 'You should both pack a portmanteau.' Without a further word or a glance in Portia's direction, he strode out of the door.

She met Dorrie's wide-eyed gaze with brows raised in answering surprise. In silent consensus they both rushed to watch his departure from the drawing-room window.

'What on earth did you do to him?' Dorrie asked in wonder.

Portia hesitated, but gave in to the awe in her companion's eye. 'I kissed him.'

Dorrie gasped. 'You didn't!'

Oh, but she had. She'd waited a lifetime for that kiss and it had been every bit as sweet and darkly seductive as she'd dreamed.

'But, Portia!' Dorrie still gaped at her. 'How could you?'

She raised a brow and swept a hand towards Mateo's retreating form. Her appreciative eye ran again over his broad shoulders, narrow hips and long legs. 'How could I not?'

She'd quite amazed herself, finally reaching out for what she wanted, and the pride she'd felt had only enhanced the pleasure of at long last being in Mateo's arms. A thrill went through her at the mere remembrance. It was heady stuff, being kissed by Mateo Cardea.

He'd kissed her mindless, breathless, until the shabby office, the livery, indeed all the world had dropped away. There had existed nothing in her universe save the two of them and the spiralling heat of their desire. She'd forgotten Stenbrooke, her people, herself. She'd been ready and willing to follow wherever he and their mutual passion led.

For make no mistake, it had been mutual. J.T. might have had occasion to mock her womanly skills, but she knew enough to recognise when a man was in the throes of sexual desire.

Dorrie still stared. Poor thing, she looked utterly perplexed. 'But what did he do?'

'He enjoyed it,' Portia replied firmly. *Thoroughly.* 'Until he recalled that he enjoys running Cardea Shipping even more, and that the running of it will not be nearly as profitable if he allows a "dalliance" to slow his return.'

'I'm sorry,' Dorrie said. She sounded puzzled, but sincere. 'Aren't I?'

'I'm not,' Portia answered with resolve. 'I didn't plan it, but it happened. I took a chance, something I've never done, except here, at Stenbrooke. And it's something we both must become comfortable with, my dear. It's a chance we are taking, setting ourselves up to live alone here. And though it didn't work out with Mateo, I am determined that it will for us, for our home.'

'Of course it will,' Dorinda said stoutly. 'But I still don't know what happened with the solicitor!'

Briefly, Portia sketched an outline of the morning's events.

'Well! Eventful indeed, and still you found time to press yourself on Mr Cardea?' Dorinda's disapproval rang clear. 'You have had a busy morning.'

'Oh, don't scold me, Dorrie,' Portia pleaded. 'Mateo did the job for you.'

'Well, I am glad that he did.' Her gaze was troubled as she pulled Portia away from the window. 'Do not mistake me,' she said. 'Of all people, I know that you deserve some happiness at last.'

She led Portia to the couch and kept a hold of her hand, stroking it gently. 'But I worry for you, dear. It has been long enough—were you discreet, no one could fault you for seeking a little pleasure. But you must be careful.' She hesitated. 'There is something in your eyes when you look at Mr Cardea—and it is in no way discreet. I think your heart is more involved in this that you might realise.' She sighed. 'I don't wish to see you hurt again.'

Portia bit her lip to keep it from trembling. Now she *was* beginning to be sorry she'd ever looked at Mateo Cardea with desire. And the worse part of having to listen to everyone counsel against a liaison was the knowledge that they were right. And not because she would be difficult to leave, although it had been sweet of Mateo to insinuate such a thing. She knew better than to believe it, though. Clearly she was not the sort of woman who could tempt a man away from his other interests. Her husband had proved that point, repeatedly.

She swallowed against the sour taste in her mouth. No, Dorrie had the right of it. Her feelings for Mateo ran too deep. She was supposed to be seeking her independence, not handing her heart over to someone with the power to destroy it.

'You know I appreciate your concern, Dorrie dear, but you may relax. Mateo possesses a plethora of reasons why we should not become more intimately involved. Not the least of which is that he has no wish to prostitute himself while getting his company back.'

'He said that to you?' Dorrie asked, shocked.

'Right before he asked me to turn Cardea Shipping over to him. Now. Before we have Stenbrooke back in our possession.'

Her companion glanced back in the direction of the window. 'I am beginning to rethink my favourable impression of the man.' She turned back, looking troubled. 'What did you answer?'

'I said no,' she said flatly. Was she supposed to just trust him to keep his end of their bargain? Lord, but she'd wanted to. She'd looked down into those pleading, dark eyes and she'd wanted to please him, to ease his worry. Even after he'd rebuffed her advances, even after the repeated offences he'd dealt her, she'd wanted to say yes.

But she'd stopped herself in time. She could not risk it. Every man she'd trusted had put his own concerns before hers. Nothing Mateo had said or done so far had convinced her that he would act differently. His priorities were firmly fixed on himself and his business.

A loudly clearing throat distracted her. Vickers hovered on the threshold, a tray in his hands. 'The post has arrived, Mrs Tofton.'

She knew before he'd crossed the room what was on the tray. She could see the worry and distaste he tried to hide. She glanced at the single letter once, and then tossed it back on to the tray.

'Burn it,' she said.

Dorrie had gone tense. 'Is it from…Reading, then?'

Portia nodded.

Dorrie jumped to her feet. 'Oh, that horrid woman! I felt sorry for her once, you know.'

Portia did not answer.

'Is there nothing to be done about her? It is harassment she's subjecting you to! Perhaps a magistrate—'

'Just burn it,' Portia instructed Vickers. 'Right away.' She turned back to Dorrie, fierce with determination. 'We have to look after our own interests. For if we don't, no one will.'

A sea captain intimately understood the value of patience. Frustrating as it might be to wait out bad weather, he knows to keep his vessel close-hauled upon the wind and wait for fair wind and sea before he unfurls his top-gallants. Many times as a privateer, Mateo had held his breath and his crew at a stop, waiting for his enemy to be caught in exactly the right position for a broadside volley. Hell, at the tender age of fourteen, the men in his mess had lectured him on how to stall his own pleasure, to be sure of his lady's. But not once, in a long and varied career, had Mateo ever had a greater need for patience than he did right now, dealing with Portia Tofton.

She would not trust him to keep his word, but she was willing to take him to her bed? What sort of logic was that? He snorted in disgust. Women's logic—the sort tailor-made to drive him mad.

And therein, perhaps, lay part of the problem. For until she had pressed that deliciously curved body up against him, he hadn't allowed himself to think of Portia as a woman. First he'd painted her as a scheming opportunist; once he'd realised that he was mistaken, still he had not truly looked at her. Instead he'd overlaid her with a picture of the unassuming, unfailingly supportive young girl he'd once known.

In reality, she was neither. Portia Tofton was proving to be far more complex than Portia Varnsworth had ever been. She still was as he'd remembered and expected, but she'd grown, too. No, he had not expected to encounter strength, steel and determination. She'd become a woman of fascinating layers. Were this any other time and circumstance, he'd enjoy nothing more than slowly peeling them away. One by one, he'd work his way from the lovely, rounded outside to the sweet and juicy kernel within.

Dio knew he was tempted. She'd kissed him—so hot and sweet—and he'd longed to loose her hair until those sun-kissed streaks curled about him. Her arms had held him tight, and he'd ached to go further until they were snarled together in a passionate knot. But he suspected that neither of them could tangle limbs without also involving hearts and lives. In the end, she would be hurt, and he was just beginning to wonder if he might not be, too. It would not be wise for either of them to indulge themselves.

Unfortunately, Mateo was a master at indulging himself. Keeping away from her was not going to be easy—especially not now that he'd had such a tantalising taste. He'd never been good at denying himself the things he was not supposed to have. As a child he'd always filched the *buccellati* his *nona* set out to cool. As a young man eager to learn of life at sea, he'd stowed away on one of his father's ships and earned the right to be called a son of Neptune.

And now Portia had lit a great, blazing light in his mind and body. It shone unrelenting on the attraction, the desire and the possibilities between them—and he was going to have to keep himself in the dark.

He sighed. Devil-may-care, his mother had called him with affection. And now, in more ways than one, his past was coming back to haunt him. If he wanted a future, he was going to have to overcome it.

His course was clear: he would keep his distance, exercise a little restraint and do his best to keep them both off the rocks.

He was off to a good start this morning. He'd hired a well-sprung carriage for the trip to Marlborough, and though it was roomy enough, he'd also hired a hack for himself. He was glad enough for it when Portia had emerged from Stenbrooke's front door.

In a spring-green dress with a tightly fitted bodice, she made him wish he could once again don those blinders he'd been wearing. There was no doubting her womanliness today, or her pique with him. Oh, she greeted him with all politeness, but she barely met his gaze, even when he took her hand to help her into the carriage.

And though he'd just set his course for distance and restraint, he couldn't help but admire the view. The square neckline and cunning wrap-around collar of her gown exquisitely framed the creamy expanse of her chest and throat. *Dio*, but he'd been a fool not to see what was right in front of his eyes. He made up for lost time now, staring until she moved past him and all he could see was the few inches of her nape between her collar and bonnet.

And right then, for a shocking instant, he could not catch his breath. Right there. His hand convulsed around hers. He'd kissed her right there and laid claim to that sweet, tender spot. And he wanted quite fiercely to pull her back and do it again.

But then she was in the coach, and her hand left his and the moment passed, thanks be to the heavens. Mateo stood a moment, flexing his hand where it had touched hers. Hell and damnation.

'Mr Cardea,' Miss Tofton said patiently. Mateo started. Was it the first time she'd addressed him? She twinkled up at him, and he thought it likely was not. 'Do you know just how old Mr Riggs might be?'

'Dorrie.' Portia called the warning from the coach, but did not look out of the window.

'What?' her companion asked, all innocence. 'A woman should prepare herself for all eventualities, dear. And just because you have no interest in marriage does not mean that I do not.'

Mateo blanched. Miss Tofton noticed and laughed outright. She held out her hand for his assistance.

With all alacrity he handed her in. Just as he closed the carriage door behind her she held his gaze and met it with a slow wink.

For the first time Mateo began to fear he was out-matched. As quickly as possible, he made sure the luggage was loaded and saw them all off.

Fortune smiled upon them. The weather held fair, the roads were wide and well kept, and the horses were fresh. They covered the first half of their journey in good time. They made Hungerford, the halfway point, by mid-morning. His mood much improved, Mateo called a halt at the Bear Inn.

All lay quiet at this time of day, which meant there was no shortage of ostlers and grooms to come to their assistance. 'Ladies, I confess,' Mateo said as they emerged from the coach, 'despite the beauty of the day, the dust of the road has me longing for the clear wind and clean deck of my brig.' He raised an enquiring brow. 'Since that's not to be had, I'll presume to propose a substitute. I dare say you won't mind a short break?'

If anything, Portia's mood appeared to have worsened. She did not answer, but climbed wearily down, her face set and wan.

'That would be lovely, Mr Cardea,' Miss Tofton answered apologetically. 'I fear neither of us is as seasoned a traveller as you. I, for one, would appreciate a chance to stretch my legs. Thank you.'

'Come, Peeve, look lively!' Mateo had never known her to object to travelling. 'We've made dashed good time. Stenbrooke will be back in your hands all the sooner because of it.'

'Let's hope Mr Riggs will be as co-operative as the weather,' she agreed. Mateo stared at her. Her eyes were closed, her shoulders drooped. It came as something of a shock. Listlessness was not something he'd ever heard or seen out of her.

'Having doubts?' he teased. 'We'll just have to hope he has a high regard for his mama.'

She didn't respond to his sally, and he could see the strain in her expression as she looked about. 'There's the innkeeper.' She pointed. 'Shall I go and bespeak us a private parlour?' she asked.

At his nod she hurried off. Mateo watched her go, then turned his questioning gaze on her companion.

Miss Tofton didn't pretend to misunderstand his look. 'It's my fault, I fear,' she fretted. 'I should have considered that an enclosed carriage…I just didn't think…' She let her words die away.

'It's not motion sickness?' Mateo could not suppress a sailor's disgust for such a notion.

'No.' Her mouth twitched at his dismay. She glanced about at the flurry of men seeing to the horses and carriage. Stepping away, she raised her brows. 'Hungerford is such a pretty little town, is it not?'

Curious, Mateo followed her. 'Yes,' he said for the benefit of their audience. 'The thatching on all the cottages is particularly charming.'

'It is,' she agreed. 'Do you know, I've stayed at the Bear once before. If I recall correctly, there is a lovely little stream just behind the inn.' She cocked her head. 'Would you mind escorting me?'

'Not at all,' he said promptly. He offered her his arm and they strolled around the building.

There was indeed a stream in the back, and it was a pretty spot. The water was shallow, but moved steadily, echoing musically over a tumble of rocks. Sunlight fought through the canopy of overhanging trees and sparkled off the surface.

Miss Tofton was apparently enamoured of the sight. He quelled the urge to prompt her. Better to keep quiet and wait.

The question, when it came, surprised him.

'Mr Cardea, will you tell me how Portia came by that nickname you call her?'

'What? Peeve?' he asked, startled.

Lips pressed together, she nodded.

He thought back. 'It started with J.T., I suppose. My family was at Hempshaw the summer that he and his family moved nearby. All of Portia's brothers were enamoured of the initials he used then instead of his full name, and they began to do the same.'

She smiled. 'And I suppose Portia wanted to follow their example? It sounds like her.'

'She did. She told us all to call her P.V. for Portia Varnsworth. Her brothers immediately warped it to Peeve, and Peeve she's been ever since.'

Miss Tofton regarded him thoughtfully. 'Until you arrived, I've never heard anyone call her by that name, except for her husband, my cousin.' She hesitated. 'It never sounded like an endearment, Mr Cardea, but rather, more of an…insult.'

'Ah. I see.' He did, too. It sounded exactly like something J.T. would do.

'Did you know James Talbot well?' she asked eventually.

Surprised, Mateo nodded. 'I did. We saw a lot of him, both at that first visit when he'd moved to the area, and later too.'

She was quiet a moment. 'I gather, then, that you will understand when I say he was a difficult person.'

Her caution irritated him and unnerved him a little too. She acted as if she were afraid J. T. Tofton was going to jump out and berate her for daring to mention him. Mateo folded his arms. 'He was a whiny snot of a boy,' he said bluntly. 'Never content with his own lot and perpetually jealous of someone else's. I'm sorry, I know you don't like to speak ill of the dead, Miss Tofton, but there's no covering the stink of rotten fish.'

'Of course, you are right.' She sighed. 'Suffice it to say, he did not improve with age.'

Mateo curbed his impatience. 'Well, I admit I was damned shocked to hear that Portia had married him. Forgive my continued bluntness, but I believe that was the first time my regard for her significantly fell.' In fact, he'd congratulated himself on making a lucky escape, for he'd told himself that any woman who had willingly chosen J. T. Tofton would never have suited him.

'Her reasons are her own, and I'm sure I can't speak to that.'

'Then I wish you would just say what you brought me back here to say.'

She gnawed at her lip and regarded him anxiously. 'Will you promise not to reveal what I tell you?'

He hesitated. 'If you wish.'

'Portia has never mentioned it to me. Vickers, her butler, did.'

'Told you what, Miss Tofton?' he asked with exaggerated patience.

'James Talbot hated Stenbrooke,' she blurted out. 'He hated the hard work it required, and resented the money spent on it. After it became profitable, he thought that the income should go into his pocket and not back into the estate. But Portia did what she could, and her father had seen to it that she had her own money to spend.'

She paused, but it was clear that she was just beginning. He waited.

'James Talbot was not…a kind husband.'

Mateo's fists clenched.

'In fact…' her voice lowered yet again '…some would say he was quite the opposite.' She looked away, over the stream. 'He locked her up once, in the tack room of an ancient barn that used to stand at the far boundary of Stenbrooke. Portia thought it wasn't safe, she wanted it torn down. She'd stopped in there to be sure that all of the equipment had been removed. James Talbot did not want to waste money tearing down a building that was falling in on its own. He found her there that day. They argued.'

'How long?' Mateo asked past a tightened jaw.

'He came back to the house, packed a bag and left,' she whispered.

'How long?' he repeated.

'Three days.' Her eyes brimmed with unshed tears. 'The servants looked, but when she was not to be found, they concluded that she must have gone away with him.' She swallowed. 'He laughed when he came home and found her still there. He said it had only been a prank.'

Mateo wished then that J.T. would jump out at them, returned from the dead—so he would have the pleasure of sending him back to hell.

'The next week Portia had the barn torn down. She also wrote and invited me to live at Stenbrooke.'

'I see,' he said. And he did.

'It was a long time before I noticed that she avoids tight spaces, and I never considered that a carriage…'

'I'll take care of it, Miss Tofton,' Mateo interrupted

her. 'Thank you for telling me.' He retrieved her hand and they started back.

'There's another reason I've told you this, Mr Cardea.'

He'd already seen that, too.

'I care for Portia deeply. She means as much to me as a sister.' She gave a bitter little laugh. 'Lord knows, she's been kinder to me than my real sister.' Her voice firmed. 'She's been hurt enough. I would not see her hurt again. By anyone.'

'Nor would I, Miss Tofton.' And he meant it. 'Nor would I.'

Chapter Seven

Portia shifted the cold ham on her plate to a new position. Her adverse reaction to being in the carriage had caught her by surprise. Had she been in a coach since... Well, just since? No, she normally rode everywhere, and hadn't had occasion for a longer trip. And truthfully, she hadn't stopped to consider that she might be affected. Foolishly, most of her resources had been focused on Mateo, while the rest were absorbed with her plans to get Stenbrooke back.

And just perhaps, without those two evils, she might never have been affected at all. But the gloom and sense of confinement in the carriage had merely echoed her larger situation. She was effectively trapped by her dependence on Mateo Cardea. His word and his willingness to help her were all that stood between her and homelessness.

Well, not homelessness. She could have a home with Anthony, or perhaps eventually with one of her other brothers. But when she thought of returning to that life, to feeling extraneous and beholden, to existing at the mercy and whim of her family and expected to feel grateful for it, that's when she truly started to feel sick. The air in the coach had grown thick and her throat had begun to close. She'd struggled to hide her distress from Dorinda, but truthfully, if he had not stopped here at Hungerford, she might just have hung out of the carriage door and broadcast her anxiety all along the Bath road.

She cast another look towards the parlour door. 'Where do you suppose Mateo has taken himself off to?' she asked. She was torn between dreading a return to the coach and wishing to get the day's travel over with.

No, she reconsidered wearily, she wanted it *all* over with. She wanted to be back home, with Stenbrooke safely hers, and Mateo Cardea gone from her life again. Then, and only then, would she be not only independent, but she'd also be safe. And if that was a contradiction or didn't make sense, then she didn't much care.

'He said something about needing to speak to the stable master,' Dorrie answered. 'Would you pass me the plate of scones? They are quite good.'

Portia did, keeping her eyes averted. Dorrie's appetite was in no way diminished by the trip. In fact, her companion appeared unusually cheerful since she'd come in from her short walk around the inn.

They both jumped as the door banged open.

'Are you finished, ladies?' Mateo asked with flair. 'Are we ready to get back to the road?'

'We've finished, Mr Cardea,' Dorrie assured him. 'But come, we'll keep you company while you eat.'

'No need! The landlady has packed me something for the road. If you please…' He beckoned. 'We have to make some changes and I wish to be sure they are acceptable.'

Portia shrugged in reply to Dorrie's mystified glance. Together they rose and followed him outside.

'What is it, Mateo?' she asked, sweeping the yard for a clue. There were no vehicles in sight save for some other traveller's open landau.

'As we drove in, I spied a wobble in the back end of the coach,' he explained. 'The wheelwright's been to look at it and he says there's a problem with the axle.' He frowned. 'We can't take a chance on it; he says it could go at any time.' He waved towards the landau. 'This is the only replacement available.'

He looked with concern at Dorinda. 'Miss Tofton, I worried that you would prefer an enclosed carriage, but will you mind the change terribly?'

Dorrie practically beamed up at him. 'Not at all! We'll be all right, won't we, Portia?'

Portia regarded them both with suspicion. The thought crossed her mind that perhaps she had not concealed her distress so successfully.

'We could perhaps find a local carriage we could hire, but I'm not sure how long it would take, or if we would be successful at all.'

'I think it will be all right, don't you, Portia?' Dorrie repeated. 'I did bring along my parasol, just in case something untoward should happen.'

Portia opened her mouth. Whether she meant to probe or to protest, she wasn't sure. She sensed a conspiracy. But abruptly, she shut it again, determined to let it go. The prospect of travelling in the open, with the wind in her face, was too delicious to pass up.

'Good,' Mateo said with satisfaction. 'Let's be on our way, then, ladies.'

The remainder of the trip passed quickly. Mateo still rode, but several times he brought his mount close by the open landau, so that conversation was possible. Other times Portia felt the weight of his gaze upon her, but she was too happy with the sun and the breeze to let it bother her. And when her own gaze wandered over to linger on him, well, she decided not to let that bother her, either. He looked magnificent with the sun lining the sharp angles of his face and the wind playing with his dark curls.

She loved to watch him ride; he had such a comfortable and natural seat—and as often happened, her mind spun away, creating the image of him striding easily across a heaving deck, masterful and in command of all he surveyed.

It was an exceedingly pleasant way to pass the time—but apparently not an acceptable one. Dorrie reached over and wrapped her on the wrist with her parasol.

'Dorrie!' Portia objected.

Dorrie merely raised her eyebrows. Then she relented. 'What was he like as a boy?' she asked with an understanding smile.

Portia tilted her head, considering. 'A great deal of fun,' she answered quietly after a second's thought. 'Busy, I would say. Never still, always on the go. Up to every rig and row my brothers could get into, but he always had time—and a kind word—for the girls too.'

Dorrie's brows went back up. 'Generous indeed.'

'He was, truly,' she mused. 'It was rare for a boy to be so accepting of others, at least in my experience.' She smiled in remembrance. 'When he was happy, you could feel it inside of you—and you could scarcely feel any other way.'

'It's a shame we haven't seen him really happy.'

'Yes, it is. Perhaps it is because of his heritage, but he feels things deeply.'

'Sounds familiar,' Dorrie said with a grin. She leaned forwards. 'And what sort of girl were you, Portia?'

The infatuated sort. But she didn't say it. She gave a little smile instead. 'Perhaps you will not credit it, but I was a fun sort, as well, if not in the same rowdy way as my brothers.'

Dorrie did not get a chance to reply, as Mateo drew his mount close in. 'Marlborough is just ahead,' he called.

They swept into the great wide main street of the town and Dorrie exclaimed at the crowds of people. A vendor gave them directions and within minutes they were on their way north.

It was not too long before it became clear that they had reached Longvale land. First the road narrowed to a track and Mateo was forced to ride ahead of the landau. Then the land opened up and they found themselves surrounded alternately by well-tended fields of grains and odd little plots, different from anything Portia had seen before. One was filled with large mounds of soil, out of which stretched a massive tangle of ground-creeping plants. Another had been ringed with young trees, to which a criss-cross system of rope had been strung. Immature vines climbed the rope and spread out, creating an oddly beautiful, floating green surface. Portia's curiosity was piqued long before they reached the house, and then it flared to even higher heights.

None of the attention so carefully shown on the land had been extended here. Weeds choked the gravel drive, shutters hung askew, and slate tiles sagged from the roof. Portia shared a bemused glance with her two companions as the landau rolled to a stop.

No groom came running. No one emerged from the house. An ancient post listed at one side of the drive. Mateo tied his hired hack to it and directed the driver of the landau to circle around and search out the stables.

Dorinda bit her lip as the carriage rattled away. Portia smiled encouragingly and took her hand as they followed Mateo across cracked stones to the door.

No knocker had been hung. Mateo pounded a fist upon the door and when there was no answer, he pounded again, long and hard. He'd just raised his fist a third time when the door opened a crack.

A young woman's face peered out at them, timid and puzzled, as if she'd never seen a visitor at the front door. 'Yes?' she asked.

'I am Mr Cardea,' Mateo said gently. 'My companions and I are here to see Mr Riggs.' He ended by flashing the maidservant his most charming smile. Portia had to bite back a grin when the girl blinked, flushed and then adjusted her cap.

'You're wanting to see Mr Riggs?' she repeated.

Again her brow creased as if this was a completely new idea.

'Indeed we are.' Mateo tried the smile again. 'May we come in?'

She thought about it. Portia could not determine if she was generally a slowtop or if she had been dazzled by Mateo's charm. The latter, likely, for she straightened suddenly and opened the door. 'Yes, do come in,' she invited, dipping a quick curtsy.

The three of them advanced into a dark, panelled hall in sore want of a cleaning. Dorinda huddled close.

'Wait right there,' the maid said, pointing to a gloomy corner. 'I'll see what's to be done with you.'

'What's to be done with us?' Dorrie repeated in a whisper. She leaned against a wall as if to steady herself. 'The offer of a seat, perhaps? Or a drink to clear the dust of the roads? I'm exhausted. All I wish to do is lay my head back for a moment's rest.' A look of horror crossed her face. 'But I wouldn't dare! What sort of man is this Mr Riggs, to keep such a house?'

'I'm beginning to have an idea,' Portia answered. Suddenly some of the observations she'd heard from the man's mother began to make sense.

'I don't care how old he is,' Dorrie said suddenly. 'I don't care if he is as handsome as sin and rich as Croesus—you are not to even *consider* marrying him! The thought of you living in all this disorder would drive me mad.'

Mateo smiled, while Portia regarded her with a grin. 'This disorder only drives you mad because you've no prospects of setting it to rights. Give you a free hand to wage war against it and you'd be as happy as a pig in swill.'

Her companion looked momentarily diverted by the thought, but she had no chance to respond before heavy footsteps echoed from the back of the house.

'Visitors,' declared the stout woman who emerged from the shadowed hall. She looked them over with disapproval. 'Ain't dressed for it, neither.'

Even Mateo's legendary charm had become strained. 'Indeed,' he answered non-committally. 'And you are?'

'Mrs Pickens. Housekeeper.'

'Very good,' he said with a nod. 'Would you be so kind as to inform Mr Riggs we are here? And perhaps find a comfortable spot for the ladies to wait?'

'No use waiting. There's a problem in one of the fields. He won't be back 'til nightfall.' She shrugged. 'That's if he don't decide to sleep in the barn.' She half-turned away. 'Best bet's to come back near daybreak. You might catch him in for breakfast then.'

Portia stepped forwards. 'We really must speak to him today. We have an urgent matter of business to discuss. Can he be summoned from the fields?'

'Aye, but he won't come,' the housekeeper said dourly. 'Most folks know not to come to the house. If you want to speak to the master, you'll have to go out to the fields.' She wrinkled her nose and ran an assessing eye over the three of them. 'I got boots of all sizes. Some of them will likely fit the ladies, but there ain't nothing I can do 'bout your hems.'

Beside her, Dorinda uttered a long, stuttering sigh.

'Boots for me, please,' Portia agreed. 'But please,

cannot you find my companion a quiet spot to rest and wait?'

'No decent place to be had, 'cept for the master's study.' She studied Dorinda. 'Come back to the kitchens with us,' she invited. 'More comfortable, and I just put on a pot o' meadowsweet tea. Good for the joints,' she explained.

'It sounds lovely, thank you,' Dorrie accepted with relief. But she cast an anxious glance at Portia. 'Will you be all right without me?'

'Perfectly,' Portia assured her. 'Now, I'll take those boots.' She shot a look at Mateo. 'And a pair for Mr Cardea, should he feel the need to change.'

'No need at all,' he replied. 'I've quite resigned myself that my boots will not survive my acquaintance with you, Portia.' He grimaced. 'Let's just hope they are the only casualty.'

Only Portia could contrive to look completely fetching while striding across farmland, wearing bulky work boots and an old linen wrapper dragged from the bottom of a storage bin. Mateo spent a few minutes watching her carefully, but she appeared to be fully recovered from her earlier lethargy.

He felt relieved, and restless because of the intensity of that relief. Though she'd always been quiet—at least when he was around—she'd always been full of interest and enthusiasm once you looked past the surface. But her companion had conjured an unpleasant image of what Portia's married life must have been like, and he couldn't shake the ugly picture from his mind. It disturbed him to think of all that quiet, industrious energy subverted by cruelty or negligence.

He hardly had time to dwell on it, thank goodness. The boy dispatched to guide them had been promised a slice of berry pie on his return, and he set a brutal pace. Portia literally took it in her stride, and indeed appeared remarkably at home crossing fields and jumping ditches. She never stalled until they skirted a damp meadow planted thick with tall, rough stalks, hairy leaves and drooping pink flowers.

She stopped and broke a stalk off. 'Comfrey,' she said musingly.

Mateo was far beyond the area of his expertise. 'Is that significant?'

'Only unusual, to see an entire plot of it planted,' she returned. She waved to their impatient escort. 'I'm sorry. Lead on.'

Clearly Portia had landed smack in the middle of her area of expertise. Watching her, with Miss Tofton's story fresh in his mind, the significance of Stenbrooke and all that it must have meant to her became suddenly clear. More than a childhood passion for gardening and landscape had gone into that magnificent estate. Stenbrooke must have provided both purpose and escape. To keep her home and live her life according to her own choosing—it would be the ultimate victory, the symbol of triumph over all that she had endured.

The idea added another level of commonality to their already dangerous understanding of each other. It also added another dimension to his determination to see both their goals met.

His master was just ahead, the boy told them, pointing to a field of spindly grain stalks. Mateo shared a smile with Portia as the boy left them at a run, and together they crossed to the far edge of the field, where a group of labourers had gathered in a loose circle.

The men parted as they approached, and he saw that they watched a man wielding a shovel. He was of middling years, and dressed as a gentleman, but his breeches were shabby, his waistcoat stained and the string of curses coming out of his mouth would have earned any sailor's respect.

'Mr Riggs.' Mateo stepped closer. 'I apologise for the interruption, but we'd like a moment to speak to you.'

'Not now.' The portly man spoke without looking around. He knelt down in the dirt and pulled a clump of scrawny plants up by the roots. He shook the dirt free, spraying it everywhere, and began to examine the root ball closely, grumbling under his breath all the time.

Mateo's patience had met its end. 'Sir, we've come—'

His gruff speech was interrupted when Portia laid a hand on his arm and squeezed. The wry twist of her mouth surprised him, but not nearly so much as the slow wink of her eye.

She stepped forwards and knelt down next to the obnoxious man.

'Drainage is fine, roots are healthy,' he said without looking at her. 'But just look at this barley; it's got barely a whisker, let alone a beard.'

'Too many heavy feeders?' she asked.

Riggs started at the sound of her voice, and at last his head whipped around.

Portia maintained her serious expression and gestured across the field. 'Have you tried beans?'

The man's eyes grew rounder. 'And clover,' he said grudgingly.

'Had the sheep in?'

He nodded.

Slowly she peeled her gloves off. Riggs and his labourers stared as if she'd sprouted two heads. Mateo wondered what under the deep blue sky she was up to when she looked over her shoulder and handed him her gloves.

Every man in the field held his breath as she knelt down, close to the earth. She peered at the hole Riggs had made, then scooped up a handful of soil. Cradling it, she picked through it. She closed her eyes, brought it close to her face and sniffed deeply. She squeezed her fist tight around it, and then examined the soil again. 'I can see you've added malt waste,' she said thoughtfully. She met Riggs's gaze. 'Have you tried marl?'

Mateo saw respect bloom on the man's face and surprise show on the labourers'.

'Aye,' Riggs answered her. 'It was the last thing I tried. It's been three seasons I let this field rest. I thought 'twould be ready again.' He kicked at the row of spindly stalks. 'But you see the results.' A crafty look grew in his eye. 'So then, will you make a suggestion of what I should try next?' He allowed open amusement to colour his voice and Mateo saw several of the surrounding men smirk.

Portia stood, clapping her hands together, then wiped them on the rough linen of her wrap. She took her gloves back from Mateo, but did not don them. Instead she waved them negligently to indicate the sparse field of grain. 'Plough it all in,' she said curtly. 'Now, have you a river or tributary on your land?'

'I do.' Riggs popped to his feet, as well, and Mateo was surprised at how sprightly he moved.

'Then I would dredge up a goodly amount of river mud,' Portia instructed. 'Lay in a store of fish, grind them and mix it in with the mud. Spread the whole mess over your field and plough it under, good and deep.' She grinned. 'It stinks to high heaven, but it works wonders.'

Riggs's jaw dropped. 'By God, I've never thought of such a thing—but it sounds as if it just might work.' He stuck out a grubby hand and Mateo bit back a smile as Portia took it with her own. 'Who the h—?' He checked himself. 'Who the blazes *are* you?'

'Lady Portia Tofton,' she said briskly.

Mateo stared. He had not heard her use her hereditary title since he'd arrived. Not that he'd given it much thought, but he'd supposed that she'd given it up on her marriage.

'We've come to discuss some important business with you,' she continued. 'But I'm pleased if I've been of some help.'

'Business?' Riggs eyed her up and down in a fashion that set Mateo's teeth on edge. 'It's enough of a shock to find a woman who understands agriculture. Will you tell me now that you've a head for business, too?'

Mateo edged closer. 'We want to discuss an acquaintance of yours, sir. Mr Averardo.'

'Never heard of him,' Riggs said. He also never took his eye off of Portia.

She took a deep breath. Mateo wished she hadn't. Riggs appeared to enjoy it far too much.

'Mr Riggs, I am the owner—was the owner—of property south of Newbury. Stenbrooke,' she said gently. 'Perhaps you recall it?'

'Newbury?' he beamed. 'Ah, then you're a Berkshire girl! Wonderful country, is it not? No place better than Wiltshire and Berkshire for research into important agricultural developments.' He took her arm and, turning her away from Mateo, led her a step or two to one side. 'You'll never see so many different terrains situated so close. Why, do you know that on this acreage alone I have high chalk plains, a lowland landscape and deeper-lying vales? Three separate soil systems in one estate! Not to mention the nearby river valleys, the—'

'Stenbrooke, Mr Riggs?' Mateo interrupted, following the two of them. 'You might recall sending your solicitor, Mr Rankin, to serve a deed of conveyance on the property—even though your name was not to be found on the deed.' He raised a brow. 'We were wondering how that came about?'

The man reddened. He clapped his hand to the milling, chatting men still standing about. 'You heard the lady, lads! Fetch the plough and get this blasted barley tilled under—and then we're for the river.'

The men scattered and Portia laid a hand on the man's arm. 'Please, Mr Riggs. That deed of conveyance has gone missing. I need to find it, so I can get Stenbrooke back.'

'I can't discuss it!' He seemed genuinely upset. 'It's not my business to share with you or anyone.'

'It's my business, sir,' Portia asserted. 'And you made it yours when you sent Mr Rankin to my home.'

'Would never have done it, had I known…' he waved his hand ineffectually '…had I known you.'

'I love Stenbrooke, just as you obviously love Longvale. Berkshire is indeed a remarkable country. I would be heartbroken to leave it.'

'I am all sympathy, my lady, but there is nothing I can do.'

'Of course you can. You can tell us about Mr Averardo.'

Riggs rubbed his fingers vigorously over his ears, as if he could block out the sound of her request. 'Don't know the man, I tell you!'

Mateo's frustration was building. 'Then how did the deed to Stenbrooke come into your possession? Why were you involved at all?'

Mute, Riggs shook his head.

Hell and damnation. Mateo's fists clenched. Was he to be thwarted at every step of this miserable business? He took a menacing step towards the man, determined to wring the information out of him, if need be.

But once again, Portia stalled him. She stepped in close to Riggs and wrapped her hand around his arm. She breathed deeply and smiled at the man. 'Perhaps you have not realised, Mr Riggs, that my father was the Earl of Winbury? I grew up at Hempshaw, also in Berkshire.'

Riggs stared at her, clearly not understanding what that information had to do with anything, but also clearly grateful for the reprieve. Mateo hadn't a clue what she was up to, either, but after her earlier success, he was willing to play this out her way.

'You've been to Hempshaw before, I believe, sir? At

least, I thought I recalled that you had escorted your mother there on at least one occasion.'

Horrified comprehension dawned on the man's face. Mateo could only hope it boded well for them.

'That's right—' Portia smiled '—I can see that you do recall it. My mother was the Countess of Winbury. Our mothers were the best of friends. I am still in contact with your mama, in fact.' Her smile grew slightly knowing. 'She's such a dedicated correspondent.'

Riggs gave a massive shudder. 'Well, I know it. You have my sympathies, if you are on the receiving end of her acid pen.'

Portia managed to look shocked. Mateo hid a smile.

'That's not a very chivalrous thing to say about your own mother, sir,' she chided. 'She's a lovely woman.' She paused and regarded him in a considering manner. 'But I admit she does seem to be a bit obsessed with your unmarried state.'

'Twenty years and I've heard of nothing else,' he moaned.

'Well, now that I've been to Longvale I have a greater insight into her objections. Your house is in a deplorable condition and your person is not much better. I don't mean to be rude, sir, but you could do with a bath, a hair cut and a trip to the tailor.' The mischievous smile returned. 'Clearly you are in want of a woman's guidance.' She darted a quick glance in Mateo's direction. 'In my next letter I shall tell your mama that I am in complete agreement with her. I dare say she will be very grateful to have her maternal urgings validated. *Very* grateful, indeed.'

Mateo gaped at her. The minx! He'd accused her of

blackmailing him into marriage and now she used the threat of marriage to blackmail Riggs. *Dio*, but it was a brilliant strategy. *She* was brilliant. He had to fight the mad impulse to laugh out loud, and the more insane urge to grab her up by her arms and kiss her, hard and long.

Except that her strategy appeared to have backfired. Instead of blurting out the information they were after, the repulsive man was running an evaluating eye over her. As if she was a prized filly at a horse fair. Mateo's heart began to pound.

'Well, I might actually consider my dear mother's feelings in this matter, were the chit in question one with a brain in her head and an understanding of what I'm doing here.' The lecherous devil leered at Portia. 'Damned if I wouldn't like to shock the old woman by presenting her with my wife!' Mateo watched him gnaw the inside of his cheek, considering. 'It would seem to solve your problems, as well, Lady Portia. What do you say?'

It was Portia's turn to gape. Her mouth actually dropped. Ah, but she was hoist by her own petard! Mateo had to recognise the humour in the situation, then, even though he could swear the man's words had started a red haze around the edge of his vision.

Portia recovered quickly. She threw another glance his way and then let loose with a gay laugh. 'Oh, Mr Riggs, you flatter me! Your mother will in no way consider me eligible to be your bride.'

'Certainly not,' Mateo agreed. 'Lady Portia is a widow, childless and likely too old, besides.'

This time she did not feign to look at him, although

her lips tightened. She looked absolutely lovely, even covered with mud and awash with annoyance.

'But how happy she will be to hear you are finally ready to take her well-meant advice!' she exclaimed. 'Of course you will be expected to find a fresh young bride. Your mother will likely insist that you spend the Season in London next spring, looking over the new crop of available young ladies.'

'She knows I can't do the Season,' Riggs said, aghast. 'The spring planting!'

'You'll have to count on missing part of the summer, for likely your young bride will wish to marry from her own home,' mused Mateo. 'Oh, and the autumn will be taken up with a bridal trip.'

'At harvest time?' Riggs shook his head. 'No. I've said it all along—marriage is a bad idea.'

'But imagine the rewards,' Portia cajoled. 'A lovely young woman, and likely children to follow. She'll keep your house, see to hiring more servants and make your life so much more pleasant!'

'Yes,' Mateo said sourly. 'She'll run through your money, expect you to keep regular hours, eat regular meals and keep her informed of your whereabouts at all times.' Mateo shuddered right along with their victim. 'And the people that will be about! Young hostesses must prove their mettle, mustn't they? There will be dinners and house parties and you'll have to do the pretty with all your neighbours—'

'Enough!' Riggs nearly shouted. 'I know what you're trying to do, but the devil of it is, it's likely to work! Lady Portia, I beg you, do not start my mother off on a tear. My nerves won't take it!' He sighed. 'But, truly, I cannot help you.'

'Tell us what you know,' Mateo said simply.

He drooped in defeat. 'All right, but come, you've quite worn me out. I need a drink.' He led them to the corner of the field, where an earthenware jug rested in the shade. He tipped it up and took a long draught, then offered it around. Both Mateo and Portia declined.

'It's just tea, not rotgut,' he clarified. 'It's gone cold, but it's good none the less.'

'No, thank you. The deed? Do you have it in your possession?' asked Mateo.

'What? No. I sent it on weeks ago.' He heaved a great sigh and settled to the ground, leaning back against a tree. 'There are a couple of stumps there.' He indicated with a wave of his hand. 'You're a strapping fellow,' he said to Mateo. 'Roll them over here and you two can sit.'

Mateo wrestled one of the wide remnants over and Portia perched herself upon it. He leaned against a tree and invited Riggs to continue.

'I handled the business for a friend,' he said with a shrug. 'I owed him, you see. Could hardly refuse.'

'Why not?' Portia asked.

He took another drink and wiped his mouth on his sleeve. 'It all started with Bright Early Morning.'

Mateo and Portia exchanged a look.

'Finest specimen of a racehorse I believe I've ever seen.'

'A racehorse?' Portia looked as startled as Mateo felt.

'Yes. It was a project of mine.' Riggs's expression lost focus and he gazed up into the canopy overhead. 'I thought to develop a special feed. Something to increase endurance, strengthen the bones, give a horse an advantage in a race. I proposed the plan to a friend, a man mad for racing and involved in breeding horses. I talked him into it, you might say.'

'Ah,' Portia said suddenly. 'The comfrey!'

'Yes, that was a component. We kept her on a special diet of my design. And she looked so damned healthy! Sound and strong—and fast, too. I thought we'd struck upon something big. We entered her in the Oxford races. My friend and I both bet heavy on her.'

'What happened?' asked Mateo, although the answer seemed obvious.

'She nearly did it, nearly won. They were turning into the last stretch and she started to pull away from the pack. Another jockey saw her making to leave them, and he jostled her—set his mount against her hard and deliberate.'

'Oh, no.' Portia's face fell.

'Aye. She went down in a tumble. Shattered a front leg and a back. Had to be put down right there on the track. Another colt was caught up in it, too. They tried to save him, but after a day or two, had to give it up.' He shook his head, closed his eyes and drank again. 'Worst day of my life.'

'But what does Bright Early Morning have to do with Stenbrooke?' asked Portia.

'My friend, the breeder, he lost his most promising filly. He lost a fortune. And he lost a good bit of his reputation, as well.' He turned pleading eyes to Mateo. 'You see, don't you? I owed him. Money, but more, too.

It was a debt of honour.' He looked again to Mateo for understanding.

And Mateo knew what he meant. 'So he asked this of you? That you deliver the deed to Stenbrooke?'

'Among other things, but, yes. He sent the paperwork by courier. But at the time we were having major drainage problems in an important field. So I sent the fellow on to Rankin so he could handle it for me.'

'And it was not Averardo who asked this of you?'

'No, it was Dowland—Lord Dowland, I should say.'

Mateo knew him. Had met the baron, in fact, when he had attended the festivities of his cousin Sophie's wedding to Lord Dayle. Near to Mateo's age, Dowland was full of enthusiasm for racing, and for Parliamentary reform. And he was something of a kindred spirit. Together they had cut a swathe through Dorset, mourning Charles's loss of freedom and celebrating their own.

'Who is Averardo to him, though?' Portia asked.

'I don't know. I barely looked the papers over, just sent the courier on to Rankin.' He paused. 'It was the courier's idea, now that I think back on it. He said he could see how busy I was, and suggested that the matter was straightforward, and something that could be handled by a subordinate.'

Mateo snorted. 'I've never heard of a less straightforward matter of business in my life.' He stilled. 'Nor a more inventive courier.' He fixed Riggs with a hard stare. 'All copies of that conveyance have gone missing, sir. Rankin thought it likely that this courier had brought them back to you.'

'The hell you say!' He bit his lip and shot an apologetic glance at Portia. 'Sorry, my lady, but, no, I got a note from Rankin stating the matter was done, and I've neither seen nor heard another word on the matter since.' He added with irony, 'Until today.'

'And would you perhaps recall the name of the courier?' Portia asked.

Mateo nodded. In a situation abounding with odd circumstances and unusual practices, this courier appeared to be the only common thread.

'No, that's not something I would...' He paused. 'Wait.'

He ran a hand over his brow, leaving a streak of dirt behind. Mateo declined to inform him of it and enjoyed a petty surge of satisfaction.

'I do recall something. It was an Italian name, Lawrence—no. Lorenzo or something like. I only thought twice of it because the man was so damned pretty. He looked like he'd stepped straight out of a painting from one of the Renaissance masters.'

'Is there anything else you might remember? Anything that might help us?' Portia asked.

Riggs just shook his head.

'We put a scare into your man Rankin. He's likely trying to track those deeds, as well. I doubt he'll bestir himself too far...' Mateo noted that Riggs had the grace to flush '...but if he finds a copy and files it with the courts before we can track this Averardo down, then our situation becomes more complicated.'

'I was little more than a go-between in this damnable situation,' Riggs said bitterly. 'And now I regret even that much.'

He could not regret it as much as Mateo mourned the thought of another delay. 'We'll need to speak to

Lord Dowland next, it would seem. Parliament's out, so he could be anywhere—at his seat or anywhere on the racing circuit. You wouldn't happen to have an idea just where we could find him, would you?' Try as he might to stop it, still bitterness leaked into the words as they left his mouth.

'He has a fine stud in Lambourn. He spends most of his time there, these days. You'll find him there,' Riggs said with assurance. 'We're trying the special diet again, and this time we are starting while the animal is young. He's looking over the likely candidates.'

Portia rose from her rustic seat. 'Thank you for telling us what you know.'

'You won't write to my mother?' He shuddered and climbed to his feet, as well.

She smiled. 'No.' Her head nodded towards the men behind him, hitching up the plough. 'Good luck with your field.'

'I'll call Rankin off if I can,' he promised.

'Thank you.'

Mateo flinched when she bent and kissed the man's grimy cheek. He took her arm and they started back on the long walk to the house. Portia strode along in earnest silence, for which he was grateful. In his mind he began to calculate distance, money and, above all, time. Precious days ran like water through his fingers. The harder he gripped, the more slipped away and each drip of a lost second echoed a mournful death knell for his future.

Chapter Eight

Portia watched Mateo's frown grow as they made their way back to Mr Riggs's run-down house. By unspoken consent the three of them politely declined Mrs. Pickens's gruff offer of a room for the night. Thankfully, Dorrie had only a short time to fuss over Portia's muddied hem before the landau was brought around. Her companion gazed back on the place thoughtfully as they pulled away.

'Do you know, I think we've discounted Mr Riggs's possibilities too quickly,' she mused.

Portia rolled her eyes. 'Oh, hush, Dorrie.'

The shadows lengthened as they headed towards Marlborough and the glower on Mateo's face kept apace. Guilt churned in Portia's stomach. She knew he was concerned over lost time and his need to be gone. She sighed in relief as they drove into town just as the last light slipped from the sky.

Stacks of carriages, post-chaises and coaches lined up outside the Castle Inn, but there were still rooms to be had. No private parlours were available, however, so the three of them ate a simple meal in the public dining room. Still and silent, Mateo picked at his food. Portia watched, the knot of anxiety in her stomach growing with each monosyllabic sentence he uttered. Guilt stabbed her. It was just so *wrong* to see his restless energy frozen, his ever-changing expression immobilised into one haunted expression. She could take no more.

'Excuse me, please.' She stood. 'I need to speak to the landlady.'

She pushed her way through the busy room, wishing fervently that she had never kissed Mateo Cardea. The signs were plain upon his face. She'd been in his shoes, could nearly feel his misery and increasing panic as if it were her own. He was trapped, just as firmly as she. Every time they caught a glimpse of light, the tunnel stretched out longer.

She made her way towards the back of the inn. It was quieter here, with the bustle and hum of the common rooms replaced by only the occasional tread on the stair. Portia found her way to a dark corner and covered her face with her hands. Somehow the fact that she'd kissed Mateo—propositioned him, practically—made it all that much worse. It added an element of awkwardness for him and a sense of anguished hopelessness for her.

For as stupid and futile as it might be, she still wanted him.

He'd refused her advances, made it clear that he valued his agenda over hers; he'd even ticked off to Mr Riggs all the reasons why she was unmarriageable, as if it were nothing more than a market list.

But he'd also let her shine today, in a way that her husband, her brothers, even her father would not have allowed. It had been she who had won Riggs over, because Mateo had not pushed her aside or felt threatened by her expertise. Even when her plan hadn't gone as she'd expected, together they had made it work. And she'd used her title again, she marvelled. She hadn't planned on it, it had just slipped out—and she hadn't even flinched. It had felt good. Almost, for a moment, as if she was whole again.

She'd been riding high as they left that field. He hadn't once made her feel awkward, or out of place. Instead she'd been buoyed by a feeling of success and self-worth—until she'd seen Mateo's face and realised what it had cost him.

She rubbed her brow repeatedly with her fingertips. Now all she could feel was exhausted by the emotional extremes of the day. For so long she'd kept herself insulated from exactly this sort of emotional tumult. It was safer to wrap her passion up into her gardens.

But it was also lonely. She'd managed to hide from that consequence for a long time. She'd brushed it aside and told herself that it was more than a fair trade. Until she'd burst into that inn in the middle of the night and found Mateo Cardea again.

Now all she wanted was to burrow into his arms and allow his kiss and the touch of his hands to chase the sadness, the awful, intense *aloneness*, away. Only he could do it, bring her back from that lonely edge, connect her solidly to the world once more.

But she couldn't ask it of him. So she determined to do what she could for him instead.

She brought her hands away from her face and pushed away from the wall. And froze. A gentleman stood just a few feet away, staring at her with a furrowed brow. Her heart started to pound. It was dark this far back inside the inn, and quiet.

'Are you all right, ma'am?' The stranger stepped closer. He wore a look of concern.

'Yes, of course. Thank you.' Portia stepped away, nervous. Long, dark locks framed his face, caught back in a queue. She'd seen plenty of men around the docks with hair like that, but never a man in the garb of a gentleman. The combination was incongruous.

She jumped as a bang, then a curse, sounded down the hall. The harried landlady emerged from a room, burdened with a load of dirty linen.

'Let me help you with that, Mrs White.' Portia hurried to the woman's side. She didn't look back at the stranger. 'I was wondering if you could answer a few questions for me.'

Mateo left the stables, his feet dragging as he headed back inside the inn. Tonight he missed the sea, with an intensity that only another sailor could understand. *Dio*, but he longed for the vast, empty ocean about him and a clean wind at his back. The sea challenged a man, it was true. Constantly she tested his skills and endurance, but she also gave him the sense that he was master of his own destiny. Prove yourself worthy, and she gifted you with the certain knowledge that the world was yours for the taking.

But here? Here nothing was certain, and his destination was complicated by the needs of others, and clouded by deceit. The opportunity for a simple trade with Portia had long since disappeared. Worse, his suspicion that someone was working to manipulate this unlikely chain of events only solidified as time passed and complications arose. But who would enact such an elaborate play? For truly, he began to feel as if he'd been playing a part prescribed to him by some unknown author—and he didn't even know the full cast of characters, let alone understand the plot.

Mateo had neither the time nor patience to play a pivotal role in someone else's drama. He was captain of a merchant ship, not a damned green-room dandy, and he knew what to do when a headwind tried to force him in a direction he did not want to go. He was prepared to beat an upwind course. Now he just had to inform his crew.

He wound his way through the sprawling inn, making for the back stairs. He'd just started up when he heard a door slam, somewhere deeper in the bowls of the place. A moment later he heard his name called.

'Mateo, wait!' Portia rushed from the shadows to join him on the stairs. 'I wish to speak to you!'

And was this not just what every seaman sent ashore dreams of—a beautiful girl waiting for him, eager for his company? Her skin glowed in the faint light, flushed with eagerness or exertion, and her eyes sparkled. She'd changed her gown, and although this one carried no field dirt about the hems, its deep v-shaped neckline tempted Mateo's thoughts in a very earthy direction.

'Will you come up to our room?' she asked.

'I will, if you agree to play chaperon. Miss Tofton

appears to be growing dangerously marriage-minded. I don't want to be caught in a compromising position.'

'Oh, stop.' She sounded perversely irritated. And that led him to feel perversely amused.

'I was just on my way there,' he said. 'I have something to discuss with you and Miss Tofton, as well.'

He gestured for her to proceed ahead of him, and then spent the rest of the two flights of steep stairs regretting that bit of chivalry. Her rump swayed above him, at nearly eye level and just out of his reach. His pulse quickened, his body stirred and he congratulated himself on the plan he meant to propose—one that would grant him a timely reprieve from Portia's tempting presence.

They'd nearly reached the second-floor landing when they met a couple of men coming down, carrying between them a wide, unwieldy trunk. The sweat and strain of their faces was testimony to the weight of the thing, their speed as they rounded the landing indicated their eagerness to be relieved of it. Portia pressed up against the stairwell wall to let them pass, but the damned thing shifted and swayed in her direction as the first man started backwards down the stairs.

Instinctively, Mateo reached out for her. He pulled her close, pressed her tight against the wall and shielded her body with his. The trunk thumped into him, scraping heavily across his back as the men cursed and struggled to regain their grips.

'Sorry, guv!' one of them called as they continued their descent.

He didn't respond. He was pressed full length into Portia Tofton—and he had no inclination to pull away.

Ever so slowly, she lifted her head. Their gazes met. And the world shrank, contracting mightily until nothing existed save for the two of them, and the retreating clatter of the men and their burden. Her eyes darkened, even as all the tension ebbed from her body. Desperately, Mateo wished he could close his eyes and savour this delicious sensation; her gradual moulding to the front of him.

Was this—this heart-pounding, breath-stealing moment—the reason his father had left the family legacy to Portia? Had he been so convinced that throwing them together would lead inevitably to this tortuous, physical longing? For the first time in his life, Mateo was tempted to do exactly as his father wished.

He stepped back instead, but her gaze remained locked with his, and he was damned if he could look away. The air between them had come alive. It pulsed with awareness, and pure, undeniable need.

There was no denying it. He had to kiss her. He might expire on the spot if he didn't. He reached for her, already anticipating the yield of her mouth against his, the feel of her exquisite curves filling his hands. His hands closed around her waist, cradled the generous swell of her hips. She reached up...and the slam of a door sounded above, followed by the fast approach of a set of footsteps.

Her arms dropped. He released her. They turned away from each other just as a gentleman reached the landing above.

'Good evening,' the man said with a tip of his hat. Judging by the hint of a smile on his damned pretty face, he had an idea of what he'd interrupted.

Mateo murmured an indistinct reply. He'd just indicated for Portia to precede him when a niggling memory caused him to turn and glance at the man again. But the fellow was gone already; he could hear his footsteps continuing on down the stairs. Mateo shrugged. Silent and tense, he followed Portia to the room she shared with Miss Tofton.

Her companion was comfortably ensconced there, Mateo noticed irritably. He'd asked her to come along expressly to prevent such tantalising interludes. What good did she do him, curled up by the fire like a cat?

'I was wondering where you'd got to, Portia, and was just trying to summon the energy to come and find you!' Miss Tofton said. 'Good evening, Mr Cardea. I hope you find your room as comfortable as we do ours?'

'I do.' It was the damned stairwell that had proved uncomfortable. 'I'd like to speak to you ladies about where we go from here, if you don't mind.'

'Of course.' Portia perched herself on the edge of the bed. 'I was going to ask the same of you.'

Mateo swallowed and went to lean against the mantel. 'I'm afraid you'll object to what I have to say,' he began.

At the same time, Portia had looked to Miss Tofton and warned, 'You won't like what I mean to propose.'

He met Portia's startled gaze while Miss Tofton looked from one to the other. 'Well,' she said briskly, 'let's get this unpleasantness over with, shall we?'

'I would normally encourage the lady to go first, but I have a matter of importance to discuss,' he said regretfully. 'I can scarcely believe there's been another leg added to this wild-goose chase, but it's clear we need to get to Lambourn next—and we need to get there as quickly as possible.' He paused. 'I've been enquiring into the state of the roads between here and there.'

'There are no direct routes, just a maze of narrow country lanes,' Portia interrupted. She shrugged. 'I've been asking about, as well.'

'It's not terribly far as the crow flies, perhaps twelve miles or so north-east, according to the ostlers. But a larger coach cannot travel that way. We'd have to travel back to Hungerford, take the road north and east to West Shefford, and then turn west towards Lambourn. It will double the distance and just take too long.'

'I agree,' said Portia. 'The best route is the most direct, but it must be taken on horseback, as there are places we would need to leave the roads altogether to cross over the chalk plains.'

'Yes, exactly.' He could only be grateful for her understanding. 'That's why I'd like you and Miss Tofton to return to Stenbrooke while I go alone.'

'What? No! I agree that Dorrie should return home, but the *two* of us will continue on to Lambourn.'

They glared at each other.

'Wait just a moment, both of you.' Miss Tofton sounded distinctly grumpy. 'Portia, you mentioned that Mr Riggs promised to stop that solicitor—Rankin—from pursuing this matter. If that's so, then why are we still in a tearing hurry?'

Mateo struggled for patience. 'Rankin is an unknown. Riggs may be able to stand him down. He might never even have lifted a finger against us after we left. Or he might be the mean and stubborn sort to do all he can to hurt us, despite anything Riggs says, just because we crossed him. We cannot know.'

He hardened his voice, just a bit. He wanted them both very clear on the urgency with which he needed to be done with this. 'But even if you remove him from consideration, I am still facing an important time issue. I must get back to Philadelphia soon, if at all possible. I am, of course, thrilled to even have the opportunity to get Cardea Shipping back, but if I delay much longer, this escapade will have cost me more than a few months' time and the loss of my pride. It will cost the company the rewards and opportunities resulting from several years of struggle and hard work.' Earnestly, he faced the two women. 'My family's fate is inextricably bound up with the success of the business. In a hundred different capacities, they make their livings and stake their futures on it. If I fail at this, I fail them, too.'

Portia's chin went up. 'Don't distress yourself, Mateo. I've no mind to let this linger on any further than need be, either. I'm tired of feeling as if an axe is about to fall on me. Where is that damned deed of conveyance? Who is this Averardo? Will I be able to keep Stenbrooke or be turned out on my ear? I need to know.' She gestured to her companion. '*We* need to know.'

She stood suddenly, and crossed to the other side of the bed. 'That courier… I haven't been able to get him from my mind.' She looked over her shoulder at him. 'Doesn't it begin to feel like we are being manipulated? As if this Averardo, whoever he is, doesn't wish to be known?'

'I'd reached the same conclusion,' Mateo confessed. 'I think he's purposefully putting obstacles between us.

It only adds another element of urgency to this mess we are in.'

'All right,' Miss Tofton said. Her voice rang with disapproval. 'I accept that all speed is necessary, but all the original objections to the two of you travelling alone still exist.' She sighed. 'I know I'm not a bruising rider like you, Portia, but I will do my best.'

Portia crossed the room again to kneel at her companion's feet. 'I'm afraid it will be too rough for you, dear,' she said gently.

'She's right, though,' Mateo said quietly. 'It would be easier were I to go alone.' After the stairwell, she had to have an inkling how true a statement that was. He stared down at her. The light of the fire caught in her hair and flowed, molten, through her heavy locks. Her eyes, though, were hidden in shadows. 'You can trust me, Portia.' It came out in nearly a whisper.

He wanted her to trust him, so intensely he ached with it.

She put her head down on Miss Tofton's knee, and his heart fell.

'In my head, I know that is true, Mateo.' Her voice was muffled in her companion's skirts. Suddenly her head snapped back up. 'But I've played the docile daughter, sister and wife for too long, and I'm less than satisfied with where it's got me.' She shook her head and stood. 'It's less about trusting you than it is about learning to trust in and rely on myself.' Her jaw set and determined, she met his gaze. 'I'm going with you.'

Mateo breathed deeply, waiting for his pride to pound annoyance and disappointment into submission. 'All right.'

Miss Tofton still wore a disapproving frown. 'How long will it take you to get to Lambourn and see the baron?'

'A few hours' ride to arrive. Not long to discuss it, provided we find him home. A full day, then, to see the business done,' Mateo calculated.

Miss Tofton's chin lifted. 'Well, then. I will take the carriage back to Hungerford and await you at the Bear. Meet me there once you've talked to your baron.' She let loose a weary sigh. 'Then perhaps we can go home.'

Portia said nothing, just looked to him. Mateo scowled. Should he expect the pair of them to place their trust in him at this late date? Apparently not. He gave a curt nod.

Portia reached down and gave her hand a squeeze. 'If it's any consolation, Dorrie, I promise not to ravish him on the ride over.'

Mateo snorted and pushed away from the mantel. 'You'd best get some sleep. We'll need to depart early in the morning.'

'I'll just ask Mrs White to have a maid awaken us at dawn.' She took a step towards the door and then stopped. 'I'll also be sure that *two* mounts will be readied in the morning.'

He nodded and she swept from the room. With a sigh of resignation, Mateo bent low over Miss Tofton's hand. 'I'll be sure that the driver has the landau's top up for you.'

She rose from her chair and stopped him as he turned for the door. 'I can't help but notice that you did not make me a promise similar to Portia's.'

No, he hadn't, and what he likely needed was a

damned vow of chastity. He glanced towards the doorway where Portia had disappeared, and was distracted by a sudden thought. 'Miss Tofton—does Portia normally use her title?'

The lady frowned. 'No. As the daughter of an earl, she could, of course, choose to use the honorary title, but I've not heard her addressed as Lady Portia in years.' Her scowl deepened and she regarded him thoughtfully. 'Do you mean to say you've heard her refer to it?'

He nodded. 'She used her title today, when she introduced herself to Mr Riggs.' He paused. 'Do you think it is significant?'

'Yes,' Miss Tofton said quietly. 'Yes, I do.'

'What does it mean, then?'

She frowned at him once more. 'It means that you had better make me that promise, Mr Cardea.'

He laughed and this time he kissed her hand as he bent over it. But he didn't promise.

Chapter Nine

The lane they followed narrowed further as Portia and Mateo grew close to the town of Albourne. For some time now there had been nothing to see save for the massive hedgerows on either side. But while the view was restricted, the noise was immense. The thick walls of crossing hawthorn branches provided a home for hundreds of warbling, chirping, twittering and peeping songbirds. They'd set a good pace, but the combination of hot sun, monotonous surroundings and cacophony of sound had lured Portia to a pleasant daze. When the concert suddenly ceased, it was a shock. She jerked to attention.

Her bad-tempered, piebald mount swivelled her ears, puzzled by the sudden absence of sound. They fixed forwards when a jingling of traces sounded ahead, around a curve in the lane. A squeal followed, and then a string of curses. Portia met Mateo's questioning look with a shrug, and they approached the turning with caution.

'What the devil?' Mateo exclaimed.

They were met with the curious sight of a high-balanced rig *backing* towards them.

'There must be someone coming this way,' Portia explained. 'There's no room to pass.' She studied the vehicle advancing towards them, end first. It barely fitted the lane, brushing the hedges on either side with its wheels. 'We'll have to go back.'

They retreated nearly half a mile, until they reached a wide turn that left room to manoeuvre. Patiently they waited while the gig made its slow way back and squeezed into the narrow space left. The driver, a red-faced young man, continued to swear and bemoan the scratched paint on his rig.

At last, then, they got a clear look at the cause of the ruckus—a placid-faced farmer driving a cart loaded high with stacks of hay. He ignored the cursing young blade, but tipped his hat at Mateo and winked at Portia. This last bit of insolence pushed the young man past his limit. He cracked his whip over his poor team's heads and went thundering back down the way they'd all come.

Laughing, Portia and Mateo followed at a more reasonable pace.

'I have some sympathy for the fellow,' Mateo confessed. 'That's exactly how this enterprise has felt: one step forwards and two steps back.' He shot Portia a crooked smile, the first that she'd seen since before they'd met Mr Riggs. 'I'm sorry if I've been as crotchety.'

'I think we might be excused, even if we were to curse a blue streak to rival that young man's,' Portia said, returning his smile. 'Heaven knows we've reason enough.' Her smile twisted a little. 'And heaven knows I heard worse when I tagged after you and my brothers.'

'And J.T.' He'd gone still, tense.

'And J.T.,' she agreed. She chose not to meet his gaze.

Mateo was suddenly blinded by a flash of insight. J. T. Tofton was not the sort of man who would appreciate his wife having a rank higher than his own. Had he insisted that Portia abandon her rightful title and take up his name instead?

He turned his gaze ahead. 'We should reach Albourne shortly. If you don't mind, I'd like to ride through. Mrs White packed us a huge luncheon; I thought perhaps we'd find a likely spot off the road to eat, after a while.'

She agreed. Soon the hedgerows ended, and the lane widened as they drew near the little town. They were quickly through, and the road out opened up again, and Portia gradually became aware that the quality of the silence had changed. Tension radiated from Mateo. He held his face carefully expressionless.

She waited.

Eventually he broke. 'I don't know that I've adequately thanked you, Portia, for giving me a chance to get Cardea Shipping back.'

'Of course you have. But it's I who owe you thanks, and perhaps an apology. My simple plan did not turn out as we expected, did it?'

He grunted. 'Well, neither of us could have predicted all of this.' He tilted his head, indicating the countryside about them. 'But I was wondering if getting Stenbrooke back would be enough.' He paused delicately. 'Miss Tofton mentioned debts, a pile of them that emerged after J.T.'s death.'

She felt herself colouring. 'Thank you for your concern, but we've managed. I've met all the honest debtors who have come knocking.'

'She also mentioned…indignities.'

Portia kept her tone carefully even. 'I believe Dorrie has been talking a bit too much.'

His brow lowered and a grim light shone from his dark eyes. 'If someone has bothered you, if a man, perhaps, has been importuning you…' His voice fell away.

'No man has importuned me,' she said, telling the truth, just not all of it. 'I'll be all right, Mateo. Dorrie and I will both be all right. We'll live a happy life at Stenbrooke, I promise you. You may rest easy.' She gentled her tone. 'But thank you for asking.'

He nodded. They grew silent again. Portia tried not to dwell on how his concern warmed her. The undulating downs did not provide much of a distraction, though one loomed soon enough when they reached a ridge and the track they followed veered sharply south.

Mateo pulled to a stop. 'Now we leave the lane and head out across the plain.'

'It's forbidding, isn't it?' Portia asked. The open, rolling landscape, empty of anything save dry, waving grass and the occasional planted field, made her feel small.

'We shouldn't be out there long. Believe it or not, there's a stretch of wood ahead, the ostlers said, a thin remnant of an ancient forest. When we reach it, we turn north and should intersect another useful lane.'

They rode on. The sense of isolation was nearly complete. Occasionally her horse would shy from a breaking ground bird, but the absence of any tree cover or variation quickly grew to be as monotonous as the hedgerows. She caught sight of a dark smudge on the horizon and wondered if it might be the beginning of the wood Mateo had mentioned.

Closer proximity revealed it to be a burial mound, instead. It was quite the longest one she'd ever encountered. The most prominent feature in the landscape—indeed, the only one—she found her eye inescapably drawn to it. There were several ploughed and planted plots in proximity, but a wide swathe of undisturbed plain had been left to surround it.

Mateo dismounted as they drew close, running a curious eye over the length of the thing. 'Shall we stop? It may be the only shade we see for a while.'

'Let's,' Portia agreed. She let him see to the staking of the horses while she unpacked the saddlebags. Mrs White had thoughtfully folded a large linen square in with her hearty luncheon. They had the makings of quite a nice little picnic.

'Come, sit down,' she beckoned. Mateo was pacing around the curved end of the mound, eyeing it with interest. He obeyed her summons, and took a seat a little apart from her. Leaning against the thing, he downed a long swill of Mrs White's apple cider, then patted the turf-covered mound behind him. 'This I have not seen in Pennsylvania, though it reminds me of the ceremonial lodges the savages build. I'm sure you can tell me why the English would fashion a hill in such a desolate spot. Does it serve a ritualistic purpose?'

She smiled around her sandwich. 'It's a burial mound.'

'As in, filled with the dead?' He wore a slightly horrified look.

She nodded. 'There's no need to be frightened, though. I've heard of the occasional ghostly figure at these sights, even unearthly spirit hounds, but I believe they mostly show up during the solstices.'

His hand hovered over the food, deciding. 'I'm not frightened. I just hate the thought of them, trapped in the dark, mouldering in the earth, drying, decaying.' He shuddered.

She put aside her sandwich. 'Thank you so much for that vivid description.' She looked at him closely. 'So no burial for you, then?'

Juice dripped down his chin as he bit into a peach. Portia found herself licking her own lips. *Stop.*

'Aye, but it'll be a burial at sea, like any good sailor.'

She shivered. 'So you'd prefer being devoured by sharks and crabs? I don't see as that has any more appeal.'

'Ah, but it does. For I'll become part of the great, living sea.' He sighed. 'Free in the vastness of the ocean.'

His eyes unfocused and she took the opportunity to drink in the sight of him. Someone should paint him, she decided. His constant energy had been harnessed for the moment as he leaned back, one arm propped on a raised knee, wearing a contemplative expression on a face turned up towards the sun... She sighed.

'I'll be the wave that slaps against the shore, the breeze that lifts the sail of some lucky brig.' His tone vibrated with intensity.

'The hurricane gale that sinks ships,' she said wryly.

'Only my competitors, perhaps.' He laughed.

She turned away from the beautiful picture of him smiling at her. He was stealing all the pieces of her heart, one smile, and one touch at a time. It frightened her, but it also stirred her temper—towards him, for staying resolute in pursuit of his goals, and towards herself, because she did not.

'I was wrong, then. You make a good case.' She sighed. 'Crossing the ocean was one of my favourite parts of visiting your family in Philadelphia. I loved the ship at night, when all grew quiet. I would stand at the rail and feel as if I were alone with the wind and the stars and the sea.'

Reaching out, she ran a hand over the rough turf. 'Perhaps these men have become part of this land,' she suggested. 'It seems likely that they might have loved this place as much as you love the sea.'

'If they wished it, then I hope it is so,' he said quietly.

She looked out over the plain. Suddenly the place did not seem so sad and desolate, not when the sun shone brightly as she sat in the blowing grass, amidst the buzz of insects and with the sky so brilliantly blue overhead.

'It really is lovely here, isn't it?' she asked with wonder. 'It's hard to believe, while sitting here in such tranquility, that someone might be scheming against us.' She turned back to him. 'It does seem so to you, too, though?'

'We've had only a hint here and there. I suppose we cannot prove it, but I feel the truth of it.'

She understood just what he meant. It almost felt like a tickle, at the very edge of her consciousness, a hint of a forming pattern taking shape in her mind.

Their dark thoughts had broken the spell of the place. Mateo shifted restlessly and climbed to his feet.

'I'll pack the rest of this away,' she told him. 'Let's go on.'

They rode companionably close, without speaking. It was to be found in silence, too—that connection she'd been craving. It rippled through her, setting her alight, making her very aware of how close his leg was to hers. He rode just a stride ahead of her. If she nudged her horse just a little, then their legs might brush. She didn't do it, though. Instead she looked her fill, following the solid curve of his booted calf up to his muscular thigh, and climbing higher to where he sat firmly in his saddle.

Firm. A very good word.

'What did you mean to do, Mateo,' she asked, mainly to distract herself, 'if I had refused to sell my interest in Cardea Shipping?'

'Hmm? Oh, I had a few ideas.'

'Such as? Or are you not comfortable sharing them with me?'

'Packet boats,' he said. 'The *Lady Azalea* is my own ship, not the company's. I thought to use her to start up a business with a regular schedule of packets from Philadelphia to English and European ports. There are a few very successful enterprises out of New York; I thought to give them a run for their money.'

'You've family here in England. I know Papa told me your cousin Sophie had married into the aristocracy. Did you never consider a life here, perhaps?' She tried with all her might not to betray the blind, breathless hope that suddenly sprouted inside her.

He laughed. 'No doubt Sophie would see me set up somehow, but can you see me giving up the sea?'

Hope withered away. She sighed. 'No, I suppose not.'

'What a challenge that would have been, though,' he mused. 'To have the run of a business from the start.'

'I'm sure you would have made a success of it,' she said stoutly. 'But there'll be no need, if we can just track down the elusive Averardo.'

He looked back. 'I'd forgotten what a good listener you are, Portia. It pains me to remember all the adolescent twaddle I poured into your ears when we were young. But I always felt better after talking to you.' He turned his gaze towards the plain. 'Perhaps that is why my father tried so hard to see us married, back then.'

'Do you think this is what your father hoped for? Why he wrote his will the way he did? Was he hoping that we would be thrown together like this?'

He glanced back at her over his shoulder. 'In all likelihood. I'm sorry that he did not appear to have considered your feelings when he came up with the idea.' He sighed. 'It is just like him, though. Everything must always be his way. He knew but one way to run a shipping company, had one clear-cut vision of how a merchant gentleman should conduct himself and considered marriage the only route to happiness.'

He rode on quietly for a moment. 'Do you know, if your father were still alive, I'd suspect *him* of conspiring to carry out my father's wishes and drawing out this process. The whole mess just reeks of the two of them.'

'I'd be inclined to agree with you. Your father was at Hempshaw not long before my father died, did you know?' She sighed. 'I was married by then, of course, but I came back for a short visit. Even though Papa was mostly bedridden at that point, they were having a grand time of it. I know his visit was a great comfort.'

'I knew of it, although I believe I was pursuing contacts along the Rio de la Plata at the time.'

Her mouth twisted. 'The irony is that if my father were still alive, J.T. would likely never have gambled Stenbrooke away. He was more than a little intimidated by Papa. It wasn't until after he had gone that J.T. began to really run amok. If Papa had been alive, he would never had got himself killed so—' She caught herself.

He'd twisted around in his saddle to watch her. After a moment's pause she continued. 'If I had not needed your help with Stenbrooke, Mateo, I would have just handed Cardea Shipping right back to you.' She stared ahead at him. 'It's what I'd do now, if so much weren't at stake.'

He checked his mount, holding him in until they were riding abreast. He met her earnest gaze with a direct one of his own. 'I know,' he said simply.

He fell silent then, and so did she. Portia felt oddly as if he'd relieved her of a burden, one which she hadn't even known she'd carried. She enjoyed the feeling, relished the peace of just being in his company, as she'd done so often in the past. She'd just noticed the dark line ahead that surely must be the wood they were watching for, when he spoke suddenly, startling her.

'Why, Portia? Will you tell me why you married a buffoon like J.T.?' He grimaced. 'Even his name was an affectation. I never understood it. What was wrong with just plain James?'

She gave a little smile, although there was no

humour behind it, and tried to avoid the first question by answering the second. 'Well, there you've hit upon your answer. You knew him. Nothing plain was ever good enough for J.T.' She did laugh then. 'Dorrie always called him James Talbot, though he hated it. He had an uncle in Virginia who'd first called him J. T. He loved it, and thought it sounded exotic, like something from the American frontier.'

'Perhaps it would have made sense, had his interests lay in that direction. But they didn't, did they? As far as I know, his inclinations centred on drinking, gambling and wenching. He never showed the least interest in anything involving hard work.'

'No, he did not.' She said it flatly. Forbiddingly.

He chose not to notice. 'And yet you married him. Knowing that about him, knowing that he'd always been envious of your brothers, of their position and rank and their life of relative ease. Still you married him.'

She maintained her stubborn silence.

He stared at her for several long moments. She nudged her mount until the piebald picked up a bit of speed and pulled ahead.

'Portia, please,' he called. 'I want to understand.'

'There's no need to go into all of that,' she bit out.

He drew abreast of her again. 'Perhaps I only feel a need to pay you back for all those times I talked and you listened. Perhaps I've just had too much damned time to think over the last few months—about my life, about my family and my father.' He paused. 'About you.'

His tone grew harder, almost angry. 'Or perhaps I just wish to make myself feel better, but I cannot fathom how you could have ended up with that bastard. Portia, please. I want to know.'

His insistence opened up something ugly inside of her. The anger that had stirred in her earlier grew, clawing its way out and up, emerging from her suddenly tight throat in a torrent of bitter words.

'Well, that does change things, does it not? You want to know. And I, of course, will cast all my own inclinations aside to oblige you.' She sniffed. 'Every day you make it clear how much more important your wants are than my own. But I warn you—you may not enjoy getting your way in this case. For you see, I married J.T. solely to get what *I* wanted.'

She'd shocked him. Good. She *liked* shocking him. Forget Stenbrooke—as of this moment her only goal was to continually and increasingly shock the hell out of Mateo Cardea.

Unfortunately, she's also spooked her mount. She shied, sidling sideways. Portia settled herself deeper into her seat and brought her under control.

Mateo's face hardened. 'Calm yourself,' he ordered.

But she was in the grip of madness and pique and the sudden urge to push him away, just as he'd done repeatedly to her. And what better way than to reveal all the dirty truth behind her marriage?

'No. You asked—repeatedly—and now I shall answer. No doubt you wonder what I could have wanted enough to make me marry a man like J.T.? I'll tell you, Mateo. I wanted a *life*.'

The incomprehension on his face only fuelled her anger.

'I was one and twenty years old. My mother was

gone, my father was failing. His health had been growing worse for a long time, but he was full of male pride
and mortally determined not to let the world know it.
I was the only one left at home—and so it fell to me to
help him. Land steward, secretary, nursemaid, I did a
little of it all while my brothers pulled mad pranks at
school and revelled in low living in London.'

She paused for a breath and reached down to soothe
her skittish horse. The forest loomed closer now. She
could clearly see the mixed line of oak and chestnut at
the edge of the plain.

'When it became impossible to hide Papa's illness,
Anthony moved home. My brothers gathered and one
of their main topics of conversation was what they were
to do with me.'

Mateo made a sound of protest and she gave a bitter
laugh.

'Anthony was betrothed, and did not believe that
his new bride would wish for me to be hanging about,
interfering with her control of the house and her new
role. But none of the others wanted me—having an
unmarried sister about would interfere with their pleasures. They'd nearly convinced Anthony he had no other
choice when J.T. offered up a new solution. "I'll take
her off your hands", was his exact wording, if I recall
correctly.'

Mateo's grim expression lightened just a bit at that.
'Eavesdropping again, were you?' he asked.

She lifted her hand in a gesture of futility. 'What else
was I to do? They were deciding my future over drinks,
as if I were the leftover runt of the litter.' Resentment
spilled out of her. 'I suppose I should have been grate-

ful that none of them thought to put me in a bag and drown me.' She took a moment to gather herself. 'They took J.T.'s offer to Papa. At first he flatly refused, but I badgered and bullied him until he agreed.'

'You *wanted*—ah, you knew Stenbrooke would come to you on your marriage,' he said quietly.

'Yes. It was a plan that worked for everyone. My brothers were rid of me. J.T. elevated himself from a country squire's son to the son and brother-in-law of an earl; he took my dowry and used it to run with my brother's set, to live the fast town life his father refused to finance. And I didn't care, because I got Stenbrooke—my own home, my own life and the chance to live there alone for much of the year.'

They'd nearly reached the edge of the forest. Without comment, Mateo urged his horse north. She followed and for a few moments they travelled parallel to the wood line in silence. But this time it was an uneasy stillness, and it did not last.

'One thing I don't understand,' Mateo said eventually. 'Surely you had other choices. You did have a Season, did you not?'

Her anger had ebbed a little as she finished her story, but now it surged anew and quickly rose to new heights. 'Choices,' she said flatly. 'Do you really not understand how few of those a woman in my position possesses? Yes, I did have a Season. It's hard to believe I didn't take, isn't it? Me, with dirt under my fingernails, more interest in landscape and horticulture than fashion and flirting, and brothers to torment anyone who might look past all that?'

She glared at him and furiously fought back the

sudden tears that threatened to flow. 'Do you profess to be surprised that no man wanted me, Mateo? I don't know why you should, when you've shown repeatedly that you do not!'

Her fury set her mount off again. The piebald reared, dancing on her hind feet. She clamped down and held on until the horse settled and then she launched herself out of the saddle. Furious, she tossed the reins at Mateo, not even waiting to see that he caught them. Then she stomped the few paces remaining and entered the sheltering embrace of the forest.

Only instinct allowed Mateo to snatch her reins out of the air. Shock actually held him rooted to his seat for a moment afterwards. He stared after her, his mind frozen under the onslaught of a veritable gale of emotion.

Guilt blew at him the hardest. The men in Portia's life had indeed failed her, and, judging by her last remark, he ranked high in their number. It was a truth he'd been avoiding, but the sudden certainty of it sent him reeling off balance.

He slid down to the ground, craning to catch a glimpse of her while he tethered the horses, but she'd disappeared into the murky distance. Impatient, he called her name as he followed her into the dense covering of oak and chestnut. 'Portia!'

No response. He shook his head. Distance—it was exactly what was missing between them. It seemed it should be there, a natural blockade resulting from years apart, their awkward past and the innate differences in their personalities. Instead they'd stepped without a hitch into the old closeness they'd shared—and the distance between them felt as if it was shrinking by the minute.

He went further into the wood, noting the change in atmosphere. The light broke through only intermittently here, and the air felt several degrees cooler. The constant breeze that swept across the plains did not reach this far in, it only set up a constant rustle in the tops of the trees. He could hear nothing else, in fact, save for the crunch of his footsteps on the bracken-covered forest floor.

'Portia?'

Indeed, this must be the remnant of an ancient forest, for some of the trees were massive. Mateo began to feel ridiculous, as if they played at children's games once more.

'Portia! *Cara*—come back!'

'No.'

Well, it was a reply at least, and it came from ahead and to the right.

'Go back, Mateo. Better yet, go on. Wait for me at the road.' Her voice sounded thick, with an embarrassed, nearly pleading note colouring her words. 'I need a few moments alone.'

Ah, he was close. He thought she might be behind the oak ahead.

'Now, Portia,' he said. 'I may have proved myself a prying lout and likely an overbearing pain, as well, but I am a gentleman. I cannot leave you here alone. You might be eaten by wolves.'

'There are no wolves in Wiltshire.'

He *was* close. He could practically hear her blink. He

crept up to the massive tree on silent feet. 'Wild boars, then?' he said, peeking around the massive trunk at her. 'Ferocious badgers?'

She cut him a scathing glance. 'No, and no.' She pushed herself away from the tree, away from him. 'And I'm not one of your dockside doxies in any case. I'm a country woman—I can take care of myself.' She raised a haughty brow at him. 'And clearly that is a skill I must fully develop.' Her gaze fell away. 'You're more of a danger to me than any wild creature.'

He sucked in a breath. 'Portia. *Cara*, I …'

Her hand hovered over her chest, as if she were in pain. 'No. You cannot cover this with laughter or fix it with glibness. I am not a child to be jollied out of my ill humour.' Her eyes narrowed. 'You were the first one, Mateo—the first man to break my heart.'

His heart sank. 'But I thought… All those years ago… When I wrote you, you were as incredulous as I at the idea of a marriage.'

Disappointment weighed down her expression. 'You knew. I will not believe you didn't know how I felt about you.'

He had, of course. 'I'd hoped it was a childish infatuation, one you'd got over.' He'd wanted desperately to believe it, so that he could carry on with his chosen course without an added burden of guilt.

'I had to be grateful—you rejected me in the nicest possible way, giving me a chance to salvage my pride and hold my head high.' She sighed. 'I was young, a naïve girl who'd spent most of her life tearing up her father's gardens. I knew I didn't have anything to offer you, to hold your interest or compete with the excitement of a privateer's life.' She turned away. 'But it still hurt. My feelings for you were real and it took me a long time to get over them.'

She humbled him with her honesty. 'I'm truly sorry, *cara*, for the hurt I caused you.'

'And then you came back, and I discovered that I had not fully banished those feelings—they were still there, buried deep inside. But I couldn't trust either of us enough to let them out.' She shook her head. 'I thought losing Stenbrooke, getting involved in all of this—' she gestured '—was the worst thing that could have happened to me. To either of us. But now I'm beginning to think it's been a gift.'

He snorted. 'You'll have to explain that convoluted theory.'

'Truly—the situation has forced us to step back and evaluate, to reaffirm what is important to us. And it's given us a chance to get to know each other again. For a long time you were an ideal to me, but now I feel as if I am growing to know the man underneath.' Her chin rose. 'And I'm happy to have shown you the woman I am now. I have flaws and foibles.' She grimaced. 'But I have strengths, too—far more than the girl you used to know.'

Tenderness welled within him. 'Portia, you are a lovely, incredible woman. I hope you will never let anyone tell you otherwise.'

She took a step closer to him. Her eyes went dark as they locked with his. 'Say it again, Mateo,' she asked. 'When you say such things I begin to believe them.'

Almost involuntarily, he stepped back. 'Portia…'

'What? When we are done with this business, whether

I have Stenbrooke back or not, I'll be starting a new life. I'm no longer a girl, a daughter, a wife. I'll be my own woman and I'm not going to hide away any longer.'

Mateo swallowed.

'I find a certain justice in the thought that the man who broke the girl's heart should help shore up the woman's,' she said, her voice gone husky. She took another step closer.

'That's enough,' he said. He had a sudden empathy for her skittish mount. He was feeling unaccountably unsettled himself. 'Aside from all the pain that I've already dealt you, there are too many other reasons for us not to contemplate...' His sentence trailed away.

'Contemplate what?'

'Whatever you're contemplating,' he said firmly.

Her dark eyes glittered in the dim light. 'What are the other reasons, again?'

Did she think to mock him? 'You know what I mean.'

She stilled. 'Ah, yes,' she said. 'Your profits.'

'Yes,' he ground out. 'Such matters are important to me, I cannot deny it. Largely because they are important to my family and their legacy. But there is more to consider. I also think of the future.' He reached out and took both her hands, and was surprised at how cold they felt. 'Not just the future of Cardea Shipping, but of my own future. And yours, too.'

Her chin went up again. 'I'll take care of my own future, thank you.'

'Yes, you will. And you'll do it at Stenbrooke, should we ever see this business through.' He sighed and enclosed both of her chilled hands inside his. 'We are very different people, *cara*. The story you just told and nearly every word you've said to me since I arrived have proved that.'

'I don't know what you mean,' she said unsteadily.

'You longed for nothing more than your own home. You fought for it and you won. It was a victory and you celebrated by putting down roots, and making Stenbrooke part of you.' He shook his head. 'This is something I could never do.' He met her gaze and let the regret he felt show. 'Our futures lie down very different paths.'

'I thought I had made it clear.' She pulled her hands from his. He found out how successfully he'd warmed them when she placed them squarely on his chest. 'I'm not asking for your future.'

He pulled away and let loose a bitter laugh. 'So you think now, at this moment. And I think I've already done enough damage.'

She closed her eyes. 'Perhaps you are right. We are different. I need Stenbrooke and you need to be free. But it feels as if we've stumbled into this place out of time, a spot between our pasts and our futures, where we can just be. And we can *be* together, if we wish it.' Her eyes opened again and her gaze connected hotly with his. 'I spent my past alone, Mateo. I'll likely spend the future the same way. I don't want to be alone here, too.'

He stared at her, standing in a dappled pool of sunlight and shadow, naked hope and desire on her lovely face, and he was frozen in an agony of indecision.

What should his next move be? He knew what he wanted it to be. He wanted to make her happy for once, here in this moment. He wanted to bury his hands in her hair, lay her down on the forest floor and prove to her once and for all how lovely she was, inside and out.

He moaned in frustration. There was no good choice. He would hurt her now or hurt her later.

She reached for him, burying her fingers in his cravat and pulling him close. 'You cannot deny that there is passion between us,' she whispered. 'I can feel it in the beating of your heart.' She brushed soft lips across his. 'And it matches the rhythm of my own.'

Her boldness captivated him. *Layers.* There they were again. And this was the sweetest, most tempting layer of Portia Tofton he'd seen yet.

'Damnation,' he said. All objection, all thought of right and wrong and consequence, was lost in a haze of desire. He gave up, gave in and pressed his mouth to hers.

Willingly, happily, her heart filled with joy, Portia lost herself in Mateo's kiss. *Yes.* This. This is what she'd ached for, for nearly half of her life, it seemed. His arms came around her, wrapping her tight and she was gone.

No, not gone. *More.* With Mateo she was a brighter, better version of herself. He looked past the tight, contained picture she showed to the rest of the world and gave her the beautiful gift of acceptance.

His kiss grew more demanding and she abandoned thought and answered with her own fierce need. Her hands moved, measuring the breadth of his chest and shoulders, dragging into the dark abundance of his curls, and at last, digging beneath layers of linen and camlet to touch silky hot skin underneath. At last.

He shuddered beneath her hands. 'Dear God in

heaven,' he moaned, and then he returned the favour, burying his face in the sensitive curve of her neck while he busied himself with the fastenings of her habit.

She gasped when he spread the fabric wide. Impatient, he tweaked her straining nipples through the fabric of her chemise. He urged her several steps back and she went willingly, until she came up against the thick tree trunk that she'd hidden behind a few minutes ago. That delicious feeling of connection swept over her again. She was part of him and he of her and somehow they both belonged in this strange place at this exact time. His fingers flew through the ties and tiny buttons of her shift and stays and at last all barriers were gone and suddenly she was bare to his touch.

Except that he didn't touch. He put his hands to her shoulders and pressed her back against the rough bark of the tree. An inarticulate growl of pleasure rumbled through him as he looked his fill. The cool forest air caressed her and her breasts swelled. Her nipples rose stiff with longing for him to do the same.

'So beautiful,' he whispered. And then he was bending down, hovering over her while his breath, hot and sweet, teased one tight peak. His finger drew tempting circles about the other.

She arched her back, silently begging for more.

'Tell me, *cara*,' he said, his voice gone rough with desire. 'You started this, damn you. Now tell me what you want.'

And she did, because with Mateo she knew that she was safe, and that he would hear her.

'Touch me,' she asked in a voice that she barely recognised. 'Do it now, Mateo.'

His tongue darted out, flicked over her and she nearly wept with pleasure. For long moments he kissed and laved and sucked while she moaned and sighed in incoherent, ever-increasing need.

Suddenly he stood and pushed himself between her thighs. Instinctively her legs widened to admit him. The hard, iron-hot length of him pressed against the intimate spot between her legs, and she moved against him in anticipation. Reaching down, he began to lift her heavy skirts up and out of the way.

'Wrap your leg around me,' he ordered.

She did. A pang of unease rippled through her. It had been a long time since she'd been so open and vulnerable to another, on many levels. But then he smiled down at her and she knew. She could risk anything with him.

His fingers traced a soft path up her leg, and the last of her anxiety vanished. At the top of her garter he lingered, teasing her soft skin and making her breath come quickly. Slowly his fingers climbed, ever higher, until they found the hot, wet core of her.

Their simultaneous groans echoed through the trees.

He slicked a finger deep inside of her, and then up to the swollen centre of her desire. Back and forth in her silken folds he stroked.

Her breath began to come in gasps. Lightly he rubbed and deeply he plunged, winding the spring of her need until she was ready to explode.

His fingers eased higher, danced faster over her. Her hands came away from him, her arms flattened behind her, against the rough tree trunk. She sobbed his name as her body strained towards him.

He answered with a firmer stroke. With his other hand he reached up and grasped her nipple. And that was the end of her. Light flashed behind her eyes as her universe broke apart. Wave after wave of pleasure and relief racked through her. Again she cried his name, and she reached for him, clutching tight lest she be spun away by the violence of her release.

He held her tight until she ceased trembling. Over and over he peppered her brow and temple with soft kisses. 'Beautiful,' he murmured. 'You are beautiful, Portia.'

It was a gradual process, but slowly up became up again, and down, down and she returned to herself. She felt light, happy and utterly content with the world around her. Straightening, she met Mateo's mouth with hers. He kissed her deeply, greedily. She welcomed him and reached for the fall of his trousers.

Frustration mingled with regret in his expression as he set her hand from him.

'But, Mateo—'

He shushed her. 'I am content. I am happy to have given you pleasure,' he said softly against her hair.

She pushed back and stared up at him. 'I know enough of men to recognise that for the lie it is. Why won't you let me—?'

'*Dio*, you are making this more difficult. God knows I want to, it's practically killing me not to!' He gathered her in again. 'But the risks are too great.'

'If you worry you might get me with child, you needn't. I never conceived during my marriage. Yet another failure,' she said bitterly. 'The doctors said it might never happen.' A stab of longing shot through her womb at the idea of a baby, but she sobered when she considered what a pregnancy would mean to him—a snare at worst, an obligation at best.

'That is not what I meant, although it is a valid concern. You are like the plants that you love so much, *cara*—at last you've found the perfect spot and you've sunk your roots deep. You will thrive at Stenbrooke.' He gave a self-deprecating laugh. 'But I am the albatross; I need a strong wind and miles of space around me.'

He took her hand. 'So if I'm given the choice to hurt you now or hurt you more later…then I have to choose now.' Frustration throbbed in his voice as he cursed again. 'You've given me so many things, Portia. Your friendship, my company, and now a moment I will treasure for the rest of my life. All I can do in return is to make the choice that will cost you the least amount of pain.'

She supposed it made sense, if you looked at the world through the warped lens of a man's eyes. He was doing as he'd done before—appeasing her pride, taking the blame on his own shoulders. Was she supposed to feel grateful? She did not. Perhaps he was right and gratitude would come later, but right now she was fully occupied fighting off the cold, familiar shock of rejection. Again.

Chapter Ten

The door to the stable office stood propped open. Inside, a group of men hovered around a table. From the grubbiest stable boy to the richly dressed baron in their midst, as one they ignored the dim light and pored over scattered, dog-eared copies of the *Racing Calendar* and the *Stud Book*.

'Topgallant is out of Three Sheets by Easy Breeze,' one of the men said soberly. 'That's top blood—and the rumour amongst the legs is that he's fast. We might find him hard to beat.'

Another man stabbed his finger at the open *Stud Book*. 'Too bad she wasn't covered by Into the Wind, or it'd be no problem,' he cackled.

To a man, they all groaned.

'Catch that?' he grinned. 'Three Sheets Into the Wind? A horse like that'd be lucky to find the finish!'

Reluctant laughter swept through the room even as a sense of nostalgia rippled through Mateo. There was something to be said for this—the camaraderie and bonding of men from different walks of life by a common purpose. He'd spent many a similar happy moment in the company of his crew.

He stepped out of the doorway and forwards into the room. 'I'm of the mind, my lord, that a horse with a grand name like Topgallant is bound to come out the victor in any race.' He smiled at the man seated at the centre of the group.

They all looked around in surprise. Lord Dowland stood, then grinned in pleased recognition. 'Cardea! You sea dog! I haven't clapped eyes on you since Dayle's wedding! What in hell's blazes brings you to Whitcourt?'

'Well, there is a matter of an outstanding bet between us. If I recall correctly, you still owe me money.'

'I most certainly do not!' The baron smiled through his mock outrage. 'That poor devil only fitted twenty-four sausages in his mouth, not twenty-five! I believe it is you, sir, who owes me!'

'You were too lost in your cups to count correctly, my lord,' Mateo said with a quirk of his lips. 'And for that matter, so was I.' He sobered a little and stepped forwards to clasp Dowland's hand. 'But I haven't come to call in a wager; instead I'm here on a bit of business.'

'Come in, then, man! Come in! Let me introduce you to my men—the best bunch of trainers, jockeys and grooms in the south of England!'

'Thank you, I'd like that, but perhaps I should first introduce you to my…associate.' Mateo reached behind him into the shadows at the doorway and pulled Portia forwards. 'My lord, may I present Lady Portia Tofton?'

He met the slight lift of Portia's raised brow with a wink and gave her a little push.

There was a scramble as men and boys straightened or hastened to stand. Portia dipped a curtsy and graced them all with a lovely smile.

'Tofton?' a dirty young man said, mouth agape. 'But ain't that the gent who done got himself killed racin' carriages? The one who—'

His words were abruptly cut off as someone clapped a hand over his mouth and pulled him roughly to the back of the group. Mateo stared at Portia's whitening face.

Lord Dowland stepped smoothly into the breach. 'Lady Portia.' He bowed low. 'How pleased I am to meet you. You are welcome at Whitcourt, as well.' He gazed at her, his face carefully composed, considering.

'Yes,' she answered his unasked question wryly, and ran her gaze over the room full of curious faces. 'That was indeed the gent I was married to.'

An excited murmur broke out. The baron waved it down. 'Forgive us our ill manners, my lady.' He slapped a hand to Mateo's shoulder. 'Well, then, if the two of you will spare me just a moment, I'll give these louts their instructions and they can get back to training my horses. Then we can retire to the house and discuss your business.'

'Thank you,' Mateo said quietly. He pulled Portia closer. 'We'll just await you outside.'

They retreated to the expansive courtyard. Curiosity ate at him. Something had definitely passed between Portia and Dowland, something they all knew about J.T.'s death. Something that he did not.

Yet he did not think he could ask. He had no right to expect one level of intimacy when he'd so thoroughly rejected another. She strayed from his side, left the cobbled court and walked over to watch the yearlings in a nearby paddock. She was quiet now, as she'd been all afternoon, since they'd left the wooded site of their tryst behind.

And he? He'd been quietly frantic, more impatient to find this elusive stranger and finish this business than even before. The image of her in that enchanted glade, gorgeous in her half-dressed state, glorious as she came undone, had been branded for ever into his mind. Portia might be content with their slow progress and time for reflection, but he feared he might not ever be content again. Nor was he so eager to shine a light on his past mistakes. He'd rather make up for them and move on.

He stared at her, slim and straight at the fence, a candle lit by her amber-in-the-sun hair. The distances between them were insignificant on one level, and insurmountable the next. It would be unconscionable of him to take advantage of her without committing fully on all of them. But, damn, it would be the best ride of his life.

Sighing, he moved over to stand beside her at the rail.

'Look at them.' She gestured towards the frolicking colts. 'Constant, joyous motion. It reminds me of you.'

He laughed. 'Standing still was never my forte.' Not in a physical, mental or emotional sense. He liked motion. He craved progress in pursuit of his goals. And perhaps even more valuable, he'd found a moving target was much harder to hit with veiled criticisms and barbed judgements.

They stood in silence for a few moments more. 'While we are here, it would be best, I think, were you to stick close to me. It's been a long time since I've been in Dowland's company, but even years ago he had a certain…reputation.' He grimaced. 'Not that I mean to disparage our host, but he is one who is also constantly in motion—from one woman and on to the next as quickly as possible.'

Her face stayed carefully bland. 'I don't believe there is cause to worry. I can't even tempt the men I throw myself after.'

Incredulous, his gaze snapped to hers. 'Is that what you think? That I am not tempted?' He snorted and a bay colt nearby answered him. He and Portia both grinned, lightening the tension of the moment.

Ridiculous, truly, that she could entertain such an idea. Where was that steely core of confidence that had got her so far on this bizarre venture? He leaned in close. 'You may put that idea straight from your mind, Portia Tofton. Have you not looked in a mirror and seen yourself in that habit? Do you tell me that you did not choose that golden frogging because it brings out the gold flecks in your dark eyes and the sunny streaks in your hair?'

She flushed and he continued. 'You've tempted me nearly every moment since I've set foot back in England. You'd tempt the dourest vicar, let alone an acknowledged rake like Dowland. Now *stick close*.' He tucked her hand under his arm and cursed himself for a damned fool for letting her know the truth of how she affected him. But at this moment, her shaken assurance seemed more important than his pride.

He lowered his voice. 'If our circumstances were the least bit different, I would have had you up against that tree quicker than a flash. I would have buried myself in you and likely have knocked the damned tree down with the force of my desire.'

He took satisfaction from the deep flush across her fair skin and the surprise in her eyes. Then he turned them both to meet the baron as he emerged from the stable office. He ignored the curious look the man tossed between the two of them.

'Now then,' Dowland said with a smile, 'shall we go on to the house?'

This was a working stud farm, not Dowland's no-doubt-impressive seat, but it was attractive and welcoming none the less. When he and Portia had left the high plain behind, they'd reached the downland of rich, green turf—and here it flowed right up to the stone manor house. A few outbuildings flanked the manor in a pleasing arrangement and Mateo could see that someone had begun a garden in the back. But the stable buildings were the centrepiece here. Built of the same stone as the house, they were immaculate and fully occupied. Box stalls looked out to a clean, cobbled yard. Fenced paddocks and freshly raked training rings completed the picture.

Dowland took them on a brief tour, pride and pleasure ringing clear in his tone, but at last he directed them towards the house. As they approached, he veered off on a path leading towards the side of the house.

'You won't mind if we skip the front entrance and

enter directly into my study, will you, ma'am?' he asked Portia with a sheepish expression. 'My son is teething and was up half the night. He's likely asleep and my wife, as well. There will be less fuss and bother—and less chance of waking either of them—if we just sneak in the side.'

Stunned, Mateo stopped dead in his tracks. 'Incredible! Dowland, you've married?' He ignored Portia's pointed grin.

The baron laughed. 'Yes, old man, it happens to the best of us.'

'My congratulations, of course. I hadn't heard a word of it.' He had to hurry to keep up as Dowland opened a wide a set of double doors.

'Sorry, Cardea, but you'll have to carry the bachelor's torch on your own now.' He waved them into his light and comfortably furnished study. He held out a padded leather chair for Portia. 'Cardea and I cut a wide swathe through the ladies of Dorset when first we met, Lady Portia, but I confess I'm quite content to tend the home fire now.'

He waved Mateo towards a matching chair and seated himself behind a handsome cherry desk. 'I also confess I'm quite curious to discover what has brought the two of you here.'

Portia spoke up. 'Your friend Mr Riggs advised us to speak to you, my lord.'

'Ah, Riggs.' Dowland leaned back in his chair. 'Brilliant man, if a bit barmy, eh?'

'We found him very helpful...' she paused '...if a little eccentric.'

Mateo would have used a stronger word himself, but Dowland seemed content.

'Well, I shall endeavour to be as helpful and less eccentric, shall I?' The baron looked to Mateo. 'What is it, Cardea? Are you ready at last to trade your clipper in for a thoroughbred?'

'Not in this lifetime, lubber.' Mateo laughed, but then settled into a more serious tone. 'Actually, we're here to discover what you can tell us of a man named Averardo.'

The baron frowned and Mateo sat forwards. Something moved behind the man's eyes. 'Averardo? It's not a name I recognise right way. Is there a particular reason that I should do so?'

Portia's heart fell. Not again.

She'd come to the realisation this afternoon—after the worst few minutes of her life fell so closely on the heels of the best—that Mateo was entirely correct. It would be best if they found this stranger quickly, made their bargains and completed their transactions in as little time as possible—before she made an even bigger fool of herself.

That meant that now was not the time for another stumbling block, and yet another person who'd never heard of the man who threatened Stenbrooke.

Mateo's expression mirrored the exasperation she felt in her gut. 'Incredible,' he muttered again.

She sighed deeply.

'Lord Dowland,' Mateo said with exaggerated patience, 'you appeared to be somewhat familiar with Lady Portia's husband. Perhaps you will not be surprised to hear that he apparently gambled her estate away—to a man named Averardo. A man whose existence we begin to doubt.'

'I knew nothing of it,' Portia said. 'That is, until a solicitor showed up with a deed of conveyance with Averardo's name on it. A solicitor sent by Mr Riggs, who in turn says he did so at your request.'

Understanding blossomed on the baron's face. And something else—remorse, perhaps? Just a twinge of anxiety. He kept his silence, but stood and quietly crossed the room to close the door.

'I gather you've recalled the matter?' asked Mateo.

'I have, now that you explain.' When he was seated again, he crossed his fingers in front of his mouth. 'I do not know how much help I'll be, but I'll tell you what I know—' He held up a hand. 'Provided you promise not to mention the matter to my wife.'

'Agreed,' Mateo answered without hesitation. He and the baron both looked to Portia now. Disappointment and reluctance warred with her need to know.

'Portia?' Mateo's brows flagged his disbelief.

She nodded and shifted uncomfortably, wondering just what she might be asked to hide.

The baron mimicked her uneasy movements. 'Yes, well, it is somewhat of a delicate matter.'

Mateo's mouth twisted. 'Let me take a stab in the dark. You agreed to handle the matter for someone else, a friend, perhaps.'

Dowland shot him a look of surprise. 'Almost. I did—but not a friend, exactly. For the Countess of Lundwick.'

The name meant nothing to Portia. She looked to

Mateo and saw incredulousness creep in. 'You didn't!' he exclaimed. 'I've heard of the woman—even seen her in action. She's a better strategist than most military officers I've met. You don't mean to say...' His words trailed away and he stared at his friend.

The baron nodded.

'But she's married!'

Dowland glared at him.

'And near old enough to be your mother, besides!' Mateo remonstrated. But Portia saw the grin dancing at the side of his mouth.

'Yes, but she's a beauty none the less, and quite the most determined woman I've ever met. Her husband is a member of the Jockey Club and heavily involved in racing. She is left alone and to her own devices—'

'Far too often for society's comfort!' Mateo laughed.

'And once too often for mine. I was drunk—a good three days beneath the mahogany.' He ducked his head. 'My dear Lady Portia, I do apologise for the coarseness of this conversation.'

'As you've shown you knew my husband, I'm sure you realise that none of which you speak is new to me.'

The pain she felt at uttering this must have shown. He hurried to add an assurance.

'Oh, no. Please do not think this a recent development. My...liaison with the Countess was long before I met my wife.'

'A fact for which she is eternally grateful, I am sure.' Her tone was as dry as her mouth.

'That is the point; I don't wish her to become aware of it at all. Unfortunately, I left the Countess in possession of some rather...damning information. I never gave it a second's thought, though, until just months ago, when she thoroughly enjoyed rubbing my nose in my carelessness.'

'So she blackmailed you,' Mateo said flatly.

'I suppose you could call it that. Though it was done very prettily and in the sweetest tone imaginable. She assured me that she would *not* whisper such choice tit-bits in my wife's ear if I handled a delicate matter for her.' He glanced apologetically at Portia yet again. 'I'm sorry, but after the scandal of your husband's death, I was not in the least surprised to learn that he had also gambled away your home. The Countess told me the man who had won the estate was unable to claim it himself. She claimed that the timing was important and asked me to see it done.' He looked away. 'I was not inclined to refuse. I am quite fond of my wife, you see, and hated to think that something so unimportant to me might be dreadfully painful to her.' He sighed. 'In truth, I was relieved that what the Countess asked was not more…unsavoury.'

Portia kept her gazed fixed firmly on her hands in her lap. Nothing about this episode in her life had been savoury.

'Dowland,' Mateo said in a strange, strangled voice, 'did the Countess give you the papers right then?'

'What? Oh, no. She sent them later.'

Portia did look up then, and straight into Mateo's eyes. 'By courier!' they said together.

Mateo leaned in towards the desk. 'Tell us about the courier.'

The baron frowned. 'He did ride an exceptionally fine mare,' he mused. 'Fifteen hands, I'd say, well developed and the softest grey colour, like the breast of a dove.'

Portia could not help but laugh. Mateo cast his eyes heavenwards.

'Anything you can recall about the man himself, Dowland?'

'He had an unusual name. Foreign. Wait, I'll have to think a moment.'

Portia met Mateo's gaze again. Breathless, they stared. And waited.

She couldn't stand another second, of anticipation or of Mateo's warm regard. 'Might it have been Lorenzo?' she suggested.

'No.' The baron leaned back in his chair, his face a study of concentration. 'Stranger than that. Cormi... Corsica...' He sat straight up. 'Cosimo—that is it!'

'Cosimo?' Portia repeated, disappointed. Was it not the same man, then?

'What did he look like?' asked Mateo.

'Hmm. Tall, if I recall correctly. Well done up, for a servant, I thought. His clothes were plain, but of good quality. Well-favoured, I would have to say. I remember thinking that the Countess might have turned in a different direction for her pleasures.'

He sat straighter. 'I also remember thinking that I wanted the job done as quick as possible. My wife is in a delicate state again, you see, and at that point she was feeling particularly unwell. I didn't wish to be gone from her for long, nor did I wish to answer many questions as to what I had to do. We were fresh out of all the trouble that occurred with Bright Early Morning—I assume Riggs told you about that?'

Portia nodded.

'Suffice it to say that I was steeped in enough misery and not looking forward to bringing it on to someone else—on to you, in short. That's when I hit upon the idea of having Riggs handle it for me.'

'It was your idea?' Mateo asked. 'This Cosimo did not suggest it?'

'No, it was my notion. Riggs was feeling particularly guilty and I thought he might be better for something to do. The man needed something else to think of besides the accident. So I wrote him a long letter and asked the courier to continue on to Longvale and make his delivery there.'

He scrubbed a hand across his jaw, clearly thinking. 'The man appeared struck by the notion. I thought it was because he knew his mistress intended me to carry out the deed. I assured him it would be taken care of.'

Mateo stood. Portia watched him as he walked over to the double doors and stared out. She knew he wasn't seeing the afternoon sun falling softly over the lush green landscape.

'Do you think that *he* might be Averardo? This courier?' she asked suddenly.

Mateo turned. 'It's possible, I suppose. But why? Why place so many barriers between you? Why would he not just tell you himself that he was taking over Stenbrooke? It's almost as if he's toying with you.'

Her mouth twisted bitterly. 'Perhaps he is a former friend of J.T.'s. It does seem like something his crowd would do, out of sheer malice.'

He stared at her for a moment. 'Perhaps it is as I said before and the conveyance is a fake.'

'That would be the best possible outcome,' the baron said. 'Although the documents appeared to be correct. It would be a lot of trouble to have witnessed accounts and everything else made up or forged.'

'And what am I to do? Sit at home and wait for someone to show up and throw me out? Or not, because it is all a hoax?' Anguish stabbed through her. 'I cannot do it. How could we live with such uncertainty?'

Mateo slammed a hand against the door frame. 'Then why all the subterfuge? None of this makes a damned bit of sense!'

'Lord Dowland, would your Countess be likely to know what all of this is about?'

Wry, he said, 'If there's the smallest bit of skullduggery afoot, then the Countess is *highly* likely to know about it. That is, if she's not thoroughly entangled in it.'

Before Portia could reply, the study door swung open.

'Reginald!' sounded a bright, happy voice. 'Your son has something to show you!'

A pretty woman with tired eyes stood on the threshold, a toddling child clutching tightly to her hand. They advanced into the room and Portia saw the moment when she realised her husband was not alone.

'Oh! I do apologise. I had no notion you had company.'

Lord Dowland's face had changed, softened. It cost Portia a pang to see it.

'Come in, dear,' the baron said, standing swiftly. 'An old friend has come to visit. This is Mr Cardea, and this is *his* friend, Lady Portia Tofton.'

'How do you do?' The baroness dipped a curtsy. She

was hampered when the child at her side objected to the presence of strangers and hid behind her skirts.

The baron coaxed him out and took him up in his arms. 'Cardea, Lady Portia, this strapping fellow is the next Lord Dowland. Now come, my boy,' he wheedled, 'take your finger from your mouth long enough to say hello!'

The boy opened his mouth, but kept his finger firmly in place towards the back. 'Ungh!' he said.

His father was able to correctly interpret this. Obligingly he peered into the boy's mouth. 'By George, look at the size of that one! Well done, my boy! It's no wonder you've been wearing your mother's nerves to a frazzle!'

The boy, reminded of her existence, reached for his mother. Smiling, she took him and he snuggled close, emitting a sigh of utter bliss before laying his head on her shoulder. From his perch he granted his father a sloppy baby grin and turned a magnanimous eye to the rest of them. A chubby king, surveying his domain with satisfaction.

They made a beautiful picture. The three of them, complete and happy. It seemed almost a sacrilege to witness their moment of contentment. Portia glanced away, looked to Mateo to gauge his reaction to the family's tranquillity—and caught him in an unguarded moment. He stared, white-faced at the scene, an odd intense emotion washing pale his tanned complexion. If Portia had been forced to label it, she would say it looked like… pain.

But the baroness had spotted an incongruity in her perfect world. 'Reginald!' she scolded. 'You haven't even sent for a tray? Your friends must think us incredibly inhospitable!'

'It's quite all right, Lady Dowland,' Portia assured her. 'We've come on business, truly, not a social call and we won't intrude much longer.'

'Nonsense, you must stay for tea at least.'

'I wish we could, ma'am,' Mateo replied. His expression had cleared. 'But our business is pressing and it sounds as if we'll have to be setting out for London.' He looked to the baron. 'Am I right, Dowland? London is where we'll find the answers to our remaining questions?'

A worried frown wrinkled the baron's brow. 'I should think so, but you'll have to be fast. The…men you seek should be there now, but they are racing enthusiasts. They'll be leaving for Doncaster soon for the running of the St Leger, and then back to Newmarket.'

Portia stood. 'Then we must be off.' She smiled. 'It was lovely to meet you all.' To the baron she said, 'Thank you for your help.'

He shifted his stance. 'It was nothing, really, the least I could do.'

The baroness glanced outside. 'But there are only a few hours of daylight left. Perhaps you should stay the night and set out in the morning.'

'They are pressed for time, dear.' Her husband went still, pondering, and then his head came up suddenly. 'Of course! I can loan you my post-chaise. It's very well sprung and my teams are the fastest you'll find on the roads. I'll be happy to send one of my men along as postillion.' He clapped Mateo on the back. 'You'll be halfway to London before the night is out.'

'That is very kind of you, but we've left my companion in Hungerford and must meet up with her when we leave here. A post-chaise will likely not seat three comfortably.'

'No.' The baron's face fell. 'It has just the one front-facing bench on the inside.' He glanced at Mateo. 'But there is the outside seat in the back, over the rear wheel.' He shrugged. 'It's by far the fastest option.'

Questioning, Portia met Mateo's gaze. He turned away and looked out of the doors again. She could almost see him weighing their options, calculating time and distance and measuring days in his head. He turned back.

'It's enclosed. Will you manage?'

She thought about it. 'A post-chaise?' She turned to Lord Dowland. 'Is it the travelling chariot sort? With the glass panel in front?'

He looked startled at the question. 'Yes, it is.'

'Then I should be all right.'

'I would feel better if you would allow me to help you in this way.' The baron meant it, she could tell.

Mateo's gaze held hers first, then moved to Dowland's. Grimly, he nodded.

Chapter Eleven

Damned if Dowland hadn't been right. Mateo marvelled as the post-chaise moved smartly along, especially once they reached the well-travelled roadway in West Shefford. The beautiful Berkshire countryside passed by in a blur. They'd likely reach Hungerford in less than an hour's time.

It had been a long day. Portia sat next to him on the bench seat, far enough away so that the bounce and sway of the carriage did not jostle her against him. Out of the corner of his eye he watched her, and tried hard not to be caught at it.

The line of her limbs, the way she sank into the padded bench—they spoke of her weariness. Even as he watched, she tilted her head back to rest and closed her eyes. She wouldn't sleep, though. Her trust only extended so far, and she was too noticeably *not* touching him to be truly relaxed. A sigh escaped him.

Her hair was falling again. Did it ever stay put? The strands lay, a delicate adornment to the slender column of her neck, pointing the way to *his* spot. The spot he loved to kiss, longed to taste again. When he touched his tongue to her there, she made the most delicious sounds in the back of her throat.

He closed his eyes and sought to distract himself before he began to think too hard about touching his tongue to all the other delectable parts of her.

That stable boy's outburst rang through his head again. And the carefully blank faces of all those other men. What did they all know about J.T.'s death? It seemed wrong, a disgrace that the world should know something so basic about her life while he did not.

He opened his mouth to ask her.

'You had a very strange look on your face today,' she said into the silence.

He resigned himself to waiting a little longer. 'Did I?'

'You did—when Lord Dowland and his wife and son were grouped together, looking like an artist's rendering of the perfect young family.' She rolled her head on the cushion to look over at him. 'You looked as if it hurt, seeing them like that.' After a moment she continued. 'I wondered…were you perhaps thinking of your father? Of the problems you had with him?'

'No,' he was surprised into answering. It was a difficult subject, his family, one he never spoke of, nor often allowed himself to dwell on.

But Portia was the one person, perhaps, who would understand. It felt important, suddenly, that she did understand.

'It's just that—it struck me—the way that boy lay his head down on his mother's shoulder. That little sigh.

Such peace. I felt it, right here.' He pressed a fist to his gut. 'And I knew, suddenly, that I hadn't felt such a thing since my own mother died.'

She nodded. Quiet fell over the carriage again. Except, of course, for the rumble of wheels and the pounding of hooves and the jingle of harness and trace.

'Have you been seeking it, do you think? For peace?' She wasn't looking at him any longer.

He pondered his answer. 'No. My father used to ask me much the same thing. He'd get so upset with my wandering, pursuing new imports and markets and contacts. What was I doing? Why could I not stick to the tried and true? What was I searching for? He'd ask it with such exasperation. I used to answer him quite truthfully: nothing.'

He set his own head back against the cushion. 'I don't think I've been searching. Instead I've just been keeping busy…distracting myself. Perhaps so I wouldn't have to think about what I was missing.'

Her gaze had fastened on him again. He could feel the weight of it, a substantial thing that made his skin flush with warmth. He kept his own gaze directed towards the glass panel in the front, where the road unravelled over the steady rise and fall of the horses. 'It shames me when I think of what we spoke of yester-day—about becoming part of the vast ocean. Suddenly I'm thinking about what I've done with *this* life—and I realise I've wasted so much time. I think I've only been skimming the surface of life, afraid to look too deep.'

Her head shook in disagreement and she followed his gaze forwards. 'I don't believe that at all. You delved deep enough all those years ago, enough to see a young girl's loneliness and offer her your friendship. You looked hard enough to notice her feelings and treat them gently. You weren't skimming when you worked so hard and long for your family and their legacy or when you acted as a good friend and example to my brothers.' She reached out then, and touched his face with gentle fingers, forcing his head to turn, his eyes to meet hers. 'Perhaps it is only your own needs that you are afraid to look too closely at.'

He stared, unable to even begin to summon a response to that.

Her hand fell away. She stretched and yawned. 'Now, I am extremely weary. We have a short while before Hungerford, yes?'

Still silent, he nodded.

'Then I think I'll take a quick nap.'

And to his amazement, and utter gratitude, she did.

Portia did sleep a little, lulled by the rhythmic sway of the carriage and the warm feeling of having returned a little of Mateo's kindness. Her last thought, before she drifted off, was that perhaps he should be happy that she did not repay some of his more painful lessons.

The postillion's calls as he pulled his team to a stop awakened her. The Bear Inn loomed, large and hulking in the last of the day's light. They left the horses in their harness and went in together to fetch Dorinda.

They found her, looking very smug and awaiting them in a private parlour.

'I hope you've no room reserved for the night,' Mateo warned before Portia had even fully withdrawn from her companion's embrace. 'We must go on tonight.'

Dorrie's face fell. 'Must we?'

'I'm sorry, but we do. I've nearly given up on making it home in time to see my ships fitted for the Orient.' His face hardened. 'Months of work, this has cost me, and perhaps the best chance for my family's future. But by God, I am going to see this through, and quickly, before he has a chance to throw even more obstacles in our path.' He waved a beckoning hand at Dorrie. 'The horses are standing. We're to London as quick as we can manage.'

Dorrie sighed, but looked resigned. 'I'll assume, then, that your mission did not go well?'

'It went exactly as well as last time,' Mateo said sourly. 'Which is not saying a great deal.'

'Then you'll be happy to hear that I accomplished something here,' she announced, 'although not as much as I'd hoped.'

'What is it, dearest?' Portia asked. 'You look like the kitchen cat that's just lapped a whole bowl of cream.'

Her companion squared her shoulders and drew herself up to her full height. 'I believe I've met your mysterious courier.'

Portia gasped.

'What?' Mateo nearly shouted. 'What did he say? Where is he now?'

Dorinda winced.

'Dorrie, please, tell us what happened. How did it come about?'

'Of course, but should we not speak in the carriage? I thought we were in a hurry.'

'We were, we are, but you'll have to tell us now.' Portia could hear that Mateo was losing patience.

'We have new travelling arrangements, dear. Mateo will be forced to ride outside. Come, let's have your bags loaded while we hear your story. Then we'll go on.'

'He arrived before me,' Dorrie said after the luggage had been dispatched and they had all settled uneasily about the room. 'He'd just bespoke the last private parlour. I was understandably dismayed when the landlord told me there were none left; I'd said I'd meet you here and I was not going to wait in the public room.' She shivered. 'I'd just decided to take a bedroom when he spoke up. He was still lingering and must have overheard me talking to the innkeeper, because he offered to share his parlour. He said he would not need it for long in any case.'

'What did he look like?' Portia asked, more than a little curious.

'He was very handsome,' she answered on a little sigh. 'Tall, with hair even darker than yours, Mr Cardea. Cut too long for my taste,' she told Portia, 'but a very dashing fellow, none the less.'

'Did he give you a name?' Mateo asked.

'Yes, that was my first clue as to who he might be. He used another exotic-sounding name: Giovanni.'

'He used yet another with Lord Dowland,' Portia told her.

'What makes you sure it was him, Miss Tofton?'

'I was not sure at first. He made pleasant, unexceptional conversation. He asked where I was from and I told him I lived now in the vicinity of Newbury. He said he'd been there, but knew it very little. We talked of London and the foreign places he had travelled. We had a light meal brought in, it was all extremely pleasant.' She made a face at Mateo. 'I'm getting there, Mr Cardea, don't look so impatient.'

'I do apologise.'

Portia was glad to hear a twinge of humour in his reply.

'I had told him earlier that I was awaiting friends. We'd just finished our tea when he asked if we would be returning to Stenbrooke once my friends arrived.' She paused and shot them a significant look. 'I had never mentioned Stenbrooke by name, you see.'

Admiration flooded Portia and she allowed it to show. 'That was so quick of you, Dorrie! What did you do?'

'I pretended that I did not notice. I answered his question and told him I wasn't sure of our plans. Then I asked him if he wouldn't mind a small fire to chase the evening chill. When he went to see to it, I slipped some laudanum into his drink.'

Portia gasped again. 'Dorrie! You didn't!'

Mateo only laughed, but Dorrie was preening at the approval in his face.

'You know I always carry a small vial, dear,' she said. 'A lady never knows when she's going to need it.'

'And did he drink?' Mateo asked.

'No,' she said with chagrin. 'I'm afraid I must have given it away. Perhaps I watched him take up his cup a bit too avidly.'

'There's a lesson for you,' Mateo said. 'The next time you think to poison someone, you'll know better.'

'Mr Cardea! Laudanum is not poison. I merely

thought to put him to sleep, so he would still be here when you arrived.'

Portia could barely contain her impatience. 'But what happened?'

'He raised the cup to his lips, but then he hesitated. He met my eyes over the rim and then he set it down. He smiled brilliantly at me. Then he arose and took my hand, kissing it in the most improper fashion.' Her tone had grown a little wistful. 'He told me I was a woman to be reckoned with.' A flush spread across her face. 'Can you imagine? Me?'

'Certainly I can,' Portia said stoutly. 'It was a wonderfully brave thing to do.'

'He left then, most cordially, but not before he asked that I be sure to give you both his regards.' She heaved a heavy sigh. 'I'm sorry, Mr Cardea.'

'There is not the slightest need for you to feel sorry, Miss Tofton. I applaud your ingenuity. It would seem none of us is as crafty as our nemesis.'

'It must be Averardo—they must be one and the same. There's no other explanation for the way he's playing with us.' Irritation grew hot in Portia's chest. 'And if he is, there is still no explanation for it!' Her fists clenched. 'I suppose I should just be grateful that he did you no harm, Dorrie, but I am growing wretchedly tired of being manipulated!'

'I know, dear.' Dorrie's tone was comforting. 'Have you any idea what he's about, Mr Cardea?'

Mateo did not respond. His gaze had lost focus. Portia exchanged a glance with Dorrie. He stared into the fire, his mouth moving silently.

'Mr Cardea?'

'I'm sorry,' he said distantly. 'All of those exotic names—surely they mean something. I'm trying to recall...Lorenzo, Cosimo.' He looked up suddenly. 'And, yes, Giovanni! Medici!'

Portia stared. 'Excuse me?'

'Yes, I'm sure I'm right. Prominent Medici names, all!'

'Medici?' Dorrie's face twisted in confusion.

'Yes, yes. It's been nagging at me and I finally remembered. It's something my father spoke of. It was when he was trying so hard to convince me to—' He stopped, flushing. 'When he tried to convince me to abandon the idea of a privateer's cruise.'

And suddenly Portia flushed too, because she knew just what else his father had been trying to convince him of, at the same time. Marriage. To her.

'They planned for us to move to Portsmouth, do you recall?' His voice sounded only slightly strangled.

She nodded. She couldn't have forced an answer past her tightened throat if her life had depended on it.

'I was to open the office there. When I...when it did not work out, he hired someone else to do it, a man named Salvestro. He praised the man's performance repeatedly throughout the years and always made specific mention of his name because it also belonged to the first prominent Medici.'

'They were merchants, as well, yes?' Dorrie asked, frowning in concentration.

'They were a family who started out in trade and grew into one of the greatest dynasties in Italian history. It was my father's dream to see his family prosper in that way. I drove him mad because I would not co-operate.'

'But you worked long and hard for Cardea Shipping!' Portia protested.

'Eventually I did, but never in quite the direction he wished to go. And always without the proper degree of seriousness,' he said with a wave of his hand.

And that was likely another reason why he needed so strongly to prove himself now, she realised.

He stood abruptly and his chair nearly tipped over behind him. 'I knew that this had the taste of my father's handiwork smeared all over it! But how? Why? I'm tired of the manipulation, as well, and I'm damned tired of being one step behind.'

He started towards the door. 'We should go, ladies.' He halted. 'Or should we, at that? Perhaps we are just playing into his hands?'

Portia stepped up beside him and laid a hand upon his arm. 'What choice do we have, truly?' She squeezed. 'Let's see this thing through. All of us, together.'

'You're right, of course. But damn it! You know I've always been one to lay my own course.' He shook her off, then held the door and gestured for them to proceed. 'Let's go then. The postillion says his teams can make it to Reading tonight. We can get a short night's rest and we'll be in London early tomorrow afternoon.' His tone grew grim. 'Just in time for a social call.'

They'd reached the narrow hallway. At his words, Dorrie came to an abrupt halt. Impatient, Mateo pushed past her. 'I'll just be sure everything's ready.'

'Reading?' Portia winced as Dorrie grabbed her arm and stalled her. Her companion's whisper sounded harsh in her ear. 'We're stopping in Reading? Do you think that's wise?'

'This is the first I've heard of it,' Portia said, trying to calm the sudden racing of her heart.

'But *she* lives in Reading. Every time those horrible, impudent letters arrived, they were posted from Reading. And all the papers, when they wrote of her origins, they called her an *innkeeper's daughter.*'

'I know that, Dorrie.' The thought of running into… *her* was bad enough, but to do it with Mateo at her side… She shuddered.

She struggled for composure. 'But we'll be getting there late and only stopping for a few hours' rest.' She grimaced. 'There are at least three inns in Reading that I can recall. We're not likely to run into her.' She frowned. 'And even if we do, what can she do? I've done nothing wrong.'

Dorrie sighed. 'As if we weren't facing trouble enough.' She folded her arms stubbornly. 'It's asking too much of you, I'll just explain to Mr Cardea—'

'And tell him what?' Portia's chin lifted. 'Lord, Dorrie, I would like to keep just one of the many humiliating episodes of my life to myself! Does the world need to throw evidence of every one of my shortcomings in his face? Please, I cannot stand the thought of him looking at me with…with pity and with…*knowing.*'

'But, there's a chance—'

'It's a chance I'll take,' she said firmly. 'Because the odds have got to be higher that nothing will happen at all.'

Chapter Twelve

It was late when they arrived in Reading and the streets lay dark and quiet. Dorrie clung to her side as Portia climbed wearily down from the post-chaise. Mateo had already completed his transactions with the postillion and the stables, now he went ahead of them into the inn to make arrangements for their short night's stay. Portia watched him go, in the torchlight only an indistinct form topped with broad shoulders and a tangle of dark curls, and considered how different her mood might be right now, had Dorrie done as she'd suggested and gone home.

Ouch. Dorrie was still very much present, as evidenced by the vice-like grip she was maintaining on Portia's arm. Her head bobbed and swivelled like a weather vane, searching corners and shadows with nervous, darting looks.

'Relax, please, Dorrie. It's late. No one is about at this hour.'

'No one we'd wish to meet,' she returned.

'Come, let's go in then.' They followed in Mateo's footsteps and found him finishing with the innkeeper.

'Is she all right?' Mateo leaned in close as the land-lord called for their baggage to be carried up to their rooms. He nodded towards Dorrie, who had steered Portia as far from the public taproom as possible and was now scanning the darkened hallways. 'What is she looking for?'

Portia shivered. Fatigue seeped into her very bones and undermined her defences. The warmth of his breath on her cheek only served as a reminder of everything she longed for and could not have. 'I think we're all just tired,' she said, crossing her arms in front of her.

'Indeed we are.' Dorrie had come back. She claimed Portia's arm once more. 'Thank you, Mr Cardea, but I'm taking Portia straight up to our room.'

'Goodnight, then.'

His gaze followed them, a palpable sensation down the length of her spine as they climbed the stairs. Portia wanted to turn back, to meet his eyes and allow him to see all the turmoil and fervent desire seething inside of her. She did not. And not just because she feared the lack of a similar conflict in his eyes. Though it took all of her will, she kept her face turned forwards, towards the future. Because soon enough this would be over and that's what she'd be left with. Her future, alone and independent, just as she'd wished.

She did as Dorrie bade, kept her gaze down and followed her companion's swinging skirts into their small room. Just the one bed, big enough to share, an empty wash stand, a small table and one chair before the unlit fireplace. Dorrie shut the door with a sigh of relief. Portia stared at the bed with a mix of longing and regret.

Had she ever been this tired? Had any woman ever been subjected to a day so filled with soaring highs and despairing lows? And would she ever stop wondering what might have been with Mateo, had circumstances been different?

With a sigh she sank down on to the foot of the bed. She smelled of horse, of wind and sun. And passion. She wondered if Dorrie could detect it, if she already knew what she had begun with Mateo today, in that dark, secluded wood. She thought of tomorrow, when she would see London again, wear a pretty day dress instead of this increasingly heavy habit, when she would meet a wicked Countess and perhaps discover the reason they'd been sent on this frustratingly wild ride.

She leaned her head against the bedpost. What she truly longed for—quite inexpressibly—was a bath. A long, steaming bath in which she could close her eyes and examine the triumphs and soak away the humiliations of the day—and prepare herself for the gains and losses of tomorrow.

Not a practical wish in the middle of the night. Abruptly, she stood. 'I'm going back downstairs, Dorrie, to request some hot water—enough to wash in, at least. I can't even begin to imagine climbing into bed in this condition.'

'Poor dear,' Dorrie crooned, 'you've been through half of Berkshire today.' Her companion sat beside her on the bed. Sympathy and a perhaps more disturbing understanding showed in her face as she reached over to tuck a stray curl behind Portia's ear. 'I'll go; you stay safely here and rest. I'll ask for coal for the fire, too, so you won't catch a chill.'

It wasn't worth an argument. The door snapped shut behind Dorrie and Portia closed her eyes and leaned again against the bedpost. Mateo's room was right across the hall. Was he falling straight into bed? She hoped he dreamed of her tonight. She hoped all the wicked, erotic sensations of the day—the sight of her bare breasts, the damp feel of her, and the sensuous sound of her release—had been burned into his brain. It was no less than he deserved. No less than she had already suffered, locked for hours on the inside of that post-chaise, reliving the taste and feel of his hands and lips and tongue all over her.

She jumped as the door opened again. 'Hot water and coal are on the way,' Dorrie said from the doorway. 'The landlord's sending a girl right up. Since we are not retiring right away, I'm going back to the kitchens to see if I can find us a bite to eat.'

'Thank you, Dorrie.'

'Sit down, dear.' Dorrie nodded towards the comfortably plush chair in front of the fire. 'You look exhausted. I'll be right back.'

Portia pushed away from the post. She had to stop this. She could not continue daydreaming over Mateo. Their paths were clear and separate. He'd made his stance plain. She would only make herself miserable and him ill at ease. They had enough trouble to contend with, without her rampant desire adding to everyone's discomfort.

She curled into the chair, staring into the empty hearth. But that was the trouble, wasn't it? She didn't feel uncomfortable with him. She only felt right, happy, at home in his regard for her.

They'd crossed a boundary today, and not just in a physical sense. She'd been deliberately prickly since he'd arrived, had worked hard to show him only the strong, determined, independent side of her. Until today. Today she had cracked. She'd let him see her soft, flawed interior—and he'd met it with the same simple acceptance and admiration that he'd shown before.

Heady stuff, that. She felt a sudden pang of sympathy for some of J.T.'s opium-eating friends. She could easily come to crave something that felt so good.

More significant, perhaps, Mateo had gifted her with a glimpse inside of him, as well. For all of his insouciance and charm, she knew him for a deeply private person. Laughter and smiles were his shields and he'd allowed her to slip past them today. It had felt like a beginning, a tantalising glimpse of the deeper, more meaningful rapport that could exist between them. Except that it never would exist. Instead, tomorrow they faced the end. One way or the other, they'd go their separate ways.

The thought nearly stole her breath.

But life was short and full of hardships. And truly, Portia knew herself for one of the fortunate few. Whether her plans for Stenbrooke were granted or not, she'd been given the gift of a new beginning—and this time around she was determined to do things differently. She'd reached for a way out last time. She'd accepted the least evil of all her options and tried to make the best of it—or so she'd told herself.

But was it the whole truth?

Now was the time for truth-seeking, was it not? Now, at this time, when her future poised, teetering, on the brink of what might be, perhaps she should look deep and accept her own truth.

She did not want to—but she feared she was to be given no choice. All the platitudes and excuses she'd used to reassure herself were flaking away. She dropped her head in her hands, tried to block out the comprehension that rose like the sun within her. But there was no escaping it. She'd accepted James Talbot because she'd been afraid. Afraid to stand up to her brothers. Afraid they were right and she wouldn't ever be anything but a burden to the people she loved.

And that wasn't all. She delved even deeper into the ache that lay buried at the heart of her and winced at what she found. Mateo had hurt her, and her unsuccessful Season had frightened her. Before she'd fully recovered, her brothers' disregard had wounded her further. And she'd given in to that hurt and fear. She'd been afraid that no other man would ever want her. She'd been afraid to even try—she'd never fought for her chance at happiness.

It was an ugly, painful realisation—but worse was the sudden thought that she might be doing it again. Was she fixating on Mateo because it was easy? Because he was here? Was she dredging up old feelings because despite all of her talk, she was afraid to be alone?

The door opened with a bang behind her, startling her out of her bleak thoughts. Peering around the high back of her chair, she saw a servant girl backing into the room, burdened with an armful of towels, and a pitcher of hot water, with a heavy coal bucket hanging off one arm.

'…inconsiderate…out of bed…heating kettles in the dead of night…' The girl kept up a continuous, discontented rumble as she made her way into the room.

Portia started out her chair. 'Let me help with that.'

'Oh, no!' came the sharp, indignant reply. 'You want hot water in the middle of the blasted night, you'll get it. My papa runs the best inn in Reading, with the best service! Anyone will tell you. A thousand times a day I have to listen to it, on and on…'

Portia shrank back in her chair. Her nerves were too frazzled to deal competently with such blatant disrespect, her emotions too raw. The woman's grumbling continued as she deposited her burdens at the wash stand. Carrying the coal, she crossed the room to the hearth. Portia curled tight into the chair, out of the way, and watched the back of her head as she quickly built up the fire.

'Thank you,' she said quietly as the coals flared to life.

'Not at all,' the girl returned, her voice heavy with sarcasm. She shot Portia a quick glance of dislike over her shoulder. 'If you suffer a longing for fine French cuisine, just say the word, my papa will have me on the first packet to Calais.'

But Portia sat frozen, arrested by what she'd just seen.

The woman finished, rose, and managed to dip a curtsy that oozed mockery. By the growing light of the fire, with the woman in full view now, Portia could see it all: the ruin of a once-pretty face, marred by a network of reddened scars that ran across one side of her face and disappeared under the wilted linen of her cap. The girl noticed her changed manner and shot her a look of scorn. Head high, she flounced across the room to the door.

She paused on the threshold. Portia's nails dug into the padded arm of the chair.

It couldn't be. But it was.

After all of Dorrie's precautions—Portia bit back the sudden, mad urge to laugh.

It was her. Moira Hanson. Her husband's mistress.

Behind her, one hesitant footstep sounded, back into the room.

'It's you, isn't it?' The girl's voice rang low now, incredulous. Slowly she retraced her steps, stopping at the side of Portia's chair to stare down at her. 'It is! I've seen you, once before,' she said wonderingly. Then she laughed, an ugly, brittle sound. 'It was at the theatre. You were with your fine, fancy friends. Me and J.T. had a box, not far away. You never even saw us...' her mouth twisted '...or what we got up to, right there under your nose.'

Portia kept her gaze locked on the fire. 'Thank you for the water.' She gestured. 'And for the fire.' She had to work to keep her voice neutral, flat. 'That is all I require.'

'Oh, no!' Moira said, low and vicious. 'You'll not get off that easy. Did you think to come here and lord it over me? Is that why you're here—making demands in the dead of night?'

Portia looked up then, focusing on her narrowed,

mean eyes, and pointedly not on her disfigurement. 'I had no idea you were employed here.'

'I'm not *employed* here, Miss High and Mighty. My father is the landlord.'

It was the scorn in her voice that did it. Dread and chagrin began to turn to anger and indignation. *She* had been the victim in this mess, not this greedy little harpy. It had been a horrible, humiliating, tragic episode—but none of it had come through Portia's actions.

She stood. 'That would be *Mrs* High and Mighty, as you would have good cause to know.'

The other woman's eyes narrowed. 'You've come to gawk at me, haven't you? Have a laugh at my expense?'

'Don't be ridiculous.'

'Me? You're the ridiculous one, so fine—you think you are.' Moira stepped forwards. Her voice rose. 'I don't care who your father was, you weren't woman enough to keep your husband happy.'

'That is enough. Just please go.'

'You think you're better than me?' the woman shrieked.

Portia shook her head.

'Why haven't you answered my letters, then? Tell me that.'

Portia raised her chin. Her heart ached at the thought of the wicked taunts and hurtful accusations that had been in those letters. How she'd love to give as good as she got, just this once. Make this vulgar strumpet eat every one of the hateful words she'd spewed at her, in writing and in person. But they had each paid a steep price already, and Mateo slept just across the hall. She shrunk at the idea of him being witness to this woman's vitriolic hatred. It would be her last, greatest humiliation.

The door opened again. Portia flinched, but it was only Dorrie, carrying a covered tray. She stared. It took a moment for her to recognise the confrontation taking place in the room, and then all her colour drained away. 'Oh, no,' she moaned.

Moira laughed. 'Oh, yes, I'm afraid so. You thought to humiliate me? You've done enough already!' She gestured towards her marred face. 'You ruined my life! And it's time you paid.'

'Please,' Portia asked. 'This is neither the time nor the place. Just go.'

'You don't know how right you are, *my lady.*' The girl nearly choked on a sob. 'This is not the place, not *my* place. Do you know how long it took me to get out of here? To make my way to London and break into the right circles? But I had done it! I was on my way to becoming one of the most glittering courtesans in history! I had my own rig, my own servants. And now here I am, back again, fetching and carrying for every loose screw on their way in and out of Town.'

She slammed the coal bucket down with a horrendous crash. 'It's all gone now!' A harsh, broken sound erupted from her chest. 'You *owe* me!'

'I'm sorry for what happened to you.' Portia firmed her voice. This woman had to be made to understand, finally, here and now. 'Truly I am. But your misfortunes came about due to your own actions. They've nothing, *nothing* to do with me.' She glared at her. 'Do you see me endlessly blaming you for the loss of my husband?

Let us not speak of who owes whom! We've both paid enough. It's over.'

'It's not over for you, is it, you spiteful, prideful bitch?' Moira's voice rose to a screech. 'You've got a future, haven't you? You can find another poor, unsuspecting sod to marry you. Look at me! No man will touch me! What am I supposed to do?'

Suddenly Mateo's form filled the doorway. Hair tousled, his eyes heavy with sleep, he scowled at Portia. 'Damnation,' he grumbled. 'What's going on here?'

Cold despair washed over her. Mute, Portia watched Moira take in his loose linen shirt, tight breeches and bare feet.

'Is this him? The next one?' the other woman spat. 'Don't be taken in by her.' She pointed a spiteful finger. 'Her heart is cold, but the rest of her is worse. If you've a wish for a warm bedmate, then keep looking.'

Portia clenched her shaking hands and raised her chin.

'Portia? Who is this little shrew?'

Mateo came further awake and quickly recognised the danger of his position. The only tom in a cat fight? Not a good place to be. He rubbed the last bit of sleep from his eyes and began to tally the butcher's bill.

One down, it would seem. Miss Tofton slumped against the wall next to a tray-covered table, her hand in front of her eyes. The remaining two combatants still faced off. Portia—looking rumpled but lovely with colour flaring high in her cheeks—shot daggers at someone who appeared to be a serving girl—one whose pretty face had been marred some time in the recent past.

'I'm sorry,' he said to Portia's opponent, 'but you appear to be upsetting Lady Portia. This, you understand, is a sacred duty that has apparently fallen to me. I can't have you interfering.' He raised a hand and beckoned. 'Come, then. I'm sure you understand. I'm afraid you'll have to go.'

'I'm not going anywhere until I've had my due,' came the snarled reply.

Clearly the serving girl was unhinged. Or didn't know when she was bested. Or both. 'Portia?' He turned to the only reasonable-looking person in the room. 'Who is this…person?'

Her chin high and her eyes blazing, she answered. 'She's the woman who killed my husband.'

The servant girl gasped and reared back. Her face went bright red, and then deathly pale. Mateo knew just how she felt.

'No!' she gasped. 'That's not true. It was your fault, you cold bitch! If you'd been any kind of wife, he'd never have chased after me! And if you'd given him the money he needed, we never would have made that bet, never been in that street…' She broke down, sobbing, and threw herself against Mateo's chest.

Other guests were beginning to gather in the hallway behind him. Mateo tried to put the girl away, but she pounded at him with her fists. 'Just look at what she did to me!' she cried.

'Please, miss. I mean, ah, madam? Pull yourself together.'

Instead she collapsed in a heap at his feet. Mateo

reached down to lift her up. She fought him. He dropped her and she attacked his legs, clawing and scratching in time with her sharp, sawing breaths. 'Not my fault,' she moaned repeatedly.

Portia turned away. Mateo was desperate for help. He turned to her companion. 'Miss Tofton,' he pleaded.

The girl clutched his ankles and sobbed harder. 'Miss Tofton, please!'

Portia's companion took pity on him. Her face shifted, a mask that wavered between anger and pity as she knelt down, captured the girl's hands and pulled her in close.

Mateo heaved a grateful sigh. Carefully he eased away and went to shoo the audience away from the door and back to their rooms. When he returned, Miss Tofton was assisting the girl to her feet. The fight had gone out of her. She leaned into the older woman, her face turned away.

'I'll just take her downstairs,' Miss Tofton said quietly.

Portia still faced the fire, her back to them all. She did not respond.

'Will you need help?' Mateo asked quietly.

The older woman shook her head. The girl's sobs had quieted now. The rasping catch of her breath faded as Miss Tofton steered her into the hall and towards the stairs.

Quiet settled over the room. Mateo waited.

And waited. Portia neither moved nor spoke.

'Portia,' he began.

'Just go, Mateo.'

'But I—'

'Please, go. I cannot take any more tonight.'

At a loss, Mateo fell back on the tried and true. He summoned a smile. 'Come now, Portia! Don't fret. You're the clear winner in this skirmish.'

That got her moving. She rounded on him, eyes wide and clearly aghast. He winced. It was not the effect he'd been hoping for.

'Winner?' She'd gone from aghast to incredulous. Not a far trip, and not one that favoured him in any way. 'Is that what you see here? A battle won?' She whirled again and began to pace, as if she could not contain her outrage. 'I cannot decide if it is because you are a man, or if you merely possess your own particular brand of obtuseness.' She threw him a scorching look. 'Would that I were a man, then, to see things in black and white.' She snorted. 'Most of us, and women most of all, know that life is lived in all the grey areas in between.'

She folded her arms and glared at him. 'And in a horrible, dirty grey area such as this, there are no winners.' She turned away again. 'We are all losers.'

'Perhaps I might see better if I knew what I was looking at,' he said quietly. 'I think it's time you told me just what this was all about.'

Silence again.

He was not going to be put off. 'Clearly it involves J.T. I may be a clown, Portia, but I'm not stupid. I know there's something I haven't been told, something about his death that everyone else seems to know.'

'It's no secret,' she said bitterly. 'It's a sordid tale that made every paper and a hundred broadsheets across the kingdom. I'm surprised you didn't hear of it in Philadelphia.'

'Tell me.'

'I'd rather not.' Her shoulders slumped. 'I don't think I can.'

He let out an explosive breath. 'Of course you can.' He crossed the room, stood between her and the obviously fascinating fire in the grate. Tenderly he cupped her face in his hands. 'I'm beginning to believe you can do anything, Portia Tofton.' He let his hands drift down, over her shoulders, down her arms. He grabbed up her hands. 'Come. We're going to talk, but not here.'

She was distracted enough not to object. 'Where, then?'

He stood in the hall, her hand warm in his. His palms itched, tingling from that brief touch, eager for more. Looking about, he considered his options. His gaze slid past his own door, and kept on sliding. The lower part of his anatomy stirred, pointing in that direction. No.

'Aha!' He pulled her down the darkened hallway, to the stairs. Faint light drifted up from below, along with the sound of masculine merriment from the public rooms. He swept an extravagant hand, indicating the top step. 'Your seat, my lady.' He raised a brow. 'As long as you promise to behave. I recall what happened the last time we were in a stairwell alone together.'

'Nothing happened!' She was blushing, he knew it. He wished he could see it clearly.

'Only because we were interrupted. You were going to kiss me, though.'

'Is that how you recall it?' She settled down on

the top step and glanced archly up at him. 'Strangely enough, I remember that *you* were on the verge of kissing *me*.'

He dropped down next to her, leaned in close. 'Oh, that's right, *cara*—I was going to kiss you. Damned thoroughly, too.' He retreated, rested back on his elbows in a completely non-threatening pose. 'But I promise—no kissing tonight.'

Dio, was that a look of disappointment on her face? Suddenly he was grateful for the dim light. It was better if he didn't know.

Footsteps sounded below. Slow and methodical, they climbed steadily upwards. 'At least we'll know if we're to be interrupted,' he whispered. They slid over towards the wall, leaving a path open.

Miss Tofton wearily rounded the turning below. She stopped, surprised to see them there.

'How is she?' Mateo asked softly.

'Sleeping.' Portia's companion gave a wan smile. 'I told you, you never know when you might need a little laudanum.'

Portia let loose a great sigh.

'The landlord sends his apologies. I explained, and he understands the situation, but still asks if we could leave early, before she awakes.'

Mateo nodded.

'Shall we head back to our room?' Miss Tofton asked Portia pointedly.

'I'll have Portia back to you in a little while,' Mateo answered for her.

A silent communication passed between the two

women. Miss Tofton sighed. 'Come soon. You need your rest.' She climbed past them. 'Goodnight, Mr Cardea.'

'Goodnight.'

After a moment the door closed behind her and they were left in the comforting darkness. Portia had tensed up again beside him; he could feel her unease radiating through the small space that separated them.

He kept silent.

And at last she relented, slumping against the wall beside her. 'I don't know where to begin,' she said.

He shrugged. 'At the beginning?'

'No,' she said definitely. 'There's too much hurt between now and the beginning. I'll just stick with the end.'

He nodded. Her head turned, tilted questioningly.

'I'm nodding,' he said.

She laughed, but it turned into a sigh.

'She was his bit of muslin?' he prompted.

'Yes, she was his mistress, obviously. Not his first— he made sure I was fully aware of that—but without a doubt she was his most notorious. They were together quite a while—I wondered if they didn't have real feelings for each other.'

His fists clenched. A sound of protest slipped out. 'Sorry,' he said. 'Go on.'

'It was quiet enough at first, and I was preoccupied with Stenbrooke, and with my father's health. But then the rumours and scandals began. I found out later it was because she wasn't content just to be his mistress, she wished to be famous, acclaimed, sought after.'

'Ah, but don't we all?' he murmured.

'No, we don't,' she said firmly. 'Some of us just wish to be left alone.'

And if that wasn't a telling statement, then Mateo had never heard one.

'At first he appeased her by getting up to mischief *with* her,' she continued. 'He dressed her up like a man and tried to sneak her into his club, but they were both tossed out before they'd barely made it past the door. He bought her a gleaming white high-perched phaeton with blue trim and a matched white team to pull it—and she had their manes and tails dyed blue, as well. He gave her lessons and she drove it all over town, always with a little blue-grey greyhound beside her on the bench.'

'Ah, yes, she sounds an exact match for J.T.'

'I think she was. They might have been happy together indefinitely.'

'Were it not for money?' he guessed wryly.

'J.T.'s lack of it, more specifically. She became more demanding. She wanted a certain, expensive, diamond necklace and he didn't have the blunt for it. Perhaps it was just an excuse—for she announced that she was moving on to a new protector with deeper pockets.'

'Poor J.T.,' Mateo said mockingly.

'He was desperate to keep her. He came to me, demanding money, but I hadn't any to give him—and I wouldn't have given it, in any case. He went back to town and made a bet with her. He would race her through the streets of London, each in a high-perch phaeton. If he won, she would stay with him. Should she win, he'd buy her a necklace *and* let her go with his blessing.'

'Oh, Lord,' he whispered.

'They set the reservoir at Green Park as their destination. All their low friends and members of the *demimonde* gathered to cheer them on.'

Mateo's teeth ground together. 'Were your brothers there?'

'No, thank goodness. I like to think that they would have tried to talk some sense into him.'

Mateo was not so generous, but he let it rest.

'They barrelled down Curzon, then he took Half-Moon Street and she took Clarges. They met at Piccadilly and were racing towards the end when they came upon a carter carrying a load of wooden faggots. His nag had broken down. They never had a chance. The carter was killed outright.'

'And J.T.?'

'He was crushed under someone's wheels. He lived in agony for a couple of days. Long enough for me to arrive—at which point he soundly berated me for ruining his life.'

'Consistent to the end,' Mateo said bitterly.

'The papers reported every dirty detail. And while all of England rebuked him for his careless disregard of safety and consequence, he blamed me for all the shortcomings of his life. Had I been a better wife, he would have been happy in Berkshire. Had I not been the dull, sturdy type more interested in playing in the mud, he wouldn't have had to stray. Had I not poured all of his money into the wreck of the estate, he could have lived happily in London.'

Hate this hot and potent must be a sin. Mateo couldn't help it; he dearly hoped that J. T. Tofton currently occupied a particularly nasty corner of hell. He clenched his fists and struggled to breathe evenly.

'A futile, meaningless death,' she finished bitterly, 'that in true Tofton fashion, managed to hurt a great many people.'

She sighed. 'You can see what happened to her. I suppose she's been here since the accident. About six months afterward, she began to write to me, demanding money.'

Mateo sat up straight. 'You didn't give it to her?'

'No, though she threatened to take her case to the courts, since she had lost her livelihood.'

'Ridiculous.'

'I still had my hands full paying off all of J.T.'s legitimate creditors. But I did take in the carter's family, brought them to Stenbrooke. Somehow she heard of it and her letters increased in number and malevolence.'

'My poor girl.' He gave in to overwhelming temptation at last and touched her. Softly, he stroked her hair, ran a slow, comforting hand over the gloriously thick mass of it, then on into a deliberate caress down the delicate length of her neck.

She tucked her legs up and ducked her head away, pressing her forehead to her knees. 'So there you have it,' she said, her voice a bit muffled. 'Now you are privy to every last humiliating moment of my life. Every hurt, every tragically wrong decision, every mistake I've ever made. I've done it all in one day—laid myself bare before you, both physically and emotionally.' She turned her face away, towards the wall. 'God knows what you must think of me.'

He froze. Reached out a hand, then let it drop. 'I

think you are the strongest woman I've ever met.' He said it quietly, fervently, with all the conviction he could summon.

Her head shot up. 'Well, you couldn't be more wrong!' Her tone rang cold and sharp. 'I'm selfish, not strong. If I were strong, I would never have married J.T. in the first place.' Tears ran down her face. They glistened, catching the soft light and stabbing him straight through the heart.

Perhaps she was right. Perhaps she was not strong yet, but she damned well was on her way to getting there, after oppression and hardship had done its best to beat her down.

'You are not selfish.' His voice registered barely above a whisper. 'You are incredibly brave, and I am awash in admiration of you. Life is hard. But you don't run. You don't hide. You meet it head-on, you take your blows and, by God, you keep on fighting.'

There were those layers again. He'd been judging her on the tough, outer layer she'd developed in the years since he knew her. The one she'd needed in order to survive all the blows life had thrown her way. And he had delivered some of the worst, he realised with horror. But at her core still lived an uncertain girl. A little bruised. Most definitely alone. Such strength and hope it must have taken for her to risk herself again— with him, who hurt her first and perhaps most of all.

He'd done everything wrong. Hurt her again and again with practically every word, every encounter. Now was his chance to make it up to her.

Yet he hesitated. It was terrifying having such insight into another person—because it was never one-sided. He could see through the window they'd opened between them, straight into her soul—and she could see him just as clearly.

A delicate, dangerous situation. One he'd spent his life carefully avoiding. To allow someone full view and sincere knowledge of your true self? He shuddered. It granted them such power, such ability to do real harm. His mother's death had proven how horrendous the pain could be when you were left alone at the window. His father had shown that it was just as bad when the window was deliberately closed.

And in his and Portia's case, the pain was a certainty. Their lives were too different, too separate for the window to last. The wrenching hurt of separation was inevitable. He would have to leave soon. And this would make it so much harder. There would be no deflecting this hurt, no outrunning it with a quick wit or a busy schedule or even a fast ship. It would live with him, inside of him. Already he missed her impudent mouth and her stubborn independence. The sweeping curve of her nape and the feel of her breasts spilling out of his hands and into his mouth. If he took this step, he'd have so much more to haunt him, so much that he knew would be impossible to forget.

But for her he would face it. She'd shown such bravery, risked so much, and she needed to know how beautiful she was—how good and strong and lovely—on the inside and out.

He'd been silent too long. She'd turned her head on her knees and was watching him.

Abruptly, he stood. He reached a hand down towards her. 'Come with me.'

She stared up at him. 'Where?'

Impatient, he beckoned again. 'There's a gorgeous view waiting for us—and we need to see it together.'

Chapter Thirteen

Just what she'd expected to happen after wrenching her emotions out and displaying them for Mateo, she wasn't sure, but Portia knew it hadn't been this.

Her hand gripped tightly in his, he pulled her away from the stairs and down the hall. He paused in front of his room. Shook his head. Then he dropped her hand and pushed her to the wall. 'Wait here. Just for a moment.'

Bemused, she watched as he left her. She was grateful for his kind words. Intensely so. He'd listened to her without judgement, responded with sensitivity and generosity. Just as he always did. Her shoulders slumped. When would she learn? Why could she never stop wishing for more from him?

And just what was he up to now? Gingerly, he tested the knob on the door next to his. 'Locked,' he whispered. Taking a step back, he cast a measuring look up and down the hallway.

'Mateo,' she said low. 'I should go back...Dorrie will—'

'No! Stay here,' he hissed.

He headed down the hall, passing one door by, stopping and listening at another. Finally he hovered in front of the last door on the opposite side. He pressed his ear against it. Ever so slowly he turned the knob. The door swung open. Holding a commanding finger towards her—a silent order to stay put—he disappeared inside.

She waited. Several quiet moments passed, then a soft glow of light emerged from the room he'd entered. He leaned out of the doorway and beckoned her.

She shook her head and raised questioning hands at him.

With a huff of exasperation that she could hear from this distance, he stalked down the hall towards her. 'You never backed down from a single challenge your brothers threw at you,' he whispered. 'Are you going to turn craven now?'

She reared back and stared into the challenge in his face. 'No!'

'Then come on, Peeve.'

She balked at the nickname, digging in her heels.

Very seriously, he turned and gripped her by her shoulders. 'I can only begin to imagine what you might feel at the sound of that nickname, but do you want to know what it does to me?'

Did she? She wasn't sure. She only looked at him beseechingly.

'It takes me back, to a blissful, happy time in my life. It brings to mind a stubborn little girl in plaits and a pinafore, a girl who never once backed down from any challenge her brothers could dream up. It conjures up a shy, pretty adolescent, who could none the less pull off elaborate pranks that boggled the mind, a young woman who listened, without judgement or recrimination, in a way that I've never encountered since. It reminds me of you, Portia, and all the laughter and anger and joy and tears that we've shared.'

Each word was a gift, a surprise that burst inside of her, utterly defeating the cold insecurities dragged up by the night's events. Portia blinked back tears.

'So I will stop using it out loud, if you insist, but you should know that you'll *always* be Peeve to me.'

He wrapped a warm arm about her and guided her to the open room, while she struggled to regain her equilibrium.

It was another guest room, but clearly for a different level of guest. This one loomed spacious, with a high, wide bed, a screen and a standing mirror in the corner and an elaborately carved wardrobe along one wall. He'd lit several candles and placed them on the mantel. She folded her arms. This room did lack one important thing.

'Mateo?' She turned to find him closing the door after them. The click of the lock sounded loud in the quiet. 'There are no windows in here.'

'I know.' He went past her to the corner of the room.

'Then how exactly are we to share the view?' She suppressed a wry grin. 'You aren't going to ask me to view your sketches, are you? My mother did warn me about such things, you know.' She ran a finger along the thick down coverlet on the bed. 'If you are not careful, I'm going to think you bent on seduction.'

'I don't have any sketches,' he said. His voice strained as he lifted the large mirror. She stared. The thing was as tall as he. He placed it carefully in front of her. 'I had something altogether more lovely in mind.'

He came to stand behind her, placed his hands on her shoulders and turned her so that she squarely faced her reflection. 'And I am absolutely bent on seduction.'

'You are?' It came out as a squeak. She swallowed past the sudden lump in her throat and met his gaze in the mirror.

'Of course.' He waved a negligent hand and sat on the foot of the bed. 'But first, I want you to look—' he gestured towards the mirror '—and tell me what you see.'

Her heart tripped, then took off at a run. 'Mateo, I—'

'Ah, ah…' He wagged an admonitory finger, then pointed at the mirror. 'Tell me.'

His nonchalant declaration had left her whole body a-tremble, but in no way was she going to give him a chance to change his mind. She bit her lip and did as he bade.

'What do you see?' he asked again, softly.

Her fingers went to her collar. 'Buttons undone and red, puffy eyes?'

'Look again,' he ordered. 'Look deeper.'

She rather liked this autocratic side of him. She definitely liked what it was doing to her insides. She tore her gaze from his and looked again. 'A dishevelled widow lady who has just had a shouting match with her dead husband's mistress,' she said ruefully.

He sighed. 'I'm disappointed in you, *cara*. Clearly you need a lesson.' He stood, stepped behind her and pressed his body close to hers. 'Shall I tell you what I see?'

His breath stirred her hair, seared her scalp and the top of her ear. She shivered, delighted with the delicious feel of it. Gooseflesh travelled down the length of her arm and her nipples tightened. 'Yes.'

He reached up, plucked a pin from her hair, and cast it on to the bed. 'I see courage,' he breathed. 'The sort that never backs down from hardship, but isn't afraid to ask for help when it's needed, either.'

Another pin followed, then another. Her hair sagged, heavy and loose. 'I see a good mind and a saucy spirit—a combination that makes every moment in your company a joy.'

Her spirits soared, even as her hair tumbled down. He watched it fall in the mirror, and she caught the blaze of excitement in his eyes. He moved closer still and buried his face in the length of it.

Intent and aroused, she stared at their reflections. Almost, she could see herself through his eyes. Certainly she did look different, with her hair tumbling down over both of them and her body pressed back into his.

He inhaled, a great, gulping breath as if he were a drowning man and she a sky full of clean, fresh air. 'I see a great heart.' He breathed into the heavy mass, his eyes meeting hers in the mirror's reflection. 'One that is able to forgive the callousness of an old friend and even the misplaced wrath of a shallow, deluded woman.'

Oh, Lord. The warmth of him sent the blood rushing to her skin. His scent engulfed her, so rich and exotically different from her own. *Man.* It spoke to her and awakened long-neglected yearnings. *Mateo*, it said. Longing and heat spiralled inside of her, pooled in her belly and sent her answer back to him.

So long it had been—but, no, that was not a thought she could finish. She'd never felt like this. Mateo's body awakened hers, his sheer physical presence sent ripples of excited sensation all through her.

But his words—his words flowed over her, inside of her. They were a balm to her cracked soul, soothing hurts she'd scarcely been aware of.

His hands clutched her hips, steadied her against him as he nuzzled her neck. 'I could sing your praises all night long, if you'd like,' he whispered.

'Touch me instead,' she answered. 'Show me, Mateo.'

Against the small of her back she felt him stirring, growing in response. 'See?' he said. 'Clever enough to know what she wants—and courageous enough to ask for it.'

'Stop talking now,' she said, turning in his arms. Rising up, she traced her finger softly over those lovely, tiny lines at the corners of his eyes. 'I love these,' she whispered. He smiled and they deepened under her touch.

She claimed his mouth with her own. He tasted of wine, vibrant and rich, of hot lust and wild desire. Or perhaps that was her. Her mouth slanted over his, their tongues danced and their souls tangled.

His fingers drifted up, over her curves and into her hair. They dug into her scalp and she arched in pleasure. He accepted the silent invitation and buried his face in the nape of her neck. Then suddenly he was working at the intricate fastenings of her habit. He'd got most of them undone and reached inside before she'd caught her breath.

'Wait,' she gasped. She smiled up at him. 'It's my turn.'

She stepped back, and trailed a teasing finger across his chest. She moved slowly, inching her way until she stood behind and to one side of him. She met his gaze in the mirror and cast him a slow, sultry smile.

'Minx.'

She stood on her tiptoes and pressed her mouth close to his ear. 'Only with you,' she breathed.

He moaned.

She didn't waste her breath on words. Instead she let the press of her body and the soft whisper of her caress tell him of her gratitude and of her desire. Lightly, she ran the tips of her fingers up his sides, across the expanse of his chest. His nipples pebbled, tiny echoes of her own arousal, and she brushed a light caress there too.

In the mirror she watched him. His avid gaze followed the sensuous path of her fingers. Suddenly his eyes lifted and locked with hers. 'Are you going to tell me what you see?' he asked hoarsely.

Her hand stopped at the edge of his trousers. Beneath it, his belly heaved and the heat of his flesh seared her.

'You, Mateo. Only you. That's all I need to see.'

He stilled. Time slowed and an incredibly long moment passed. 'Portia,' he said quietly and in a voice full of regret, 'I want you, more than you could possibly imagine. But we cannot go further until we both acknowledge that this can only be temporary.'

She pressed a kiss against the hard muscle of his

arm, then stepped in front of him and snuggled into his arms. 'Do you remember what I said—?' She closed her eyes and shook her head. 'Was it only earlier today?' She chuckled and smiled up at him. 'We're in a unique position, caught between our pasts and our future. We'll likely never see another time like this in our lives.' With a raised brow and a challenging grin, she reached down and cupped the fullness of his erection. 'We might as well make it memorable.'

Mateo groaned and thrust himself further into her hand. Memorable? Every second he'd spent with her in his arms had already etched itself into his soul.

He reached out and quickly finished the job he'd started earlier, plucking and pulling until her habit was undone and falling to her waist. She wriggled her hips and it dropped, leaving her feet buried in a puddle of fabric and the rest of her clad only in her undergarments.

He made short work of them, too. In mere seconds, it seemed, she stood naked, unveiled before him. Candlelight flickered over her curves, shadows danced over her high, pink-tipped breasts. He let his gaze wander lower, over the thatch of her curls, darker than the honey-and-amber locks on her head.

She bit her lip and smiled at him, grabbing the waistband of his trousers. 'Play fair, now,' she admonished. Swiftly, her fingers moved over the buttoned placket and at last his erection spilled free, leaden with arousal.

She sighed in appreciation and touched him with delicately dancing fingertips. An erotic path she traced, over the top and down the length of him. He swelled impossibly high.

This, then, was why he'd spent so long denying them this. Her strokes grew firm; he grew—incredibly— harder and he knew that her touch had become a necessity, like air for his starving lungs.

Dio, yes. He wanted to breathe her in.

He kissed her again, open and intense. Excitement surged through him. He was going to learn her every curve, every contour, both inside and out, and he was going to start right here, exploring her mouth with abandon.

But soon enough, he needed more. Bending his knees, he lifted her and placed her on the bed.

She laughed. He caught his breath again at the sight of her hair in the dim light. A glorious welter, it slid over her shoulders and around her breasts. They called to him, teased him with the smallest glimpses of tightened nipples and darkened areolas as she moved.

He answered. He pursued her on the high bed, approaching with all seriousness until he loomed over her. And then he dipped his head and ran his tongue over a shyly peeking bud. The room shrank as he suckled, first one gorgeous breast, then the other, until nothing existed save for the caress of her hair, soft against his face, the little gasping sounds of her pleasure and the feel of his hot breath against her wet flesh.

At last she dug her fingers into his hair, lifting his face up to hers.

'Come to me, Mateo. I've waited so long.'

No man could resist such a sweet summons. But incredibly, he hesitated. He had to be sure.

He pressed a kiss on her mouth, then turned over on to his back. A hairpin jabbed him and he fished it out, then threw it aside. He laid his head back against the pillows and his mouth quirked. Her fascinated gaze was locked on to his straining erection. Impressive already, even to his own eyes, it jumped a little, stretching impossibly under her regard. 'Come and take what you want, Portia,' he rasped.

She glanced at his face, puzzled, then her brow cleared. Her eyes widened. And she smiled.

She crawled up and over him, her eyes alight with excitement. Leaning down, she tantalised him with a long, hot kiss, and then she positioned herself, open and inviting, over him.

Already she dripped, hot and silky with need. She teased, touching down on just the very tip of him, and a groan travelled up and out of him.

Without any further warning, she sank down. And down and down.

God help him.

There were no words to describe the sensation. He was harder than iron and she was giving way before him, her inner passage clenching, then relaxing as she took him in.

Easy.

But she was hot and tight and he was greedy and nearly beside himself with pleasure. He couldn't do it, couldn't wait. In a flash he had her lifted off the bed, and then underneath him. And he did it without breaking their incredible, intimate contact. 'All right?' he asked, while he still had enough sense to comprehend her answer.

She moved, wiggled, adjusting. Her sex pulsed, coaxing him further, higher, longer. And then she nodded.

Thank God. Gripping her hips, he began to move.

She met his thrusts with eagerness, hunger. He adjusted slightly, lifted his hips and settled into slow, rhythmic strokes.

'Mmm,' she said, and arched her back. Her fingernails carved little wounds into his shoulders. He had it right, then.

In the shifting light he saw her face sharpen with need. 'More,' she whispered.

Yes. His body echoed her. Almost against his own will he began to thrust faster. She tightened, pulling him even deeper.

'Portia.' It was a question. An order. A prayer.

'Yes,' she answered. Then she let out an exultant, strangled cry.

He was gone. Over. Lost in a tumult of surging, throbbing joy. Almost, it was too much. He hung, balanced on the knife's edge between madness and bliss—and then came down hard on the side of bliss.

He could heartily recommend bliss.

Slowly, he returned to himself, happy to find Portia just as thoroughly boneless and content as he. Her head lolled. She gave him a sleepy, satisfied smile and a huge sigh. It was the most beautiful sound he'd ever heard in his life.

He disengaged, rolled them into a comfortable position, and buried his face into the sweet curve of her neck.

'There,' he said into her damp flesh. 'Try to forget that.'

Chapter Fourteen

Portia had worn her finest day gown, a lovely striped linen in varying shades of green and ivory, but she realised with sudden certainty that it was not near fine enough for an audience with the Countess of Lundwick.

She stood, staring like a country yokel at her surroundings, at the immense marble hall, at the collection of priceless curios and the grand, sweeping staircase. And this was just the entrance hall.

She was an Earl's daughter herself, for goodness' sake. She'd grown up on a large estate with a big, rambling, ancient house. She'd danced at balls, drank tea, listened to music and dreadful poetry at some of the most prominent houses in Town, but never had she witnessed such an ostentatious—but somehow also flawless—display of wealth.

A stiffly reserved butler handed them off to an only-slightly-less-rigid footman, who escorted them to a drawing room where they could await the Countess's pleasure.

Dorrie entered first. She came to a dead halt just a step into the room. Portia crowded in behind her, and was forced to go around to make room for Mateo. She followed Dorrie's gaze around the opulent room and her mouth dropped open.

'It's as if we're inside a pastry,' marvelled Dorrie.

'Or a boudoir,' Portia answered, taking in all of the laces and flounces and rich pastel fabrics.

She flushed. Perhaps, after last night, she just had boudoirs on her mind. And who could blame her? She glanced at Mateo, to gauge his reaction.

He said nothing. Loath, no doubt, to add to the meagre number of words he'd allotted to them this morning.

He met her gaze suddenly, and she was taken aback by the bleak shadow that crossed over his features. 'Portia, I'd like a word with you, if you please.'

'Of course.'

He held out his arm, an oddly formal gesture, and she took it, wondering where he meant for them to go. But he only crossed to the window at the far end of the room. They stood there a moment, while he gazed back at the decadent décor and out to the street below, anywhere but at her.

Her heart began to thrum in sudden panic. All of last night's laughing charm had converted to pensive silence. Why?

Perhaps it was her—though she was a widow, her experience was not extensive... No. She cut loose that thought almost as soon as it blossomed. Last night had been wonderful—in his eyes, as well as hers. His tenderness had told her so, as had the joyous urgency of his touch.

Did he know something, then? Or suspect something about what they might learn today? Brow furrowed, she waited.

'There's something I should tell you, *cara*, though it's not easy for me to say.'

She nodded.

'God only knows how this will turn out today.' Each word emerged reluctantly, like a tooth that must be tugged out by the root. 'But if something happens, and we are not able to save Stenbrooke, I won't expect you to give up Cardea Shipping.'

She jerked back a pace. 'Mateo, I—'

'No. I didn't bring this up for discussion. I'd rather not talk about it at all.' He paused. She could practically see him gathering fortitude. 'But I want you to know that I believe that all you'd need is a little coaching, and you'd do a good job with it. You've proved yourself several times over. You've a good head on your shoulders. More important than any of that, though, I want you to understand how much I value your kind and generous heart.' He lifted an ironic brow. 'You'll acquire more Cardeas than you'll know what to do with—all those uncles and cousins are still employed as agents and clerks and captains and mates.' He faltered a little. 'I know you would do your best for them and take care of them as if they were your own.'

He'd shocked her. Never had she been so taken aback, or so deeply, deeply touched. Tears welled in her eyes. She bit her lip. 'No one has ever paid me a bigger compliment, Mateo.' Her voice fell to a whisper. 'Thank you.'

He reached for her hand and gave it a squeeze. Across the room, the door swung open again. Together they turned to face the future.

The Countess of Lundwick stood poised on the threshold, prettily framed.

In direct contrast to the room they occupied, she was clad in the sort of simple elegance that only an abundance of money could buy. It was a brilliant manoeuvre, and one that only enhanced the stunning perfection of her beauty. For a beauty she still definitely was, for all that she was old enough to be Portia's mother.

She swept a beaming glance across the room, shining joy indiscriminately upon them all. Then her gaze settled on Mateo and she stilled.

'Mr Cardea.' She nearly floated across the room, her arms outstretched.

Portia bristled. The expression in the Countess's eyes as she ran her gaze over Mateo could only be deemed *hunger*. The older woman clasped his face in her hands and kissed both of his cheeks.

Her irritation fled, turned to bemusement, really, when the Countess then turned immediately to her—and with the same avid interest. It was not a sensation Portia was used to—to be gazed upon with something that looked almost like…covetousness.

'Lady Portia.' Portia's cheeks flamed as she found herself greeted in the same continental manner, and also subject to a soft caress over her brow and along the line of her jaw.

'My darlings,' the Countess breathed enthusiastically. She reached out a hand to them both. 'I am so glad you've come to me at last.'

Portia shot a quick, baffled glance at Mateo. He looked just as dumbfounded as she felt.

'Lady Lundwick.' Mateo sketched a bow. 'Clearly you know who we are. Might we also assume you know why we've come?'

'But of course!' The Countess turned a beguiling smile on him. 'At least, I presume you are here to discuss Averardo, no?'

Portia stared. Her heart sounded suddenly loud in her ears. It gave her such a jolt of pleasure and relief—to have someone actually verify the man's existence. She'd almost come to believe he was a myth.

The door swung open once more. She turned, almost expecting, in this day of surprises, to see the elusive Averardo himself. But it was a different entity altogether who rather absently entered the room.

'Lundy!' the Countess exclaimed brightly. 'Just see who has come!'

'Can't! I'm off, my love!' The Earl, for Portia assumed 'Lundy' to be the Earl of Lundwick, was the very image of a life lived hard and well. Wide, where he had once been broad and soft where he had once been firm, he still possessed a degree of handsome appeal. 'I've just come for a proper goodbye, then I'm to Tatts for...' He faltered as he took in the trio of visitors. 'Well, now! Look at this. They've come at last, have they?'

'Yes, they've only just arrived.' The Countess crossed the room to greet her spouse with a fond kiss. Together they turned and smiled upon their bewildered guests. 'Aren't they lovely?'

Portia felt befuddled, as if she'd stepped into a waking dream. After all the trials, hardships, horses, carriages and questions, this elegant, affable couple was not what she'd been expecting to find here. She reached over to reclaim Mateo's hand.

'Very happy to have you all,' boomed the Earl. 'Sorry I can't stay.' He leaned down and kissed his wife once more. 'Enjoy them, my dear, and I will see you tonight at the Ashfords' ball?'

The Countess waved him off and opened the door wider as a maid came in, wheeling a cart spread with a lavish tea. 'Now, my dears, we will have tea. You can introduce me to your friend…' she indicated a wide-eyed Dorrie '…and then, we shall talk.'

Torn between amusement, frustration and impatience, Mateo waited. He waited through tea and sandwiches and cakes, through awkward silence punctuated by stilted small talk, presided over by an inexplicably delighted Countess. And when their hostess at last set down her dish of tea, he leaned forwards.

'Averardo, my lady?'

She laughed, an appealing little trill of good humour. Nearly everything about her was appealing, in fact. He could well understand the Earl of Lundwick's choice, although if he recalled, there had been a buzz of scandal at the time, due to her age and her obscure background.

'Yes, Mr Cardea. All in good time. First I would like to offer my condolences on the loss of your father.'

He blanched. 'Thank you.' He sharpened his gaze. 'Did you know him?'

'I did.' Her bright countenance faded a little. 'A very

long time ago.' She turned troubled eyes towards Portia. 'And your father, as well, dear. His death was such a shock, being the first. It quite frightened me, I confess, for I am not in the habit of contemplating my own mortality.'

No one seemed able to conjure an appropriate response to that. After a moment she straightened. 'Well, then. I know you must be anxious indeed to hear what I can tell you. But first, I would ask a favour. I want to hear something from you.'

'What is there about us that could possibly interest you?' Portia asked her. 'Forgive me, my lady, but I find myself quite at a loss here.'

The older woman gazed at her fondly. 'I long to hear about your journey, dear.' She sketched in the air with her hands. 'How you got *here* from *there*.' She smiled. 'Though it is a loathsome prospect, I have been forced to acknowledge that I have reached a certain…maturity in my life. Though it's a slight compensation, with age does come a little wisdom.' She smiled. 'I will share with you some of the most important lessons I have learned.'

Intent, she leaned forwards. 'It is true that destinations are important. People need goals to achieve satisfaction. But more important than even achieving your goals is the *journey*—the path you take in pursuit of your ambitions.' She glanced slyly at Mateo. 'And most crucial of all? The people you travel with. Those are the things that make life worthwhile and reaching your objective palatable.'

Mateo stared at the woman. She sat, her head tilted in earnestness, her toe pointed, hair still dark and face still largely unlined. A fey, gorgeous creature. She radiated contentment, like a cat curled before a fire. He greatly resented being her plaything.

She glanced askance at him, with her wise, knowing eyes and sudden suspicion bloomed. A *snap* echoed in his head. His brain had just sorted the pieces of separate puzzles and realised they fitted together into a breath-taking whole. It seemed an impossible notion.

He returned her look, and then, quite deliberately, he decided to give her what she wanted.

'I, for one, have experienced an incredible journey on my way to your drawing room, my lady. It started in anger—but ended in something else altogether. Along the way I've experienced frustration, exasperation—' his eye fell on Portia '—but also laughter and admiration.'

'Tell me,' the Countess urged with a smile.

So he did. He told her of Rankin and his disgruntled clerk, of Riggs and his wasted field, of Lord Dowland and his horses and his young family. But mostly, he spoke of Portia. He waxed enthusiastic over her passion and skill for landscaping, over her incredible knowledge, over her sensitivity and quiet strength. And when he was finished Portia sat with a reddened look of bash-ful joy, Dorrie gazed at him with a thoughtful, worried expression and the Countess—she watched him closer still, with undeniable cunning, but also extreme satis-faction.

'Is that what you wished to hear?' he asked her gently.

'It is indeed.' She drew a deep breath. 'And so I shall tell you what you wish to hear.'

'Averardo?' asked Portia.

The Countess nodded. 'That is one name by which he is known. There are others.'

'Like Lorenzo and Cosimo? The names of the Medici?'

She laughed delightedly, but it was respect that shone in her eyes. 'Very good, Mr Cardea. And why not? The Medici were self-made men—they worked and schemed their way into prominence. They made themselves great, but they also lifted others—men of art and science and architecture—into greatness.'

'My home…' Portia swallowed and Mateo winced at how difficult this was for her. 'This man won my home, in a card game with my late husband.' She glanced over at Mateo. 'We wish to buy it back.'

'I do not think he will take your money, Lady Portia,' the Countess said gently. 'But I also do not believe that he will take your home.'

Portia looked stunned. 'But…but why?' She swept an encompassing arm. 'Why put me—all of us—through all this?'

The Countess regarded her kindly. 'I cannot say. You will have to ask him that yourself.'

'I'd be happy to do just that.' Portia's eyes flashed with anger and Mateo wondered if perhaps he should warn the Countess about the danger of underestimating her. 'Do you know where we can find him?'

The older woman shrugged. 'I do not know, precisely. He is a mysterious figure.' She flicked her fingers. 'He comes in, he goes out. One never knows when one will see him next.'

Portia stared at her. She threw down her napkin and started to stand.

'To your knowledge, my lady,' Mateo interjected, 'has Mr Averardo ever gone by the name of Salvestro?' He asked the question smoothly, as if the answer were of no consequence whatever.

She met his gaze directly. 'Yes, Mr Cardea, I believe he has.'

Click. Another piece of the puzzle snapped home. The revelations were coming fast, but he could see that Portia followed his line of thinking, at least to a degree. 'But, Mateo, you said that Salvestro was your agent in Portsmouth…that means…your father knew him, hired him… He's been *working* for you, for all these years…' Her face hardened and she turned to the Countess with determination. 'I'm sorry, my lady, but surely you know more. We must see this man, and straight away.'

Calmly, the Countess poured herself another dish of tea. 'Do not fret so, my dear. He will come to you when the time is right.'

'The time *is* right—right now. Mateo stands to lose too much if we delay any further.'

'Then perhaps you must give Averardo reason to come to you.'

Portia was on her feet. 'This is preposterous. Do you think this is some sort of game? The course of all our lives is at stake here.'

Mateo's mind was racing. He stood. 'Come, ladies. I think perhaps our journey is over.' He levelled a hard look at their hostess. 'Sometimes life's journey takes you to places you've no wish to see.'

Portia tried a last time. 'Please.' She turned a pleading gaze upon the other woman. 'Won't you tell us what we need to know?'

The Countess patted her hand. 'All will be well, dear. You must trust me.'

Portia drew back. Her face set, she walked away.

Mateo bowed low over the lady's hand. 'Thank you. I understand that you have said what you can.' He paused. 'And, perhaps, done what you can.'

'You are very welcome, Mateo,' she said softly. She gazed after Portia's retreating form. 'I hope she will forgive me. Will you bring her to visit again?'

He stared down at her, made note of the wistful tone she allowed to creep into her voice. 'Eventually, perhaps.'

Outside they waited for the post-chaise to be brought from the livery. Several times Miss Tofton opened her mouth to speak, but each time she closed it again and shook her head. Portia stared blankly out at the traffic for several long minutes before she turned to him.

'Mateo—the same man, all along? All through this… wasted excursion, but further back, as well? We suspected Averardo and the courier might be one and the same. But I'm afraid I don't understand. Was he also the same man your father mentioned, the one he hired—to take your place here in England?'

She reached out. Proprietarily, she grasped his hand. 'Perhaps he's been after your dream all along,' she said as if she were thinking out loud. 'Perhaps he's after your legacy.' She stared up at him. 'Perhaps he thinks I will make the trade with *him*, Stenbrooke for Cardea Shipping.'

He blinked. 'I confess, I hadn't even thought of that.'

'You hadn't? But something occurred to you in there, I saw it in your face. What does it all mean?'

He tugged his hand free and captured both of hers. He kissed them tenderly, even as she stared in amazement.

'Peeve, I'm going to ask you do something. I ask it, knowing full well that it may be the most difficult thing you've ever attempted.'

She breathed deep. 'Of course. What is it?'

'For both of our sakes, I need you to trust me. Completely. Implicitly.' He feared that she would realise how everything inside of him hovered, awaiting her answer. 'Can you do that? Will you?'

Her hands spasmed, clutching his. Silence grew thick between them. 'Yes. Of course I will.'

His heart lurched, his chest expanded. Beside them, the post-chaise rolled to a stop.

'Where are we going?' she asked, not taking her eyes off his.

'To see someone I've journeyed with in the past.'

Chapter Fifteen

'The knocker's up,' Mateo said in relief. The post-chaise drew to a halt in front of the Bruton Street town-house. 'We're in luck.'

He instructed the postillion to wait. When the door swung open, he flashed his most charming smile. 'Batten down the hatches, Fisher. I'm afraid it is an American invasion.'

'Yes, Mr Cardea,' the butler answered formally. 'I am duly frightened.' He opened the door wide and bowed Mateo and the ladies in.

'Before you start counting the silver, will you inform Sophie of our arrival? It might be something of a shock,' he added ruefully.

'It would only be a shock if I were able to inform her, sir. Lady Dayle and the children are currently in Kensington.'

That did deflate Mateo a little. Sophie's help he knew he could count on. Of her husband's he was not so sure. 'And Lord Dayle?' he asked.

'I believe he is in his bookroom. I'll just go and see if he's at home, shall I?'

Mateo grinned. It took true skill to convey sarcasm through a stiffly proper demeanour. 'Thank you, but step sharply now,' he called. 'There aren't enough valuables in the entrance hall to keep me interested for long.'

Fisher's stately pace never faltered.

'There are likely a hundred inns within a mile of here, Mateo,' Portia said. Worry created shadows beneath her eyes. 'Perhaps we should just find one for the night?'

'That wasn't exactly a warm welcome, Mr Cardea,' Miss Tofton chided.

'Nonsense. Fisher expects me to light a fire under his bowsprit. It's no more than the man deserves—a name like that and do you know he's never set foot in the smallest dinghy?'

'Fisher!'

Mateo turned in anticipation. The call came from above, not from the bookroom down the hall.

'Fisher—I'll need an umbrella. The sky looks as if it's going to open up.'

Mateo stepped forwards as Charles Alden, Lord Dayle, husband to his cousin Sophie, appeared at the top of the stairwell, fastening his cufflinks as he came. 'Fisher?'

'Sorry, Dayle. I sent him off to find you.'

The Viscount's head popped up. 'Cardea?' His face lit up in shock. 'By God, Cardea, it is you, you soup-swilling son of a sea-cook!'

Mateo laughed. 'You're improving, Dayle. I could almost use that one without shame.'

'Yes, well, a man should never stop striving for excellence. In all things.'

His cousin-in-law had reached the hall. He reached out and pulled Mateo in for a bracing hug and forceful thump on the back. 'What are you doing here, Mateo? Does Sophie know you're in England?' His eye fell on the two ladies, silently watching. 'And who is this you've brought with you?' He let his arm fall from Mateo's shoulder and shot them both a blinding smile.

Mateo stepped protectively towards Portia and her companion. 'You're an old married man now, Dayle,' he objected. 'Turn it down a bit and allow me to introduce an old family friend, Lady Portia Tofton, and her companion, Miss Tofton. Ladies, this is the Viscount Dayle.'

'Tofton?' Dayle frowned.

'Yes, *that* Tofton,' Mateo said in exasperation.

Portia curtsied, and came up with a grin. 'One might just as easily say, *that* Lord Dayle. I believe I've heard just as much about you, my lord, as you might have about my late husband.'

Dayle laughed. 'I dare say that could be true. But people change, do they not, Lady Portia?'

'Some do, my lord,' she answered non-committally.

'And some are just destroyed by their own stupidity. Come, Dayle, I've been dragging these two ladies all over the south of England for days now. I was hoping you'd redeem me and put us all up for the night?'

'I hope you're planning on staying longer than a night? Sophie will skin us both if she misses you. She and all the rest of the family are up to their elbows in

Mother's latest project: an orphanage in Kensington. They'll be wanting to give you the grand tour.'

Mateo purposefully did not commit to anything. 'Thank you, Charles. I knew I could count on you.'

'Not at all. Look, here's Fisher. Where have you been, man?' Dayle called to his butler.

Fisher's eyes flicked in Mateo's direction. 'Counting the silver, my lord.'

'Not a bad idea, with a pirate in the house. But now I need you to see to these ladies.' He cast a sympathetic look at Portia. 'I'd wager they'd like a hot bath, and perhaps a tray in their rooms?'

'Oh, yes, thank you, my lord,' Miss Tofton piped up.

Mateo noted that the offer of such homely comforts had dazzled the companion where Dayle's blinding charm had not. Perhaps days spent under the influence of his own considerable charm had granted her an immunity.

'There's a post-chaise out in front that will need taking care of,' he informed Dayle.

'Fisher will see to it, won't you, man?' Dayle leaned in confidingly. 'He's the most sought-after butler in town, Cardea—he can do any number of things at once, and all brilliantly well.'

Portia looked back once as the ladies were led away. Mateo nodded encouragingly. Dayle observed this silent communication, but did not comment. Neither did Mateo.

'Come on. Let's find some brandy. You look like you could use one.' He laughed. 'You're the perfect excuse to keep me from Lady Ashford's ball tonight, and for that I owe you.'

Dayle waited until they were settled in the bookroom with cigars and brandies before he eyed Mateo's relaxed slouch with scepticism and asked, 'What sort of trouble are you into now?'

'I wish I could say it was the usual sort, but I'm afraid it's gone a bit worse than that.'

'You know I'll help, in any way I can.'

Mateo blew a smoky cloud of relief. 'Thank you, Charles.' He sat up straight. 'Here's what I'll need.'

Chapter Sixteen

Early morning light painted Mayfair with a dazzling brush, reflecting off immaculately swept steps and bright, shining windows. On Bruton Street, the sun sparkled off Lord Dowland's newly washed post-chaise and flashed amidst the jingling traces of the freshly harnessed team.

Lord Dayle worked fast. Portia ruefully eyed the carriage and then her agitated companion.

'Are you certain about this?' Dorrie asked, her tone low with concern.

'It's as good a plan as any,' Portia sighed. 'Averardo has watched us so closely all along, he must be doing so now.' She tried not to peer about the seemingly empty street, but it was a difficult urge to conquer. 'Even if he's not watching himself, he's likely hired someone to keep an eye on us. We have to make this look authentic.'

'You know I don't like leaving you.'

'It's just for a short time. I'll follow you home soon enough, perhaps as early as tomorrow if Mateo's plan works.' She gripped her companion's hands. 'We have to finish this. And when we do, Stenbrooke will be ours and we'll never have to worry about losing it again.' She smiled. 'And I will be travelling alone this time, not in Mateo's company. So you may relax.'

Dorrie lifted an ironic brow.

'I'll be all right, Dorrie. I promise.'

Her companion's mouth twisted wryly. 'Yes, I know. You trust him.' She sighed. 'And that's as good a recommendation as I'll ever hear.' She hugged Portia close, and then stared intently into her face. 'Now I wish you would begin to trust yourself.'

Portia swallowed.

Dorrie relented, and hugged her once more. 'Now, I hope to see you tomorrow.'

Portia nodded, her throat too thick to speak. Part of her returned the sentiment. She firmly squashed the other part.

Behind them the door opened and Mateo and Lord Dayle emerged, blinking into the bright sunlight. Mateo carried a travelling case in his hand.

'Well, I hope all of this sun presages an easy journey for you, Miss Tofton.' Lord Dayle bent low over Dorrie's hand. 'It was a pleasure to make your acquaintance.'

'And yours, as well. Thank you for your generous hospitality.' Dorrie curtsied and then extended a hand in Mateo's direction. 'Mr Cardea…' She stopped and gave a little shake of her head.

Portia's eyes filled as Mateo ignored the outstretched hand and pulled Dorrie in for an embrace. She forgot her tears, though, when she saw him whisper something in her companion's ear.

'I think that is precisely what I'm afraid of,' Dorrie told him tartly, but her eyes looked suspiciously bright, as well.

'Portia will be home with you soon,' Mateo told her as he handed her into the chaise.

'Goodbye, Dorrie!' Portia called as the vehicle moved away. She watched and waved until it turned a corner, and her companion was gone.

But there was no time to brood. One of Lord Dayle's grooms was already leading a saddled horse up. Mateo lost no time before strapping his case behind the saddle. Once he had it secure, Lord Dayle grasped his hand and gripped him tightly on the shoulder.

'It was damned good to see you, Cardea. I hope next time you'll be able to stay a while.'

'I will. Give Sophie my regrets.' He winced. 'And my apologies.'

Lord Dayle laughed. 'Yes, you'll have hell to pay when next she sees you. Sure you won't reconsider?'

'I wish I could.'

Portia felt the impact when his eyes slid to her.

Lord Dayle cleared his throat. 'Well, then. I'll let you two say your goodbyes.' The Viscount gave her hand a squeeze and retreated inside the house.

Silently, Portia turned her gaze to Mateo. Mere inches of pavement separated them, but in her heart she felt the gap between them widening. She jumped a little when he reached out suddenly to grasp both her hands.

'I've an idea how we can ensure this appears convincing.'

Her mouth quirked. 'Do you?'

He leaned in and pressed the softest kiss upon her. It was a feat of strength not to lean in and silently ask for more.

'I'm not sure I'm convinced,' she said when he pulled away.

A laugh bubbled up. 'Perhaps you can drum up a tear or two?' He kissed her hand and then climbed into the saddle.

Their eyes met once more. 'What did you whisper to Dorrie?' she asked suddenly.

Her favourite laugh lines appeared at the corner of his eyes. 'I promised her I would do the right thing.' And with that he nudged his horse and was on his way.

Portia stood rooted in her spot for a long time, long after he had turned the corner and disappeared into the London traffic. Her reaction came startlingly close to her companion's; she very much feared Mateo did intend to keep that promise. Tears did come then, easily. She let them fall. One last look over her shoulder at Lord Dayle's welcoming home, and then she did as she'd been bid, and walked away.

Berkeley Square was a green blur that she passed right by. She followed Berkeley Street all the way down to Piccadilly, then crossed into Green Park. She kept her directions firmly fixed in her mind and tried her best to walk casually. She was supposed to appear self-absorbed and not horribly on edge at the idea of being observed and followed.

The park was nearly empty at this time of the morning: a wide, green expanse occupied by only a rider or two, and a few children with their nurses. Portia ambled along her prescribed route, until she found a bench near the reservoir. She sat, staring over the peaceful scene.

She waited. And she tried desperately not to *think*.

A bank of clouds passed over, blocking the sun. The water before her grew nearly black beneath it, a painful reminder of storm-swept eyes that darkened in anger, and lit up in laughter, and softened in love. The tears started to fall again.

She ducked her head as a finely dressed gentleman passed on the nearby footpath. He tipped his hat to her, but came to a halt when he glimpsed her face. 'Miss? Are you in need of assistance?' He whipped out a hand-kerchief and presented it with flair.

'No, thank you. I'm all right.' She wiped at her tears, but did not take the handkerchief.

Sheepishly, he stuffed it back into a pocket. 'Don't know why women don't carry the cursed things, when they are so often in need of them.' He smiled and plopped down on the bench beside her. 'Now what's amiss? You're too pretty to be so sad.'

Portia's tears dried as she stared at him. Her eyes narrowed. 'But I know you. Don't I?' She considered his impeccable clothes, his handsome features…and his long, dark hair, which, tied tightly back, was not noticeable immediately. 'Yes. I saw you at the inn in Marlborough.'

She saw the truth of it in his face, but before he could answer a horse thundered up behind them, pulling to a stop right behind their bench. Portia turned as Mateo swung down from the saddle.

'My, that was fast, Peeve.' He cast a hard look at the

man on the bench beside her. 'I see you've met your brother.'

Her heart stilled. The gentleman jumped to his feet. But Mateo was watching him with a mock frown. 'Or perhaps he's mine?'

Mateo had never quite realised how many reactions—and at such a clip, too—could show in a man's eyes. Like the swiftly turning pages of a book he saw the rounding of surprise, the swift narrowing of anger, the hardening of calculation and, finally, a rueful easing of respect.

Fluid and graceful, the gentleman—his brother?— slid back into his seat. 'Now there's a question for the ages,' he said wryly. 'And one I wish I knew the answer to.'

Portia glanced wildly from him, to Averardo—for lack of a verified name—and back again. 'What are you talking about?'

But their adversary's gaze never left his own. 'How did you know I'd follow *her*?'

Mateo smiled and lifted a shoulder. 'One thing I do know about you—you're not stupid. Given the choice between the three of us, *I'd* certainly choose her.'

Portia still looked bewildered, and increasingly not happy about it. He noticed the tracks of tears on her face and his stomach clenched.

'Mateo, it's extremely bad manners to throw a statement like that out and not explain it. I thought we suspected this man of trying to steal your company?'

'Steal your company?' Averardo straightened in surprise. 'Oh...' he grinned '...the Portsmouth office. You worked that out, did you?'

'Somebody had better begin talking to me,' Portia said through gritted teeth.

'It's the story, *cara*,' Mateo said gently. 'The story that so occupied your father and mine through all those years. If I've put all the pieces together correctly, then the Countess of Lundwick had at one time, a very different name.' He smiled at the dawning realisation in her eyes. 'La Incandescent Clarisse.'

'But she—' She went still, then turned to the man at her side. 'Then you are—'

'Indeed. I am her son. But your father's, as well? Or his?' He gestured in Mateo's direction and breathed deep. 'We shall never know.'

'For years they searched,' Mateo said. 'But when did they find you? Where?'

'When I was fourteen years old, they found me. In Nice.' He drew a deep breath. 'When your fathers were thrown into that Naples prison all those years ago, my mother was left alone. Her home had been destroyed; she was reputed to be harmed or dead. It was then, when she begged sanctuary at the home of a friend, that she met Teodoro Donati. He was a wealthy merchant, and he was, naturally, enchanted. He offered her his protection and took her home to Nice.' He grinned. 'Quite frankly, I think my mother had had enough of notoriety. Donati sympathised with her, petted her, and treated her like a lady. She was in her element.'

'Did they marry?' Portia was clearly caught up in the story.

'Eventually. Donati was also no fool. He wed her

after she gave birth to me. She lived happily with him until his death, a spoiled, happy wife.'

Mateo had caught the undertone of tension in Averardo's voice. 'And you? Were you happy, as well?'

He hesitated. 'Yes, for the most part. Always it was clear I was part of the Donati family, but not truly of it. When your fathers approached me with their story, I was...relieved. He eyed them both solemnly. 'They were great men. I would have been proud to have been sired by either of them.'

'But why did they never tell us?' Portia said almost angrily.

'I believe your mother fell ill, soon after they found me,' Averardo said to Mateo. He shrugged. 'I suppose they did not want to upset her. After that...well, we had already established a clandestine relationship. But they were attentive and very kind. They had me tutored in English, and made sure I had a gentleman's education.'

Another surreptitious glance. 'They had expectations, as any father would. Leandro took me into the shipping business in small ways and there were other opportunities, as well. Between their patronage and my contacts with the Donati family, I have had a varied career and done very well.'

'But the will and the conveyance and all of this...' Portia waved wildly. 'How did it all come about? Why?' she asked, clearly growing upset.

Averardo put his hand over hers. Mateo told himself firmly not to mind.

'Your fathers loved you both very much. They worried for you both. Some years ago they concocted this scheme...' he laughed '...and several variations, as your circumstances changed.' He rolled his eyes at her. 'For one, I am very thankful they did not press me into challenging your husband to a duel, but it was a near thing.'

Portia's face flamed. Mateo hitched his mount to a nearby sapling before crossing to the bench and perching on the arm next to her.

'I felt bad enough cheating him out of your estate,' Averardo continued. His face lit up in remembrance. 'Oh, was he in a frenzy! I began to quite enjoy it. But when I did not immediately press my claim, he relaxed. I swear, I think he forgot all about it as the months passed.'

'Yes, he might have,' Portia said bitterly. 'Stenbrooke meant nothing to him. But it was more likely he just wanted to avoid my wrath while he could.'

'Your fathers finalised their plans just before your papa died,' Averardo told her gently. 'They told me what they had done, and asked for my help.' He took a deep breath. 'They had done so much for me, and, truly, they believed that this was their best gift to you.'

'Gift?' Portia cried. 'But Mateo has likely lost a great opportunity! When I think of the anxiety and the anger and all of the…' Her voice trailed away and she looked to Mateo for support.

'The journey,' Mateo told her. 'The chance for our lives to converge again—that was what they considered a gift.'

'You do see,' Averardo said, nodding in approval. 'I have not given you enough credit.'

Mateo glanced down at Portia. 'They are still matchmaking, the pair of devils,' he said simply.

'They sought to give you an opportunity,' Averardo

corrected. 'Your father, in particular, Mateo, felt very strongly about it. He gambled his life's work because he believed that you would make the most of it.' He stood. 'Whether you do or not is entirely up to you. I will send the deed to Lord Dayle's house.' He tipped his hat and stepped away.

'Wait!' cried Portia. 'I finally have a brother worth knowing! You can't go now!'

Averardo hesitated. He looked over his shoulder, his face softening. Then he cast a questioning look in Mateo's direction.

'I just have one question.' Mateo said.

Averardo turned. 'Yes?'

'What is your *name*?'

'Not Cosimo, I hope,' said Portia with a shudder.

His expression remained serious. 'Not many people know my true name.' He took a deep breath. 'Marcus. My name is Marcus Donati.'

Mateo extended a hand. 'Welcome to the family, Marcus.'

Chapter Seventeen

A cheery fire burned in the grate of Lord Dayle's bookroom and Portia sat before it, warmed through. Mateo's acceptance of Marcus had enabled them all to return to the Viscount's town house where Marcus had presented her with a thick roll of papers. With a flourish, he had said, 'The conveyance on Stenbrooke. I doubt it would have held up, in any case, as is it not even in my legal name.'

Portia had none the less greatly enjoyed feeding the thing to the fire and watching it go up in smoke.

Now she drowsed in a comfortable chair and let the men's animated talk flow over her. Sleepily, she let her gaze roam over the pair of them. Last week Dorrie had been the only thing preventing her from feeling completely alone in the world. Today she had a new brother. And a lover. She sighed. Yesterday she had been worried that her longing for Mateo sprang from a fear of being alone. Tonight she knew that some deeply buried part of her had thought him safe precisely *because* he was certain to leave her alone.

For so long she'd dreamed of independence, of finally having control of her own life. Thanks to these two men, she finally had it. Even more importantly, she knew she deserved it. But for the first time she feared it wouldn't be enough.

She closed her eyes against the pain of that realisation.

When she opened them again, the room had gone quiet. A glance told her that the fire had burned low. Mateo sat in a chair nearby, watching her.

'Did you know that you snore?' he asked conversationally.

She sat up. 'I do not.'

'You do. Just the tiniest rasp.' He got up, crossed over to her and cupped her jaw with his large, calloused hand. 'It's adorable.'

'I'd wager you snore, as well,' she said irritably, 'but I doubt it's adorable.' She was perversely annoyed because she didn't know for certain.

His other hand rose to frame her face. 'It's our last night together,' he said quietly. 'Everyone else has gone up to bed.'

She leaned into his caress. He kissed her then and she knew that she'd been right, this was not enough. She would miss the incredible connection they shared, miss the comfort of his company, the sure knowledge that he knew her thoughts almost before she did, and found them amusing and worthwhile. Years loomed ahead, years that suddenly seemed empty because they wouldn't be filled with him.

But he'd said it himself—they were so different. He

needed the sea, needed a sense of freedom just as he needed air to breathe. And he needed the chance to show the world what he could do. He could never be happy if he was forced to give those things up.

And was she any different? She spared a moment's thought to the idea of giving up Stenbrooke. A wrenching pain squeezed her heart, and a healthy dose of fear, but she thought she could do it. A lifetime with Mateo would be more than a fair trade.

But the same, she feared, could not be said of him. And what would happen to her heart if he refused the idea? Or worse, if he agreed and came to resent being tied to her?

'You're thinking too loud,' he said softly in her ear. 'And tonight is for feeling. You can think tomorrow.'

She sighed. But he was right. So she would savour the moments that they'd already shared and she would fill this night with more. Her arms crept up around the expanse of him and buried themselves in the tangle of his curls. She kissed him with all the longing in her past and future.

He pulled her tightly against him, as if he could not get close enough. There was a desperate urgency in them both that fuelled their feverish touches, but which somehow added another layer of tenderness to every caress.

Time slowed to a crawl. Perhaps it stopped altogether as they played, touching, tasting, laughing softly with each button that came undone and each tape that came untied. At last he was standing naked and she was left only in her stockings. She bent to undo the rosebud fastening of her garter.

He put out a delaying hand. 'Don't. I like them.' He fingered one frilly garter admiringly. 'Especially the roses.'

'Well, what did you expect?' she said tartly. 'No doubt if I were a dockside doxy I'd have fish, or anchors or something nautical on my garters.' She laughed. 'What do you suppose the Countess has on hers?'

He didn't answer. Not with words. Instead he dropped to his knees and pressed a hot kiss to the tender skin her stockings left bare.

She gasped.

Torture. That's what it was. He nipped and teased the soft flesh of her thighs, even moving behind her and paying lavish homage to the back of her legs. His hands roamed down over her calves and up over her buttocks, setting her to squirming.

'You said you trusted me.' His warm breath tickled her right through her stocking.

'I do.' It was a vow.

'Then put your hands on the arm of the chair.' His voice was soft, but there was a ring of command in it, as well. Her heart pounded, but she did as he asked.

'Lower,' he said. 'Brace yourself on your elbows. And spread your legs.'

She did, swallowing back a surge of anxiety. She was open before him, on display, exposed and vulnerable. But it was Mateo who asked, Mateo who had taken such tender care of her spirit, she could not but trust him with her body. Tense, she waited.

'You are beautiful,' he whispered. 'Gorgeous.' He slipped a finger along her woman's crease as he said it and she started, then groaned in pleasure.

She was wet and ready for him. His fingers lingered, teasing back and forth, threatening her sanity. He reached further and teased the swollen centre of her passion. Her sex pulsed with arousal.

'*Dio*, but I cannot wait. I wanted to make this last all night long, but I have to be inside of you.'

'Don't wait,' she said. And discovered that there was a power in her ability to overthrow his control.

He raised her from the chair and positioned himself behind her, between her legs, the length of him a burning brand against her. She gasped as he pushed gently across her achingly wet folds.

And then he slid home, entering her fully on one hard thrust. She cried out at that pleasure, at the wonderful stretching of her body and the incredible pressure of his.

He clutched her hips and began to move. She ached with the joy of it, with the intensity of her need, and she pushed back against him, demanding more. He gasped for breath, his grip on her tight, his thighs tense against her own.

His pace began to grow more frantic. He reached around and cupped her, his finger finding her swollen bud. It was all she needed. With a cry she went over, shaking, shuddering, her body gripping his in waves of undulating pleasure. And he followed, crying out with a hoarse voice as deep inside her he throbbed to a violent release.

Eventually they stilled. Mateo withdrew gently from Portia's body and, still holding her tight, he twisted so that they landed in the chair, with her on top of his lap. Softly he kissed the honeyed glow of her hair.

'It's not enough,' he whispered. 'I want more, all of you, in every way. I want you all night long, to make up for the nights ahead.'

'Mmm.' She gave a tiny wiggle against him, not lifting her head from his shoulder.

He laid his head against hers. 'I've come to care for you, Portia.'

Her finger drifted across his chest. 'I know.'

He pulled back, a little annoyed. 'You know?'

She smiled lazily up at him. 'You might not have said the words, but you've shown me in a hundred ways.'

'I didn't mean for it to happen,' he said testily. 'In fact, I tried damned hard to prevent it.'

'I know,' she said again, but her smile took some of the sting from her words. 'I care for you, too, you know.'

'It's incredibly foolish of us.' He sighed.

And it was. The Countess of Lundwick might spout on about journeys, but it was Portia who had come the farthest. *Dio*, but he was proud of her—of the tough determination she'd shown in the face of adversity and the extraordinary courage it had taken to allow him past it.

He'd seen the fierce joy in her eyes when that deed of conveyance had gone up in flames. She'd battled hard for her independence and now she had won it. He'd done his best to help her reach it—how could he even think about asking her to give it up now?

It would be the height of selfishness to consider it. And the height of foolishness, as well. He clenched his teeth. More than just geography and temperament kept them apart. This was Portia's chance to live her dream, bask in her triumph. She deserved the opportunity to stand on her own two feet, to discover her own strength firsthand.

'I'll have to leave tomorrow,' he said.

She nodded. 'You'll take a piece of me with you.' Her voice shook with feeling.

He reached out to caress her, stroked her hair. And ignored the fact that his hand was shaking, too. 'It's the most precious gift anyone has ever given me.' He lifted her chin and stared into her gold-flecked eyes. 'I will treasure it always.'

'Tonight is a gift, too,' she said, reaching for him. 'For both of us.'

He pressed his lips to hers. 'Then let's make the most of it.'

Chapter Eighteen

The *Lady Azalea* rocked, resisting the tug of the tidal surge. Mateo stood alone on the quarter deck, enjoying the feel of the wind washing over him, waiting for the tang of sea air to fill him with anticipation and joy. Deliberately, he faced south. The sea was there, just beyond the mouth of the harbour. A siren, she tempted him with her call. For the first time in his life, he hesitated to answer.

Over the last week he'd found one reason and then another to delay their departure. His chief mate was growing restless, his crew had begun to look at him in wonder. Still, he could not bring himself to give the order to heave anchor and cast off.

Other voices filled his head, drowning the siren's song. His father's rang loud and often. *What are you looking for, son?* Portia's often followed. *Have you been looking for it, do you think? For peace?*

He had not been looking for it. But it had found him anyway. Because that's exactly what Portia gave him:

peace and companionship, calm acceptance and uncon-
ditional trust. All the things he'd refused to acknowledge he'd been seeking as he wandered.

But the real beauty, the great, grand wonder of Portia
was that she also gave him adventure and desire, opposition and laughter. Everything that he'd embraced as a
substitute, and come to crave.

In Portia he'd found everything, all rolled up in a
saucy, delectable package.

Dio, but he was a fool to even think of leaving her
behind.

His mind churned as he stared unseeing at the busy
harbour. Perhaps, just perhaps, there was a way. Deliberately he turned from the rail and went to his cabin.
Now anticipation set his heart racing, but he held himself in check, adopting calm as he sharpened a quill and
pulled a fresh stack of paper from his drawer.

He had a lot to put down, and it took quite a while.
He had just finished, and was sealing a thick packet
of documents when his mate knocked and entered the
cabin.

'Oh, there you are, John,' Mateo said pleasantly.
'Order me up a boat's crew, please. I'm going ashore.'

The man looked at him in surprise. 'Actually, the
boat's manned and ready, Captain. We've just had a
signal. There's a passenger wanting to sign on.' He
paused, considering. 'We can fit him in if we bunk
Hatch in with the men.'

'Good, but tell him and the crew, too, that it will be
several days, likely a week before we set sail.'

'Another delay, Captain? The crew will—'

'The crew will do as I say, as always. Anyone who

wants to question that can head ashore and find berth on someone else's ship. Now go and make sure that boat is manned, John.' He handed over the sealed packet. 'And see that this is delivered. I've written down the address. I'm going to Berkshire. You'll have the ship while I'm gone.'

'Aye, sir.'

The boat weaved through the harbour traffic and Mateo fought the urge to hurry the men as they pulled. The Portsmouth docks loomed ahead, indistinct in the evening light. Mateo's mind ranged ahead, trying to calculate how long it would be until he could reach Stenbrooke, trying to anticipate Portia's reaction to his plans.

The pier was closer now, but quiet at this time of the evening. A lone figure stood there, watching them come in.

Mateo started, then rose half out of his seat. Surely not?

'Strongly now, men! Pull! Put your backs into it!' He narrowed his gaze and peered across the water. His heart nearly burst with joy as he cupped his hands and shouted across the water. 'Peeve! What in blazes are you doing here?'

She waved, but didn't answer. The boat pulled alongside and Mateo was scrambling out and on to the pier before the men had even pulled in their oars. With a laugh, he swept Portia up into his arms and twirled her wildly about. 'How did this come about?' he asked joyfully. 'And where is Dorrie?'

'Dorrie is in Wiltshire,' she said with a smile. 'I wrote to Mrs Rankin and told her we had been to call on her son. I sang Dorrie's praises and made sure to mention how struck she had been with the potential of Longvale. She received an invitation to visit, and, if I'm not mistaken, Mr Rankin and his mama are even now evaluating *her* potential.' She cast a dark look over his shoulder towards a bustling dockside tavern. 'And just where were you going?' she asked suspiciously.

'To Berkshire.'

A tiny grin fought its way through her severe expression. 'Why?'

He lifted a shoulder. 'I'm two and thirty years old. I thought perhaps it was time I started listening to my father.' He looked steadily at her. 'Would you care to travel along with me?'

'It sounds lovely, but I couldn't. I've just booked passage to Philadelphia.'

His mouth dropped. 'You're the passenger?'

'If you'll have me.'

He gathered her into his arms. 'Oh, I'll have you.' He bent to kiss her, but pulled away at the last second.

She pouted.

'I feel it's only honourable to inform you of the change in my circumstances, Peeve.' He frowned down at her. 'You may wish to reconsider your passage.'

She raised a questioning brow.

'I'm afraid I'm no longer the sole owner of a shipping company. I just turned fifty percent of it over to Marcus Donati.'

She gasped. 'Oh, Mateo! I cannot believe it!'

He smiled. 'I'm done with skimming the surface. I'm diving in and soaking up everything life has to offer.'

He ran a finger along the tempting sweep of her nape. 'And the best it has to offer is you.'

Her eyes filled. 'Still, it is a generous gesture—and I know how difficult it must have been for you.'

He shook his head. 'Not at all. I'm going to let him hold the reins for a while. He deserves a chance at the family legacy. If he hurries, he might still join the fleet to Canton, but even if he does not, with his contacts in Italy he'll make a good go of it.' Sobering, he asked, 'Well, what of it, Peeve? Will you turn tail and run back to Stenbrooke now?'

Clearly holding back laughter, she bit her lip. 'I cannot.'

'Why not?'

'Wait.' She reached down and dug into her portmanteau and held out a thick packet of her own. 'I signed a deed of conveyance, granting it to Marcus Donati.'

He sucked in a shocked breath. 'You didn't!'

'I'm nearly seven and twenty years old. I thought it was time I stopped letting fear make my decisions for me.' She bit her lip. 'I had to take the chance. I had to ask. You mean more to me than Stenbrooke ever could.'

Very gently, he reached out and took the parcel from her hand. Then he turned and with a mighty heave, threw it out into the harbour.

'Mateo!' she gasped. 'Why did you do that?'

'Because I can't let you give Stenbrooke up, after you battled so hard to keep it. And in any case, we're going to need it.'

Her shock was quickly done in by curiosity. 'We are?'

'We are,' he said firmly, then leaned down and kissed

her soundly. 'Packets, Peeve! A business of my own that I can have the running of from the ground up! We'll have the best of both worlds: earth and sea. I'll have a fleet of ships to manage, but we'll need a retreat, a place where we can get away from the bustle of the docks, the pressures of business, a place to make babies and watch them run free.'

Tears shone in her eyes again and she nodded vigorously.

'Perhaps we can live part of the year in England, and part in Philadelphia. Perhaps we'll build a new home in Le Havre or on the Rio de la Plata.' He grinned. 'You can have a garden for every climate.'

'I don't need a home in every port. All I need is you.' Her arms clutched him tightly. 'We only have one life, Mateo.' She smiled. 'One journey. I want to travel it with you.'

'One life,' he whispered. 'Let's make it memorable.'

* * * * *

HISTORICAL

Where Love is Timeless™

HARLEQUIN® HISTORICAL

COMING NEXT MONTH
AVAILABLE APRIL 24, 2012

A TEXAN'S HONOR
Kate Welsh
(Western)

RAKE WITH A FROZEN HEART
Marguerite Kaye
(Regency)

LADY PRISCILLA'S SHAMEFUL SECRET
Ladies in Disgrace
Christine Merrill
Three delectably disgraceful ladies, who break
the rules of social etiquette, each in need of a
rake to tame them!
(Regency)

THE TAMING OF THE ROGUE
Amanda McCabe
(Elizabethan)

HHCNM0412

REQUEST YOUR FREE BOOKS!

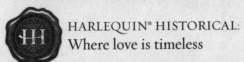

HARLEQUIN® HISTORICAL:
Where love is timeless

2 FREE NOVELS PLUS 2 FREE GIFTS!

HARLEQUIN® HISTORICAL:
Where love is timeless

SCANDAL NEVER LOOKED SO GOOD
WITH FAN-FAVORITE AUTHOR

MARGUERITE KAYE

Waking up in a stranger's bed, Henrietta Markham
encounters the most darkly sensual man she has ever met.
The last thing she remembers is being attacked—yet being
rescued by Rafe St. Alban, the notorious Earl of Pentland,
feels much more dangerous! And when she's accused of theft,
Rafe finds himself offering to clear her name. Can Henrietta's
innocence bring this hardened rake to his knees…?

Rake with a
Frozen Heart

Sparks ignite this May!

*Lady Priscilla and the Duke of Reighland play
a deliciously sexy game of cat and mouse in
LADY PRISCILLA'S SHAMEFUL SECRET,
the third and final installment of the Ladies in Disgrace
trilogy, a playful and provocative Regency series
by award-winning author Christine Merrill.*

He was staring at her again, thoughtfully. "Considering your pedigree, it should be advantageous to the man involved, as well. You are young, beautiful and well born. Why are you not married already, I wonder? For how could any man resist such a sweet and amenable nature?"

"Perhaps I was waiting for you, Your Grace." She dropped her smile, making no effort to hide her contempt.

"Or perhaps the rumors I hear are true and you have dishonored yourself."

"Who…" The word had escaped before she could marshal a denial. But she had experienced a moment's uncontrollable fear that, somewhere Dru had been that she had not, the ugly truth of it all had escaped. And that now, her happily married sister was laughing at her expense.

"Who told me? Why, you did, just now." He was smiling in triumph. "It is commonly known that the younger daughter of the Earl of Benbridge no longer goes about in society because of the presence of the elder. But I assumed there would be more to it than that. And I was correct."

Success at last, though it came with a sick feeling in her stomach, and the wish that it had come any way but this. She had finally managed to ruin everything. Father would be furious if this opportunity slipped through her fingers. It would serve him right, for pushing this upon her. "You have guessed correctly, Your Grace. And now, I assume that this interview is at an end." She gestured toward the door.

"On the contrary," he replied. "You have much more to tell me, before I depart from here...."

If you like your Regencies fun,
sexy and full of scandal then you'll love
LADY PRISCILLA'S SHAMEFUL SECRET
Available May 2012

Don't miss the other two titles in this outrageous trilogy:
LADY FOLBROKE'S DELICIOUS DECEPTION
LADY DRUSILLA'S ROAD TO RUIN